Odette Azul

Ratcatcher

Book Cover by @dkmrgn
1st edition 2026

For my magic space dad.

For my magic space dad.

Chapter 1

RAFF

"Hell, no. What the shit is this?" I ask as I look at the piece of paper tacked to the corkboard. It's two p.m. on a Tuesday. We open at six. Sunday was a shit show. We were closed on Monday.

The office is small. The lighting is stark. If Guy moves his arm one inch to the right, he'd be able to elbow me in the junk. "Ah, you finally saw the schedule," Guy says, not turning from his laptop.

"Fuck no," I say. This isn't fucking happening. No way. Never. I refuse. "I don't want one of those loud bread girls running around my kitchen."

Guy sits back with a sigh. "She's not loud."

I shake my head. All of them are loud. They reminded me of this movie, Spice World. My sister Eleni had an old VHS tape that she'd bought at a garage sale for fifty cents. The summer that we were stuck at our dad's auto body shop in Sebastopol, we'd watched it on repeat in the waiting room. That is, until dear old dad smashed the tape into pieces with his hammer. "They're all loud," I counter.

"What other options do we have?" he asks.

He is, of course, referring to Meghan, who quit mid shift on Sunday. Coward. She may have a perfect resume, but she certainly doesn't have the soul of a chef. Good fucking riddance. If you want to work on my crew, I require gumption.

Guy is now rocking his chair from side to side. Each swivel is slightly off tempo from the Pixie's song that's playing on his laptop. He would never come out and say it, but he's worried. Each move of his large frame on the vinyl seat causes a clicking noise that makes my eyes twitch.

"I don't know. Dane? Maybe Shelby?" I offer.

Halting his repetitive swivel, Guy stares at me. His mouth pressed in a firm line as if to say *really*? Fuck Guy. I hate that he knows everything about me.

Let's make one thing perfectly clear: I don't brag. I don't need to be celebrated for my conquests or some immature shit like that. If I had my way, no one would ever know. Unfortunately, Guy is my roommate. And much to my dismay, the old ranch-style house that he inherited has thin walls... and women are not usually quiet when they're with me. Shelby certainly wasn't. That's not bragging. It's just a fact.

"She moved back to San Francisco."

I blow out a breath. "Olivia," I start, but he just shakes his head.

"Raff, I'm going to save you some time. There is no one else. We are out of options," he says resolutely.

"Then I'll train someone." Leaning back against the cramped office wall, the California labor law posters crinkle behind my back.

"We already have the new girl," Guy starts.

"Perfect," I say, heading out the door.

"She's straight out of school. A total Barney, man. She won't be able to keep up with you."

I turn back. "We'll get her there."

Guy shakes his head. "And what's going to happen in two weeks when she falls in love with you and then you get bored with her?"

I laugh, but Guy continues, "You have a reputation."

That is fucking ridiculous. "What's that supposed to mean?" I ask with a snort.

Guy lifts a questioning eyebrow. "Seriously," he says.

I open my mouth, but Guy continues. "We need someone now. Business is booming. It's the perfect time to take

Silverstein up on his offer. But we can't because you're too much of an asshole." Guy levels me with a pointed look.

I flip him off, which only makes him laugh. Guy is my best friend and business partner. He is intimidating to most people, but I'm not most people. Nothing scares me. Especially not Guy. Like, I give a shit that he's an imposing, ripped, bearded mountain man. So, what if his six-foot-five frame makes me look puny, even though I'm six feet tall?

Guy is a teddy bear. I knew him way before the growth spurt. Back when Guy was a painfully shy fat kid who would follow me around the boardwalk looking for loose change to waste away summer afternoons at the arcade.

"But why her of all fucking people," I say, my voice almost a whine. I clear my throat. God, I sound like such a punk-ass bitch right now.

"Because she's fucking good," he says, rising to his feet.

"Doesn't she live in LA? Or New York? Somewhere that isn't here."

He shakes his head. "She got back last week. Asked for a job."

He lumbers past me out of the office towards the back door. I've left it open for the delivery guys. He grabs a gray plastic tote from the stack that Miguel and Chuy have lugged inside. I grab one too and follow him towards the walk-in.

“Maybe if I can convince Kimbo to come back,” I say, treading on his heels.

Guy stops, nearly letting me slam right into him. “I’m pulling my trump card, man. This destructive behavior... you’re walking a fine line, Raff,” he says, putting his tote bin down.

I exhale sharply. Fuck. Guy is right. I know he’s right. “But seriously, why her?” I say.

Guy grins. God, is he fucking enjoying this? “Because she’s the one person that I’m certain you would never *ever* fuck.”

Chapter 2

ASH

I can't believe I'm doing this. Fuck. I really am a glutton for punishment. I've found myself outside the loading dock of Princess Pizzarina, staring across the empty parking lot at the wholesale vendor unloading their truck.

A single bead of sweat trickles down my temple as At The Drive-In blares on the car stereo. Cedric Bixler-Zavala's voice sounds tinny coming out of my shitty speakers. I kill the ignition of the hand-me-down jeep. The car is still vibrating slightly even after the engine is off, which only enhances the thudding in my chest.

Show no weakness. That's always been my motto. I steady myself and take a few deep inhales. The nerves are causing my breath to catch in my throat. Whatever. I got this.

I push the car door open, using the toe of my boot to kick the heavy metal wide. Belinda is a pretty crappy car, but driving this silver fox is a rite of passage in my family. I slide down and slam the door shut behind me with my hip.

Show no weakness, I repeat. This is what I want. I can do it. I shake my hair out for good luck before tossing my bomber jacket over one shoulder and tucking my bag under the other.

I make my way to the open door, knocking swiftly on the jamb. "Hello," I say. Damn, my voice sounds a little shakier than I had intended.

"In here," Guy says.

I cross through the threshold, my eyes taking a minute to adjust to the fluorescents.

"Hey, Ash. Thanks again," Guy says, stepping out of the walk-in.

"Anything for you," I say with a smile.

A smile that quickly fades when Raffael Lambrou shoves out of the fridge behind him. God, look at him. His ridiculous backward hat and dumb mustache on his stupid symmetrical face. What an attractive asshole. I'm pretty sure my upper lip is curling into a slight sneer as we make eye contact. Raff and I stare at each other for a tense beat before Guy blows out a breath.

He nudges Raff in the ribs with his beefy elbow. "Raff was just saying how excited he is to work with you again. Right, Raff," Guy says with an amused grin.

Raff jerks his head toward Guy in surprise. He is about to say something, but then stops himself. I raise an eyebrow at the pair.

"Cool," I reply wearily. I hold up my jacket and bag. "Is there a spot where I can toss this?" I ask.

Guy closes the distance between us, ushering me further inside. Much like a petulant toddler, Raff continues to glare at me from over Guy's shoulder.

Show no weakness. I smile and wink at Raff as I continue to be guided by Guy. And much to my amusement, Raff actually huffs before stomping out the back door towards the vendor.

Guy gives me a quick tour, introduces me to the kitchen crew, has me sign a few forms, and sets me up with a black Princess Pizzarina crew neck and apron. I toss the T-shirt on over my ribbed tank top and pull my long, dark hair up into a messy ponytail. Typically, I wear clogs or vans in the kitchen, but I wasn't sure if I'd need to kick Raff in the balls. So today I'm keeping my motorcycle boots on. Thank God for gel inserts.

I roll and then re-roll the sleeves of my T-shirt a few times before Guy looks up from his laptop at me. I can hear the kitchen coming to life outside the office door. "Well, guess I'll get out there," I say.

"Give him hell," Guy says with a grin.

"Not like that," Raff snaps from over my shoulder. He's pressed so close that I can practically taste him, charred citrus and Barbasol. His exacerbated tone is palpable, and I can feel Miguel on my right wince. Jesus, no wonder he can't keep cooks for long. Too bad for Raff, he doesn't realize that I'm unbreakable.

"Sorry, chef," I reply innocently.

I give Miguel a slight smirk as I pause my prep. Raff pushes his way between me and my station. Taking the bench scraper from my hand and showing me, for the fourth time, how he prefers to measure the dough.

"Oh," I say with mock amazement, which only makes Raff's jaw tick.

"Faster. I need this to be done faster. Service starts in twenty, and I need you to help Chuy," he huffs as he shoulders his way past Miguel and me towards the front of house.

"Yes, chef," I sweetly coo at the now swinging doors that Raff has just disappeared through. I resume measuring dough just as I had before Raff came over. Miguel stifles a chuckle. "Pobrecito," I tut as I incline my head in Raff's general direction. This causes Miguel to guffaw with laughter.

As we continue to work, I nudge him with my elbow, pointing my lips at the speaker dock on the shelf above us. "Luis Enrique," I ask, already knowing the answer.

Miguel gives me a wide smile, showing off his gold tooth.

"Don't be shy, bump that shit," I say, encouraging him to turn up the volume.

He gingerly wipes his fat fingers on a kitchen towel tucked into the waist of his apron and then increases the volume. I shake my hips and sing along as Luis contemplates Mañana.

I've only been here for a few hours, and it's obvious that the kitchen staff are ripe for the plucking. I'm going to corrupt his crew. Sorry, Raff. I'm the captain now. I will have them eating out of the palm of my hand by the end of the shift. I guaran-fucking-tee it.

It's a good thing I flipped Miguel and Chuy early, because when service starts, I'm totally in the weeds. I knew that Princess Pizzarina was popular, but I didn't realize it was non-stop slammed. I'm practically panting to keep up with the two cooks who move with controlled efficiency. Several times, they have saved me from making a stupid mistake, which is good because Raff is also putting me through my paces.

Every time he has a moment to spare, he's in my face. Constantly bellowing at me to move faster, do something different, and even snatching the wooden peel right out of my hand to demonstrate for the hundredth time that I am incompetent.

I know that he's trying to get under my skin. However, this is a two-way street. Every one of Raff's insults or terse commands is met with a placid 'Yes, chef,' which I know is driving him crazy.

At this point, I would not be surprised if he hasn't cracked a tooth yet. He's been clenching his jaw the entire shift. Is this how he normally runs his kitchen? Now I get why Guy was so desperate.

It's not uncommon for chefs to get insane and controlling over how *their* food is cooked. Perfectionism is rewarded in the restaurant industry. However, Santa Luna is a very small coastal town in Northern California. Everyone knows everyone, especially in the kitchens. But how sensitive could my predecessors actually have been? I sense that something else is the issue here.

Besides, this is child's play compared to working with my family. We aren't known as a pack of she-wolves for nothing. As I clean my station at the end of the night, I smile, thinking about what other mind control tactics I'll be deploying on Raff tomorrow.

With my shift complete, I head out to the front of house. It's the first time that I've really seen what Guy and Raff have created. It's been nearly five years since I left Santa Luna. Princess Pizzarina is *the* spot in town now. Despite it being 11:30 p.m. on a Tuesday night, the bar is still packed.

College students, locals, and even a middle-aged couple press elbows, crowding the long chrome and wood bar. I recognize the bartender, Laurel, from Nat's Sunday Vinyasa yoga class. Laurel is a gangly blonde with a nose ring and gap between her front teeth. She gives me a nod as I slip behind the bar, scooping ice into a large plastic deli container.

"Need any help?" I ask as I squirt Diet Coke out of the beverage gun over my ice. She gives me a withering look, which is all the invitation I need to start taking orders. I'm by no means a bartender, but I can pour a pitcher or run someone's credit card, anything to help a sister out.

By the time everyone's been served, and Laurel has given last call before we close up at midnight, I'm finally getting to take that first sip of my crisp Diet Coke.

"How do you stand the noise?" I ask.

The overhead speakers are bumping an old Mystikal song, and a few feet away from the bar sit two vintage pinball machines, which keep chirping and ringing over the music.

Laurel shrugs. "You get used to it."

We both lean against the back bar as she begins to close out her register. I survey the front of house, watching the lone busboy wipe tables. Eventually, when I master the menu, I assume I'll be manning the humongous wood-burning pizza oven that anchors the space. Despite the long, dining-hall-style seating and the informal atmosphere of arcade games and a vintage photo booth, the food at Princess Pizzarina is practically Michelin-star dining.

A fact that is hard for me to admit... especially because Raff is such a fucking asshole. I hate that he's so talented. Honestly, it's wasted on a cocky shit like him. But damn, the food is really good. That's why I asked Guy for the job.

"Here," Laurel says, extending a twenty-dollar bill towards me.

I shake my head. "Just helping out."

She smiles at me as she pockets the tip money. All a part of my master plan.

I take a long sip from my Diet Coke just as Raff approaches with a container of hot water for Laurel to melt down her ice bins. He's smiling for the first time tonight... an expression that quickly sours when he sees me.

"What are you still doing here?" he asks, eyes narrowed on me.

"Hey, Rat."

He shudders at the old nickname as I lift my shoulders in a slight shrug.

"Just hanging out," I smile back in response. He huffs as he dumps out the boiling water.

"Well, go *hang out* somewhere else." Steam rises as the ice hisses and pops its agonizing farewell.

Confused, Laurel glances between us. "I'm going to cash out with Guy," she says awkwardly before shuffling past. I take another long sip of my drink as Raff continues to glare daggers at me.

"Anything else?" I ask when he doesn't move. I feel like he's about to chew me out, but he continues to study me, biting the corner of his bottom lip. God damn... Raff has a good mouth. A fact that I hate to admit. So instead, I attempt not to notice how full his lips are as he continues to glare at me.

These little tense moments of silence are fun. I can see Raff's brain trying to work out how to respond. I must be throwing off his usual mode of operation, and it's delightful to see how off-kilter it's making him.

I let him stew for a few more seconds before I push off the back bar. "Ok, well, I'm going to head out now, Rat," I say, making my way towards the kitchen.

I try not to glance back, but, honestly, I would give anything to see what expression is on his dumb face right now. Laurel is walking towards me out of the swinging doors. I smirk at her as I make a mental note to ask her tomorrow.

It's a few minutes past twelve thirty by the time I get home. Well, not my home yet. I'm subletting from an old high school friend, Anita. She took up with a guy in Portland and is going to see how she likes it before she gives up her studio. It's small but close to Jupiter Street and the beach. If Anita doesn't come back, it wouldn't be the worst place to stay for a while.

I haven't worked nights in a while, and I'd forgotten that the adrenaline in my body takes some time to work its way out. I turn on the faucet to the bath before pivoting to open the fridge. Yes, this is the weird type of tiny apartment that boasts a bathtub in the kitchen and a Murphy bed a few paces from the front door. Lucky for me, I have very few belongings, so the limited space isn't a bother.

There's nothing to write home about inside the fridge: my sourdough starter, leftover family meal from the bakery, and a few pieces of loose produce that Van gave me. It is ironic for someone who spends their entire day around food to have so little to eat. I settle on the leftover frittata, popping it into the microwave before returning to the bathtub to turn off the faucet. Moments later, I'm soaking in the hot water as I eat hurried bites of lukewarm egg and asparagus. I swish my tattooed thighs side to side under the surface, letting myself count the hours before I need to be awake again.

I continue to do this mental math as I slide beneath the duvet thirty minutes later. I barely register the divot in the thin mattress between the frame braces of the Murphy bed. My body is tired, but my brain is still very much alert. It's ok. I'll adjust. I'm far from fragile. In fact, I am unbreakable.

Chapter 3

ASH

I'm seriously dragging this morning. My arms are screaming as I hoist a tray of croissants onto the rack to proof. It's already been a few weeks of pulling double duty at both the bakery and Princess Pizzarina, and my body is currently in revolt.

I can already feel new muscle developing. So, I know that the overwhelming exhaustion I'm experiencing will eventually pass. After I slide the last tray onto the rack, I take a long draw from my water bottle just as I hear keys in the door behind me.

"Morning," Van calls as she enters the bakery. Her assortment of bracelets jangles, announcing her arrival.

"Morning, Mama," I nod in reply before taking another sip of water. I feel like I just finished running sprints, which, unfortunately, does not go unnoticed by Van.

"Ash, you feeling ok?" Van asks after flicking on the secondary overhead lights.

Ever the caretaker, my cousin Vanessa rushes towards me, placing a palm on my forehead. There is a reason that we all lovingly refer to her as Mama. "Do you think you're coming down with something?" she asks before turning back towards the counter where she threw down her oversized purse. She starts rummaging through its contents. Then she extends an unmarked blue tincture bottle towards me. "I have some oregano oil. That should help fight anything off."

Oh, if she only knew that the germ I've currently been fighting off is Raff. But she can't know that I've been moonlighting at Princess Pizzarina most nights. Then waking up to be here by four most mornings. Vanessa would utterly lose her shit knowing that I've only been operating on three hours of sleep. So, I just shrug. "I think it's allergies."

She shifts her focus towards starting the drip coffee pot. "Ok, well, if you need me to cover any of your shifts, I can swap classes with Nat." Vanessa and our friend Natalie Komatsu teach weekly yoga classes out of an old yurt in the woods near the college. It's all very Santa Luna hippie-dippy shit, which is incredibly fitting for my gorgeous Stevie Nicks-loving cousin.

I shake my head. "Nah, Mama. Truly, I'm ok," I reply before lifting a tray of morning glory muffins onto the rack.

Chappell Roan starts singing through the speakers. Van has just connected her iPhone to the Bluetooth. "Hell, yeah," I hear Nat's raspy voice call out as she pushes her way through the back doors into the bakery. She is followed by my little sister Lex. They shimmy their tattooed shoulders with the music. It's nearly six, which means that all the badass babes who run Mother Wolf Bakery will be arriving soon.

My grandmother, Adela Lobo, started the bakery when she first came to Santa Luna in the 1960s. At the time, it was just a panaderia named Lobos, mainly specializing in Mexican baked goods. Abuelita was a total baddie who ran a business and raised two daughters on her own. Eventually, those daughters, Marta Luz and Christina, took over. Inseparable twins, they'd both done their formal culinary training in San Francisco and then Paris, before returning to Santa Luna to revitalize the bakery.

New name. New vibe. They infused their culinary training and coastal Northern California upbringing into the panaderia. Now it was all French-inspired and locally sourced. The only item that remained on the menu from the old days was the oreja, rebranded as a palmier to match the new style.

Ever since we were old enough to stand behind the register, Vanessa and my sisters, Mac, Lex, and I, have been working at Mother Wolf. We all learned how to make the breads, pastries, and coffee that have made this bakery a Santa Luna fixture. Mother Wolf is our family legacy.

Except for "Uncle" Ray, who has been our handyman since before I was even born, Mother Wolf is run exclusively by women. And what a wild group of women we are... tattoos, shaggy haircuts, and foul mouths. My mother, Christina, and aunt, Marta Luz, who we call Cita and Lulu, are large and in charge in this kitchen.

So, it's no surprise that the Mother Wolf crew is a bunch of indie babes with attitudes. We constantly get mistaken for a motorcycle gang or punk band when we go out drinking... which is often. What can we say, we like dive bars that let us play loud music and shoot pool. The bakery has even earned the nickname 'bread and bangs' with locals because, well, we all rock some seriously cute cuts.

My baby sister Lex softly sings along with the music as she starts helping me move racks up front for opening. Her lavender French-bobbed hair is slightly damp and tasseled this morning. She's wearing a bright orange beanie that is sticking slightly off the top of her head. The way her hair and hat frame her heart-shaped face, and the absurd color combination of purple and orange, give her features a more elfish look than usual, as her bright red lips curve along with the Hot To Go lyrics.

A studio art MFA candidate at UC Santa Luna, she usually helps me with any baking in the mornings or custom cake orders before heading to class. She's truly amazing at what she does. Her signature Rococo cake design is highly requested, and there's often a six-month waitlist to order one of her wedding cakes.

"We missed you last night," she said, following me out into the front of the bakery. I shrug. The new, more demanding work schedule has meant that I have been MIA from more than a few nights at The Tide Water, our local hangout. We start to stock the racks for opening, but I can feel Lex's big green eyes on me.

"Were you with someone?" she asks, a mischievous grin twisting up the sides of her mouth. I bark out a laugh at her. I should have known my family would suspect I was up to something when I stopped going out all the time... now I know that they think I'm just hiding a boyfriend. Great.

"Like I'd tell you," I muse as I fill the wooden shelf behind the long glass guard with loaves of sprouted buckwheat bread. Except Van, none of the Lobo girls date. This is because of the Lobo Curse. Vanessa thinks it's bullshit, but three generations of broken hearts can't be wrong.

"Tell who what?" Natalie asks conspiratorially as she cleans the steam wand on the espresso machine.

"Ash has a boyfriend," Lex singsongs as she scrunches up her button nose.

"Really," Van gasps with excitement as she pauses her till count, register splayed open in front of her. "Do you need a plus one for the wedding?" she asks excitedly. I roll my eyes. Here we go.

Vanessa is engaged to Cary, a boisterous former Stanford football player turned tech bro. We were all very confused when they started dating three years ago. And even more confused when he proposed. But he did pop the question on a new moon. So, I guess he knows her well enough. Their flower-child handfasting ceremony under a harvest moon, or whatever ritual Cary is begrudgingly allowing to become husband and wife legally, is set for the end of the summer. This is one of the reasons that I moved home.

"Tell us," Lex begs in the whiny tone that only the baby of a family could dare use effectively.

"Maybe it's still new. Let's not put too much pressure on her," Van starts carefully, but I stop them.

"I'm *not* seeing anyone," I quickly snap. Maybe too quickly, because they all turn from their opening tasks to look at me. Oh shit.

Romance is a sore subject. Starting with Abuelita's mother, then Abuelita and her daughters. The Lobo women have been cursed in love. It's a long and painful reality that has been ever-present in our lives, starting back in the time of Zapata.

Raised by a heartbroken woman, Abuelita grew up without a father in Jalisco. He had tragically died in some revolutionary battle... but the details are rather hazy. And as Cita loved to point out, Abuelita liked to exaggerate, especially when it came to Mexico and love. Despite being unlucky in romance, Abuelita loved telenovelas and racy novels. Guess she had to pass the time somehow. Lulu said that Abuelita's greatest love was her skittish papillon, Suzy.

Christina and Marta Luz never knew their father. In her lifetime, Abuelita never discussed him or his whereabouts. In fact, as one distant cousin told it, Abuelita was considered a spinster in Mexico. All we knew was that Abuelita arrived in Santa Luna with enough money to start her bakery and a broken heart. She did not know at the time that she was pregnant.

Collecting broken hearts and children became a trend for the Lobo women. Vanessa's dad left when he found out that Marta Luz was pregnant with her. Our father, Erik, was a different story. He doted on all of us. We all assumed he was the outlier. Unfortunately, this was not the case.

Though I don't remember him well, some things stand out in my memories. A tall man, he was very gentle and kind. He stabilized all of us tiny women who revolved around him like a sturdy redwood tree. However, just after Lex was born, Erik Morgan met an untimely end while riding his motorcycle down the winding mountain road towards San Francisco.

I know that we were all devastated. Though I was only five at the time, I can vividly remember impressions of grief. Sitting in a sun-drenched waiting room, watching old cartoons on a black and white television while my aunt collected Erik's belongings from a police officer. Abuelita's paper-thin skin as she rubbed my bare arms while Mac and I slept in her bed that warm summer night. Hearing my mother's muffled sobs as she paced in the room above in the big blue house that he'd bought for us.

I remember the pockets of time, but I can't recall the feelings. For most of my life, I have been unable to let those feelings, any feelings really, flow freely. It's like I have a tough hide that keeps most things out. I am numb.

I should have told them about working for Guy and Raff, but things are complicated, especially regarding the bakery. Despite my immense passion for baking, I've only just been allowed to start working at Mother Wolf again.

Natalie narrows her dark eyes at me. "Is it someone we all know?" she asks suspiciously.

I shake my head. "Seriously, I'm not dating," I insist before walking through the large swinging wood door. I nearly fall over when I turn back to see that Van, Nat, and Lex have followed me into the kitchen from the front of house. They are not going to let this go.

I am about to tell them to drop it when I hear a loud slam. The back door has flown open, smacking hard against the wall. All of our heads snap up as we hear the heavy, platform-clog-footed tread of Mac. She looks pissed. "What the literal fuck," Mac growls. Her eyes narrowed in on me.

Shit. Mac knows. Of course, she fucking knows. "Whoa, take it easy, Daddy," Lex says as Mac chucks her purse over her shoulder and closes the distance between us in a few swift stomps.

Only a few months apart in age, Vanessa and my older sister Mackenzie are two sides of the same parentified coin. If Van is Mama, sweet, ethereal, and nurturing-- basically the perfect Cancerian mermaid goddess, then it only makes sense that our fierce and assertive oldest sister Mac is Daddy. Despite being the shortest Lobo at five feet four inches, the voluptuous and bespectacled firecracker with a killer attention to detail and a soft razor shag has only two settings: destroy or asleep. She's the best person to have in your corner, but the worst to go head-to-head with. Fucking Aries bitch.

"I hung out with Guy last night," Mac says, crossing her arms as she squares up to me. Fuck. Of course, Guy fucking told her. They're best friends. I didn't expect him to lie, but I also assumed they'd have better things to talk about than me. Wide-eyed and mouths agape, I can feel the other three turn to stare.

"You're *dating* Guy," Nat stammers.

Mac's eyes bug. The one person she's more protective of than us is Guy. She would probably kill me in cold blood right now if she thought that the two of us were messing around. "No, Daddy. Seriously, I would never," I say quickly before I turn to the other three, blurting out, "I'm working at Princess Pizzarina."

"What?" Lex gasps before the utter chaos of voices breaks out. The overwhelming, energetic tidal wave nearly knocks me back. All three women are talking over one another, hurling questions at me. Mac simply glares at me amidst the mayhem.

"Stop," I demand on an exhale. Mac pokes the inside of her cheek with her tongue as she waits for me to continue. "Guy was desperate to get someone... I'm just helping out," I say.

"Just helping out," Mac repeats as she studies me. It's hard to read her expression.

Mac knows as well as I do that working for Mother Wolf might not be a long-term situation for me. Not if Cita has anything to say about it. My mother and I don't always see eye to eye.

Mac takes a deep breath. Then she asks, "Why didn't you tell us?"

I shake my head because she knows the answer. "Please don't tell Cita or Lulu," I start, but Mac puts her hand up.

"They're going to find out. They should hear it from you," Mac says firmly.

I nod. She is right. However, that's a bridge I can't cross. Not yet, at least. "I will," I say, but my tone isn't very convincing.

I'm fully prepared for Mac to start chewing me out, but to my utter shock, she just nods slowly. "Ok... So what can we do to help?" Mac asks with a shrug. This is the softest my sister will ever be with any of us.

I throw my arms around her neck. "Thank you," I say before feeling the other three envelop us in a group hug.

"Get off," Mac yells from within the cocoon of our bodies.

As we all finish our opening tasks, I recount the past few weeks, how I've been ingratiating myself with the Princess crew, how I've been basically playing dumb to Raff's intimidation tactics. By the time Mac has turned the sign and unlocked the front door, I'm laying out my plan to turn everyone against him and overthrow his reign of terror.

"Damn. Never underestimate a woman scorned," Nat says on a raspy laugh.

"I'm not a woman scorned," I reply. However, I do catch my sisters exchanging a pointed glance. "I'm not," I assert.

Lucky for me, before they can push the topic further, our early morning rush picks up. Mac and Van run the pastry counter, while Nat plays barista. Lex and I head into the back to finish baking off what we need for the rest of the day and prep everything for tomorrow.

By ten thirty, we start to hit a lull in customer traffic. Lex puts on a fresh pot of drip coffee while I make lunch for everyone: thick slices of our rustic bread toasted and topped with a layer of creamy ricotta cheese, a generous spoonful of Lulu's pesto, blistered cherry tomatoes, and then drizzled with fresh olive oil and a hefty pinch of flaky sea salt and cracked pepper. "We're going to smell great," Nat says dryly as I hand her a plate. She takes a deep inhale of the pungent garlic in Lulu's pesto.

"Yeah, yeah," I say, rolling my eyes. Nat thinks she's funnier than she actually is... a major character flaw, but it is also her most redeeming quality. She's infuriatingly gorgeous with perfect skin and a toned yogi body that makes men fall to their knees. Ironically, though, fall as they might, Natalie Komatsu is only interested in women. So maybe she does have a sense of humor after all.

I nudge her with my hip as we switch places. Lex and I will man the bakery while the other three eat. Then Lex will take her food to go as she has an afternoon class. I, on the other hand, have to close down the kitchen.

Mac has all but taken over the managerial work from Cita and Lulu, but make no mistake, they are still very much in charge. They have made it perfectly clear that we will have to pry Mother Wolf from their cold, dead hands... something that I know my sister Mac has strong feelings about, too. Like me, she lives in the shadow of our family's success. It is painful that Cita and Lulu will never retire.

Despite my mother and aunt working only a reduced schedule in the bakery, their presence is always felt. Typically, they'd be pushing me out the door when Lex leaves for class, but this week, Cita and Lulu are in San Francisco staying with friends for some big Grateful Dead festival. Honestly, it's been nice to not feel them all over us for once. We can breathe a little.

I finish pulling a shot of espresso for one of our regulars, Dave, when Mac walks out of the kitchen. She angles the plate she's carrying towards me. "What's this?" she asks with a raised eyebrow. I place the espresso and a slice of lemon on the long wooden bar for Dave, before casually glancing at Mac's plate.

She's showing me a pavlova topped with thinly sliced and charred citrus and garnished with roughly chopped pistachios and a light balsamic drizzle. "Just something I was messing around with," I shrug.

Dave whistles from across the bar. "Can I get one?" he asks eagerly.

I shake my head. This would be a huge no-no if Cita or Lulu were here. They are adamant that nothing be altered or

"I'm not a woman scorned," I reply. However, I do catch my sisters exchanging a pointed glance. "I'm not," I assert.

Lucky for me, before they can push the topic further, our early morning rush picks up. Mac and Van run the pastry counter, while Nat plays barista. Lex and I head into the back to finish baking off what we need for the rest of the day and prep everything for tomorrow.

By ten thirty, we start to hit a lull in customer traffic. Lex puts on a fresh pot of drip coffee while I make lunch for everyone: thick slices of our rustic bread toasted and topped with a layer of creamy ricotta cheese, a generous spoonful of Lulu's pesto, blistered cherry tomatoes, and then drizzled with fresh olive oil and a hefty pinch of flaky sea salt and cracked pepper. "We're going to smell great," Nat says dryly as I hand her a plate. She takes a deep inhale of the pungent garlic in Lulu's pesto.

"Yeah, yeah," I say, rolling my eyes. Nat thinks she's funnier than she actually is... a major character flaw, but it is also her most redeeming quality. She's infuriatingly gorgeous with perfect skin and a toned yogi body that makes men fall to their knees. Ironically, though, fall as they might, Natalie Komatsu is only interested in women. So maybe she does have a sense of humor after all.

I nudge her with my hip as we switch places. Lex and I will man the bakery while the other three eat. Then Lex will take her food to go as she has an afternoon class. I, on the other hand, have to close down the kitchen.

Mac has all but taken over the managerial work from Cita and Lulu, but make no mistake, they are still very much in charge. They have made it perfectly clear that we will have to pry Mother Wolf from their cold, dead hands... something that I know my sister Mac has strong feelings about, too. Like me, she lives in the shadow of our family's success. It is painful that Cita and Lulu will never retire.

Despite my mother and aunt working only a reduced schedule in the bakery, their presence is always felt. Typically, they'd be pushing me out the door when Lex leaves for class, but this week, Cita and Lulu are in San Francisco staying with friends for some big Grateful Dead festival. Honestly, it's been nice to not feel them all over us for once. We can breathe a little.

I finish pulling a shot of espresso for one of our regulars, Dave, when Mac walks out of the kitchen. She angles the plate she's carrying towards me. "What's this?" she asks with a raised eyebrow. I place the espresso and a slice of lemon on the long wooden bar for Dave, before casually glancing at Mac's plate.

She's showing me a pavlova topped with thinly sliced and charred citrus and garnished with roughly chopped pistachios and a light balsamic drizzle. "Just something I was messing around with," I shrug.

Dave whistles from across the bar. "Can I get one?" he asks eagerly.

I shake my head. This would be a huge no-no if Cita or Lulu were here. They are adamant that nothing be altered or

“I’m not a woman scorned,” I reply. However, I do catch my sisters exchanging a pointed glance. “I’m not,” I assert.

Lucky for me, before they can push the topic further, our early morning rush picks up. Mac and Van run the pastry counter, while Nat plays barista. Lex and I head into the back to finish baking off what we need for the rest of the day and prep everything for tomorrow.

By ten thirty, we start to hit a lull in customer traffic. Lex puts on a fresh pot of drip coffee while I make lunch for everyone: thick slices of our rustic bread toasted and topped with a layer of creamy ricotta cheese, a generous spoonful of Lulu’s pesto, blistered cherry tomatoes, and then drizzled with fresh olive oil and a hefty pinch of flaky sea salt and cracked pepper. “We’re going to smell great,” Nat says dryly as I hand her a plate. She takes a deep inhale of the pungent garlic in Lulu’s pesto.

“Yeah, yeah,” I say, rolling my eyes. Nat thinks she’s funnier than she actually is... a major character flaw, but it is also her most redeeming quality. She’s infuriatingly gorgeous with perfect skin and a toned yogi body that makes men fall to their knees. Ironically, though, fall as they might, Natalie Komatsu is only interested in women. So maybe she does have a sense of humor after all.

I nudge her with my hip as we switch places. Lex and I will man the bakery while the other three eat. Then Lex will take her food to go as she has an afternoon class. I, on the other hand, have to close down the kitchen.

Mac has all but taken over the managerial work from Cita and Lulu, but make no mistake, they are still very much in charge. They have made it perfectly clear that we will have to pry Mother Wolf from their cold, dead hands... something that I know my sister Mac has strong feelings about, too. Like me, she lives in the shadow of our family's success. It is painful that Cita and Lulu will never retire.

Despite my mother and aunt working only a reduced schedule in the bakery, their presence is always felt. Typically, they'd be pushing me out the door when Lex leaves for class, but this week, Cita and Lulu are in San Francisco staying with friends for some big Grateful Dead festival. Honestly, it's been nice to not feel them all over us for once. We can breathe a little.

I finish pulling a shot of espresso for one of our regulars, Dave, when Mac walks out of the kitchen. She angles the plate she's carrying towards me. "What's this?" she asks with a raised eyebrow. I place the espresso and a slice of lemon on the long wooden bar for Dave, before casually glancing at Mac's plate.

She's showing me a pavlova topped with thinly sliced and charred citrus and garnished with roughly chopped pistachios and a light balsamic drizzle. "Just something I was messing around with," I shrug.

Dave whistles from across the bar. "Can I get one?" he asks eagerly.

I shake my head. This would be a huge no-no if Cita or Lulu were here. They are adamant that nothing be altered or

added to their perfect menu. I'm about to tell Dave no, but Mac slides the plate across the bar towards him. "On the house. But keep it quiet," she says in a sweet and conspiratorial tone. "It's off menu."

In a way that exaggerates his crowfeet, Dave winks at her before accepting the plate. "Meet me in the office," Mac says in a low tone. Fuck. She's definitely going to chew me out.

"I like that you're helping Guy," Mac starts cautiously. I feel my eyebrows shoot up in surprise. "But I'm not going to lie for you," she adds. I cross my arms as I lean back across from her.

"Which is probably why, I'm assuming, you didn't tell me." I nod. She gets it. "So how bad is it?" she asks, her curiosity finally getting the better of her.

"Typical Raff bullshit. He's so talented, but he just gets in his own damn way," I say.

Mac exhales a 'ha' sound. Raff is the reason that we have the informal Girls rule and Boys drool policy at the bakery. He briefly worked as an apprentice baker at Mother Wolf, so Mac is very familiar with his antics. "So what... you're going to take over if Raff leaves," she asks.

I know that she's trying to work out what will happen with Mother Wolf if I bail again. I shake my head, which I can see relaxes her shoulders slightly. "I don't think it's long-term, per se... I just want to..." I trail off.

How can I tell her? What I want is stupid. Maybe too stupid to say out loud at the very least. It doesn't totally make sense either. Right now, Princess Pizzarina is just as stifling as Mother Wolf... but it's also different... new. Unencumbered. And the harder I work to loosen Raff up, the more I feel the environment shifting.

"Ok," she starts. "I'm going to move the schedule around to make sure you don't die of exhaustion." I tilt my head back and exhale deeply. Thank God. I'm not sure that I would be able to keep this up without having a total psychotic break. However, my relief is short-lived. "Ash, whatever is going on with you, please don't make us lie... Not again," Mac says.

Chapter 4

RAFF

"Don't feed her that," Guy warns. I roll my eyes as I pull back the outstretched peanut butter pretzel that Minnie has been sniffing. He glances over his shoulder at me from the fridge inside the open garage. "Seriously, don't give her that," he says.

"Why," I say, feeling like I want to fuck with him a bit. I know his dog, Minnie, has a temperamental stomach, but I can't resist.

"She'll throw up," he says, popping the top off a Lagunitas beer and handing it to me.

"You're just worried she's getting fat," I reply, accepting the glass bottle. Minnie is a Great Pyrenees mix. She's already over a hundred pounds and mainly fur.

Guy exhales. He's used to my bullshit, and honestly, he's probably the only one who isn't shaken by it... well he was the only one. Now it seems that a certain pint-sized brunette is also unfazed. Shit. It's my day off. I don't want to be thinking about Ashley Morgan Lobo.

I certainly do not want to be thinking about the soft hair at the nape of her neck or the way her full lips roll when she's concentrating. The first thought that popped into my head this morning was how she extends her pinky fingers out when she's pulling dough. It's so strange and so specific. It makes her hands look really elegant, like the hands of a chick in a Renaissance painting. I caught myself watching her the other day. To the point where she stopped and turned to me.

Eyebrow cocked, she asked, "What's up?" I just had to pretend that she was overworking it.

Jesus Christ, I need to get laid. These past few weeks have been the longest I've ever gone without sex since I was sixteen. I should go to the bars tonight. I need to blow off some steam. I've been pent up since Guy stepped in.

"Are we playing or not?" I ask as I set down my beer and pick up the nearby basketball. It's rare for either of us to have a day off together since we opened Princess Pizzarina. However, the benefit of being roommates is that we get to shoot hoops in the driveway on the outside chance that both of us are free.

It's been this way since we first became friends over twenty years ago. However, back then it wasn't Guy's house. It was Louise's. If we weren't roaming around the boardwalk or the woods, we always hung out here. In high school, I practically lived with Guy and his grandmother.

We'd carve figure eights on our skateboards in the garage when it was raining too hard to go to the parking lot behind the elementary school. Louise let us keep our surfboards on the side of the house, even if she did lean out of her bedroom window, Virginia Slim in hand, yelling,

“Watch the stucco, you little rats.” She installed the basketball hoop when we were in middle school, so we’d stop getting into so much trouble. Louise was cool as shit.

Neither of us would say it out loud, but we missed her a lot. The money she’d left Guy enabled us to start our restaurant. Even in death, the old bird was looking out for us.

Guy puts down his beer, opening his hands for me to toss him the ball. He bounces it a few times before he shoots it up over my head towards the hoop. I try to jump, but I just look dumb as the ball sails clean over my fingertips. Lucky for me, Guy has horrible aim.

The ball bounces off the backboard and straight into my waiting hands. I jump up, tipping the ball over the rim into the basket. “Count it, suckah,” I gloat as I make a show of jogging around the driveway.

“Jesus, you’re more annoying than usual today,” Guy says as he retrieves the ball.

“And whose fault is that,” I say.

Guy shakes his head. “Your own damn fault.”

He tosses the ball in yet another feeble attempt at a free-throw. This time, I can jump high enough and swat the ball out of the air. “I’m going insane, man.”

“Seriously, it’s only been like two months,” he says with a raised eyebrow.

"How the hell do you do this celibacy thing?" I ask. I bounce the ball a few times, but Guy steals it and attempts another shot.

"Who says I'm celibate?" Guy asks.

I snort a laugh. We share a house, thin walls and all. If Guy were bringing anyone home, I'd know about it. "I never said that you needed to be celibate. Just don't fuck our employees. Have you ever thought about finding someone you like and dating them?" he replies as we both watch the ball bounce off the rim.

"Oh yeah," I say, catching the wayward ball. "How's that going for you?"

Guy shakes his head. "What about Nora?" I ask, tossing the ball back to Guy. He holds it firmly against his chest.

"Dude, no."

I'm not being serious, but Guy's response is too quick. Sure, in the past, I would have easily fallen into something with her. She's cute enough. Let's be honest, it's nice to have someone so eager to please. She started the same week as Ashley, but they couldn't be more different.

"Seriously, man. Don't."

I put my hands up. "That's the old me. The new Raff is going to find a nice girl, just like you said. No more shitting where I eat." I use my index finger to draw an X shape over my chest.

Guy makes a face. "Gross. But thanks, I guess."

I know that my bullshit is fucking Guy up. He is the stable one. He has to be responsible. Without him, we would have folded a long time ago. However, I know that it isn't his dream to keep me in line all the time. When we started Princess, my dream was to have a sick restaurant, and his was to brew our own beer. A two-phase plan... but we've been stuck in the first phase for almost five years. I don't know how much longer Guy can keep being the reliable saint that he has to be all the time.

Minnie is suddenly up on her feet. She's shaking her hips and tail in a clumsy wobble as she trots down the driveway towards a familiar pair of clogs. "Speak of the devil," I say with a wry smile. Guy glares at me as he turns down the driveway.

"Hi, Minnie, baby," Mackenzie Morgan Lobo says, crouching down to pet the dog.

I continue to bounce the ball, ignoring Mac as she straightens up and advances towards Guy. "Hey," Guy says, jogging towards her.

She hands Guy something wrapped in butcher paper. "Hell yeah," Guy says with a smile.

"Where's mine?" I ask sarcastically.

"Whoops. Must have forgotten you existed," Mac replies.

I jut out my hand. "See! This is how you act around someone that you dislike," I say.

Guy brings an oversized hand up to his face. Mac looks at him with confusion. "He's making a point," Guy exhales.

"Which is," Mac asks.

"If you don't like someone, you react. You say snide comments. Or do purposefully mean things like exclude them from sandwich deliveries," I continue.

Mac rolls her eyes and pulls another wrapped sandwich from her bag. "Here, you big baby," she says, thrusting the item into my hands.

"He's freaked out that Ash isn't being outright mean to him... which I said is normal because she's not a dick. Unlike him," Guy says, plucking the sandwich out of my grasp and handing it back to Mac. "I know that you didn't just give him your's."

Mac shakes her head. "There's more at the blue house. He can have it." I grab for the sandwich, but Guy lifts it up over his head and out of my reach. "It's alright. I can't stay long anyway. I have to go to Van's final dress fitting," Mac says.

Guy reluctantly lowers the sandwich down. I snatch it hastily. Unwrapping it, I take a deep inhale. Mac is by no means a chef, not on the same level as her sister. However, the sandwiches that she makes for Guy every Monday are insane.

I first discovered the sandwiches a few years ago. Guy had left half of one in the fridge while he was out. It was just screaming to be tasted. They're always different, but each is a near masterpiece. Today's is probably her best work yet.

Premium tuna packed in olive oil, chopped with garbanzo beans, pickled jalapeños, diced red onion, and dill pickles, minced garlic, lemon, kewpie mayo, and thinly sliced pepperonis, with a generous sprinkle of salt and pepper. There are a few thin slices of avocado and shredded iceberg lettuce that help to keep the chopped tuna salad contained on a fresh ciabatta roll. This sandwich is transcendent. She's cooking on a new level with this one.

Mac isn't my biggest fan. Not since I told everyone in our seventh-grade math class that she had the biggest boobs in the entire school. To be fair, I was dared by Ahmed Rehab to do it, and she totally did have the biggest boobs in school. Besides, Guy already gave me a dead arm for it anyway. However, despite this fact, she will on occasion bring me a sandwich. Though I am not totally sure why. These Lobo women are confusing.

I take my first tangy, chewy bite. Relishing in the satisfying flavors as Guy and Mac continue to discuss something about someone's wedding dress. When I take a sip of my beer, the lingering acid from the sandwich, mixed with the mellow, creamy flavor of the Laguinitas, is so satisfying that I suddenly blurt out, "Marry me."

Stunned, Guy whips towards me as Mac throws her head back. Her cackle is so loud that Minnie jerks up to standing from where she was lying on the smooth epoxy garage floor. "You're definitely not my type," she says.

"What," I say in response to Guy's glare. "You said I should date someone I like."

Guy drags his hand over his face with a deep exhale. "You just like the sandwich," Guy says sharply as I open my mouth.

"Then I have bad news for you," she says, her grin turning diabolical. "Ash made these." I nearly snort my beer through my nose. Mac laughs again.

"Can I get some relief from Ashley Morgan Lobo today?"

"Why are you thinking about my sister so much, you creep?" Mac asks, taking a sip of Guy's beer.

"Maybe he's got a crush," Guy says. I shoot him a look. This is a line that I don't think he wants to cross with Mackenzie here.

Fuck. I need to get laid tonight. "You guys suck," I say, heading inside.

"It was a joke. Where are you going?" Guy calls.

I just keep walking. The last thing I hear as I open the door into the house is Mac asking Guy, "Oh shit, you don't think he actually…" I let the door close behind me, unwilling to contemplate the sentiment.

Chapter 5

ASH

Cita drives an old Dodge Ram cargo van from the 90s. As the early July sun magnifies through the windshield, I can feel the skin on the back of my thighs suctioning to the blue leather bench seat with each jostling turn she takes. Besides Lulu's open window, there is very little ventilation coming through the slivered quarter-glass openings in the back of the van. And, of course, the A/C has been busted for years. The roar of the freeway is deafening as Cita barrels us toward San Jose.

We're on our way to Rudy's Bridals and Special Occasions. Cita and Lulu insisted that we carpool because "why waste gas when the catering truck is big enough." Of course, when they learned that Van was driving separately with Cary's mother and Nat was teaching, Cita refused to reinstall the back rows of bench seats. She didn't want to remove the stack of folding tables that was now sliding and crashing violently in the empty cavern of space behind us.

Cita strains forward, clutching the steering wheel as she peers down through glasses that are balancing precariously at the very tip of her nose. Lulu, on the other hand, has slipped off her sandals and propped one bare foot up on the scorching dash, letting her toes tan while keeping the other foot neatly tucked up underneath her. They're practically identical, except Lulu wears her salt and pepper he actually…" I let the door close behind me, unwilling to contemplate the sentiment.

Chapter 5

ASH

Cita drives an old Dodge Ram cargo van from the 90s. As the early July sun magnifies through the windshield, I can feel the skin on the back of my thighs suctioning to the blue leather bench seat with each jostling turn she takes. Besides Lulu's open window, there is very little ventilation coming through the slivered quarter-glass openings in the back of the van. And, of course, the A/C has been busted for years. The roar of the freeway is deafening as Cita barrels us toward San Jose.

We're on our way to Rudy's Bridals and Special Occasions. Cita and Lulu insisted that we carpool because "why waste gas when the catering truck is big enough." Of course, when they learned that Van was driving separately with Cary's mother and Nat was teaching, Cita refused to reinstall the back rows of bench seats. She didn't want to remove the stack of folding tables that was now sliding and crashing violently in the empty cavern of space behind us.

Cita strains forward, clutching the steering wheel as she peers down through glasses that are balancing precariously at the very tip of her nose. Lulu, on the other hand, has slipped off her sandals and propped one bare foot up on the scorching dash, letting her toes tan while keeping the other foot neatly tucked up underneath her. They're practically identical, except Lulu wears her salt and pepper hair in a long braid slung over one shoulder while Cita's hair is cropped in a wiry bob. They used to get mistaken for Joan Baez and Mimi Farina back in the day.

My sisters and I are squished together on one sweaty bench seat. Our hair whipping around our faces wildly, skin on our bare arms sticking together, and the scream of traffic drowning out Joni Mitchell's Cactus Tree that Lulu is blasting on the radio.

It's for the best, though. I've been avoiding Cita and Lulu since they got back into town. I know that I need to tell them. I *will* tell them. However, Cita and Lulu tend to overreact. So, with them, timing is everything.

Cita's eyes shoot up to the rearview mirror, homing in on mine. I quickly dart my gaze out the window. "What, mami?" Mac calls. Cita and Lulu have been talking this entire drive. We, of course, cannot hear a word they've said. They've been chattering happily in the bubble of the front cab. The entire hour-long trip has been punctuated by one of us yelling for clarification every few sentences. It's all been harmless, but I'm on edge nonetheless.

Cita narrows her eyes in the rearview as she attempts for a second time to say whatever it is she's saying. To my right, Lex suddenly starts to sputter. She's somehow inhaled a strand of my long hair and is gagging. This causes Lulu to spin around in her bucket seat and start thrusting half-empty, discarded mason jars of water and home-brewed sun tea towards Lex. Cita swerves slightly to get a look at the chaos behind her. To my left, Mac is rubbing her temples. "Eyes on the fucking road, Cita!" No doubt a migraine is building behind Mac's eyes.

We finally make it to the fitting, sweaty and disheveled. Apparently, what Cita had been trying to ask the entire last ten minutes of the drive was if anyone wanted to stop to get a coffee. My mother is the only person in the world who wants to drink hot coffee at any time, in any place, or at any temperature. It's alarming to see a diminutive Latina sitting poolside in the 105-degree Las Vegas sun, sipping black coffee in a bright teal tankini.

Meredith Phillips purses her lips at us as we step into the shop. She stands stoically to the side as we all envelop Van in sweaty hugs and kisses. Cary's mother is Palo Alto posh. She benevolently tolerates Van, who is demure and polite. However, she's less than thrilled to be encountering the rest of us. Especially as she takes in my sisters and I as we feebly attempt to fan the fabric under our armpits in the most discreet way possible. Classy.

Much to Van's chagrin, Lulu and Cita turn their affection towards the rail-thin matriarch. They start to hug and jostle Meredith. Each woman grasping one of Meredith's bony elbows in their hand and escorting her towards the long, champagne-colored sofas. Much to her credit, Meredith is doing a good job of gracefully enduring our family. She's gracious as my mother and aunt speak over one another to machine gun Meredith with questions about her day, where she got her stunning shift dress, if she hit any traffic, and any other random thought that pops into their heads.

Rudy herself is waiting for us in all of her satin pantsuit splendor. She's been helping Van with the entire process of choosing, ordering, and fitting her wedding dress. To Meredith's relief, she is released as my mother and aunt immediately envelop Rudy in an unsolicited embrace.

Rudy accepts this affection much more readily than Meredith had, as she is now nearly six months deep into a relationship with Cita and Lulu. This time, all three women are rapid-firing pleasantries of "how are the grandkids, how's business," and "can you believe that those lousy Giants lost to the Padres last night?" Honestly, if Van told me that the three of them had been on a secret group chat, I'd believe her, no questions asked.

Rudy is also tiny. So, she is a perfect match for Cita and Lulu. She's a cheery Filipino woman in her late sixties with a mop of overly processed curls and the shortest neck I've ever seen. Rudy's chin is essentially sitting on her chest. It's a very good thing that Rudy's short because she is effectively smiling up at everyone she encounters.

We're all instructed to sit on the long sofas positioned in front of a trifold of well-lit mirrors. Van is whisked off with Rudy as the rest of us are tended to by Rudy's teenage grandson, Trevor. "Can I get you something to drink?" he asks in a tone that is nothing short of disassociation. It is obvious that Trevor would rather be spending his summer vacation anywhere other than Rudy's Bridals and Special Occasions.

There is a stagnant pause that occurs after the grandson departs to fetch our drinks. Meredith attempts to make small talk, but it's clear she's unsure how to connect with us, commoners. "Who's working if you're all here?" she begins in an almost accusatory manner. Lulu and Cita aren't paying attention as they're both looking through Lulu's oversized purse.

Lex and I look awkwardly at Mac, who is effectively our spokesperson as the oldest. She clears her throat and says, "We close early on Mondays."

Meredith nods thoughtfully. Perhaps looking for common ground or something to compliment, she scans our outfits. In an attempt to dress for the occasion, we're all wearing some sort of summer dress. Mac is in a navy polka-dotted slip dress, an open chambray denim shirt knotted at the waist, and a pair of leather slingback platform clogs. Lex has donned a transparent pink camisole tulle dress over a brown leotard and green cowboy boots. I am positive that she spray-painted the thrifted boots that specific shade of jade herself. I am just wearing an old, oversized black backless maxi dress, which, in all honesty, might be a pool cover-up. All our tattoos are on full display. Meredith quickly darts her eyes between us. Obviously unsure of how to say something nice about our attire, she settles on, "You all look so unique."

She's attempting to think of another question to ask when Cita's hand suddenly shoots out of Lulu's purse. She's holding a disposable camera over her head and waving it around wildly. "You found it," Lulu singsongs as she claps excitedly. "Everyone scooch together," Cita demands. So, we all oblige.

"Shoulders back, Ashley," my mother hisses.

"Cita, just take the fucking photo," Mac scolds. Meredith is definitely not used to our kind of crassness and makes a sound that can only be described as a surprised mouse. I can feel Lex's shoulders shaking with silent laughter beside me. My smile tightens as Cita clicks the shutter.

She cranks the film roll and exclaims, "That's going in the scrapbook for their children."

Meredith is usually good at guarding her facial expressions, but I clock Meredith grimacing when Cita mentions Van and Cary having kids. I'm pretty sure that Lulu doesn't notice because she turns to Meredith to ask, "Should we do a silly one next?" Mac and I exchange an amused glance as Meredith echoes the word silly in a puzzled tone.

Meredith is spared from any additional group photos as Van emerges from the changing room. She looks stunning in the Bohemian style dress. Delicate lace, a flowing silhouette, deep v-neckline, and bell sleeves make Van look effortless, feminine, and timeless. Her hair is flowing in long dark waves over her shoulders, accentuating the ethereal look of the gown. Van is perfect. Exactly like herself in the best possible way.

My sisters link arms with one another, each making a little sniffling sound. This is when I should feel something. Looking at my beautiful cousin, standing in the strategic lighting, on the precipice of a major life event, is when I should feel that little lump that catches in the middle of my throat. My eyes should be tingling. I should be crying or smiling or some emotion that is linked to deep fucking happiness, right?

However, I catch a glance of myself in the oversized gold-framed mirrors. I look the same as always. Blank. A stone in the middle of a rushing river of emotion. Everyone is easily flowing around me as I'm stuck in place. Unmoved. I press my lips together and will myself to form a smile.

Everyone on the sofa next to me is feeling something. Fuck — even Meredith's face is showing her feelings. Although I can't tell if her face is expressing extreme happiness or dread. It's obvious that Meredith has had a facelift in the past ten years. Her lower eyelids don't always match the rest of her facial expression, so it's difficult to tell. However, after another glance, I'm leaning towards dread.

I look at Van, hoping that she hasn't noticed. Only she's smiling at herself in the mirror as Rudy walks around her, fluffing up the ruffly lace details on the bottom of her hem. Van is experiencing something incredible. She's decided to do something despite not knowing the outcome. She's choosing to have faith that everything will work out.

Van wants to be married. She wants to have kids. Fuck, I'm pretty sure she even wants the dog and the white picket fence, too. Although she's probably more of a rescue mutt-and-geodesic-dome-house type. She wants all that, even with all of our fucked-up family history. She's going after what she wants without any guarantee that it won't hurt like hell.

I'm quickly pulled back to reality when I hear the wail next to me. Cita is latched onto Lulu, bracing her sister as Lulu sobs. "My baby is getting m-m-married!" Van steps off the low pedestal and makes her way to console Lulu.

"Mascara," Rudy shrieks in her thick Tagalog accent, but the threat of makeup stains doesn't stop Van. She's embracing her tiny mother and stroking the top of her wavy black hair, and making a shushing noise.

I do feel something then. Pity. Mama is a joke nickname, but all jokes have at least one kernel of truth. I often wonder if Vanessa would be so caring and nurturing if she didn't always have to be. Cita and Lulu are the parents, but Van and Mac raised us. All of us.

They take care of Cita and Lulu as much as anyone else. However, you could never say this out loud to them. Cita and Lulu desperately need to keep the illusion of control. Without control, what would they have?

When the fitting is done, and the complimentary drinks are drunk. Cita and Lulu make a big to-do about presenting Rudy with their credit cards. They have taken pride in purchasing this dress for Van. The same way they felt about paying for all of our braces and bachelor's degrees. Despite their immense wealth, Cary's family has not contributed a single cent. A fact that has given Cita and Lulu great satisfaction. All of us Lobos have been chipping in to cover the entire cost of this wedding.

This was very important to Van. To all of us, really. We're not poor by any means. The bakery does well. Plus, all of us work second jobs. So, unless someone is hiding a gambling addiction, no one is hurting for money. We're just not Phillips rich. Cary and his two older brothers all grew up knowing that hefty trust funds would be available to them.

Van doesn't want anyone in the Phillips circle to think that she was trying to marry into money. This has always been a sore spot for Cary and Vanessa's relationship. She told Mac that the first time she met Cary's middle brother, Carson, he casually said, as if Van weren't even in the room, "She's pretty, but is she willing to sign a prenup?" He didn't even have the decency to look up from his phone.

So yeah. Let Cita and Lulu wave their credit cards around. Fuck I'd even pay for it with the meager wad of tips I keep stashed in a tin above the fridge. I love my cousin, and I'm glad that she's happy. My eyes dart back to Meredith, who looks like she's smelling garbage. I am certain in that moment that all of us are tolerating Meredith Phillips just as much as she's tolerating us.

The trip back up the mountain is much better than the way down. Cita and Lulu are in high spirits. They keep leaning over and nudging each other jovially as they recount how beautiful Van looked. Lex asks if either of them wants to see the photos she took with her phone, but they wave her off. Reliving the shared memory is grander than the actual experience. The two of them are working themselves into a foamy lather of excitement.

This is the time to tell them, I think.

Chapter 6

ASH

The Tide Water is in full form tonight. Pool balls crack together somewhere behind me. Dumpy, graying regulars with their gin noses and bloodshot eyes mutter and cough at the bar. Weed and cigarette smoke linger. My shoes stick to the floor as I sway in front of the Cosmic Blast jukebox. They make a satisfying pop as I lift my heels with each rock from side to side.

"Play it again," Stan or Liam says. I don't remember which one is which. They are two randoms just in town on business. They have somehow infiltrated our group. Stan, I think, is the shorter one with cystic acne on his neck and cargo shorts. While his companion, Liam, is the tall and leering type. Either way, one of them is talking right now.

"Ash, maybe we should put something else on," Van says gently. I pause my swaying and brace my forearms on the greasy glass of the machine.

"Why," I grunt out.

"Because if you play Never Tear Us Apart for the fifth time, Raj is going to stab you," Mac says bluntly from the booth next to us. I spin around and stare dumbly at the portly man with overgrown mutton chops behind the bar. He is the human embodiment of a ribeye steak, a big slab of fatty meat.

“Raj would never,” I gasp. “We’re best friends! Right, Raj.”

In wordless reply, he drags a stout thumb across his thick neck as he stares at me unblinking.

“But what about our matching tattoos,” I yell far too loudly.

To be clear, Raj and I do have matching tattoos. However, we didn’t get them together. I’ve always liked the American traditional rose tattoo that Raj has on his forearm. So as a cheeky twenty-two-year-old, I went out and got one to match.

When I proudly showed him, Saran Wrap still fresh, all he had mustered in reply was a flat, “neat, kid.”

“I’d protect you,” I assume Liam barely whispers to Lex. She side eyes him. “No, thank you,” Mac cuts in sharply. She’s definitely going to fight one of these dudes tonight. They have been hovering around for the last twenty-five minutes.

The short one was way too eager. He made a beeline for Mac straight out of the gate. He’s been showering her with backhanded compliments since he glommed on. “For a big girl, you’re actually tiny,” he’d started.

“For an adult man, so are you,” she’d replied. Surprisingly, this hasn’t deterred him yet. The spindly one has been awkwardly muttering towards Lex, who has been fighting a laugh this entire time.

“Don’t you think the beginning of this song kinda sounds like Back That Azz Up,” I say, spinning around towards the booth.

“Play that song next,” Stan demands, lifting his arms up over his head, revealing fresh pit stains.

“Genius idea,” I agree. For whatever reason (six vodka cranberries), I decide the easiest way to get to my wallet is to crawl under the table to reach the pile of purses stacked between Nat and Lex.

“No,” Mac immediately scolds as she yanks me out from below the table.

“Ouch,” I say.

She pinches my arm, pulling me to standing. “We’re going home,” she starts, but I wriggle out of her grasp.

“Why? It’s not like I have to work at the bakery tomorrow,” I protest, giving her a pointed look.

Cita and Lulu had not taken the news well. When I told them about Princess Pizzarina, the car immediately fell silent. Fuck, even the tables in the back didn’t so much as rattle. All of the air seemed to be sucked out of the van. Then it happened. Cita started yelling accusingly, and Lulu immediately started to cry. It was hard to distinguish what each of them was saying, but I got the gist.

Then, because I am dumb, and told them twenty minutes into an hour-long drive, after about thirty minutes of this behavior, they suddenly switched roles. Cita started to cry fat, cartoonish tears while Lulu was yelling about "how I could possibly make my mother cry." It carried on like this until we pulled into the driveway of the blue house. They both immediately ran inside, up the stairs, and slammed their bedroom doors behind them. Teenagers.

Seriously, it's not like I'm the only one who has work outside of Mother Wolf. Nat and Van teach yoga. Lex is an artist and a full-time student. Hell, Mac even does seasonal work as a wedding photographer in the spring and summer. They just don't like that it's another restaurant. Cita and Lulu hate that I could be successful without their permission.

When they get like this, Cita and Lulu are beyond reason. Mac had attempted to talk some sense into them while they ranted and sobbed. Much to both of my sisters' credit, they had tried to work out the logic with the pair. However, this only sparked a long diatribe about how my mother thought "maybe taking over ops management was too much pressure for Mac." Sensing that a much larger blowup was about to come of it, I steered the conversation back to my situation.

At the blue house, when I attempted to explain myself to the twins, they both refused to speak to me. "This is a huge betrayal," Cita had said through her closed bedroom door.

"Why did you even come back if you weren't going to make the bakery your priority?" Lulu had asked.

Mac had assured me that they just needed a little time to cool off. Then, forty-five minutes later, when we were huddled around the kitchen island, eating Lulu's homemade hummus straight out of the tub rather than making dinner, Mac received a text from Cita. They demanded that she remove me from the schedule indefinitely and drive me back to my own home. Fired and banished on the same day. Cool. So here we are, six vodka cranberries deep.

The weather in Northern California fluctuates wildly. The heat of the day is now replaced with a chilly mountain breeze, somewhere in the low fifties. Despite their instructions, I didn't go home after the disaster at the blue house. I just came straight to The Tide Water and started drinking. So now I'm shivering in my stupid backless cotton dress.

"Let's dance," I proclaim as I make my way back to the small opening between the bar and the jukebox.

"Hell, yeah," the little guy hollers.

"Raj, my man, I'll have another," I call out as I lift my empty tumbler, giving it a shake. Ice falls out of the glass onto the top of my head.

This definitely isn't a dance floor, but I'm drunk enough to make it one. I'm quickly reminded, as it hits me full force in the back of the head, that the "dance floor" is actually a clearing for the heavy wooden door to swing inwards. I'm just off kilter enough that I go tumbling forward onto my hands and knees, ass straight up. *Thank God this is a maxi dress,* I think. I immediately regret that Back That Azz Up is scoring this moment in time.

"Shit," the swinger says. I scramble to my feet, clumsily stepping on the hem of my dress in the process. I desperately hold up the neckline in a bunched fist. I wheel around with my finger jutted out. "What the hell," I start, only to realize that Guy is the one who opened the door.

"You ok?" he asks, steadying me.

Then, to our surprise, the door swings open again. This time, sending Guy stumbling into me and Mac, who initially stepped forward to help me up. Luckily, Guy is much sturdier than either of us. He holds onto my wrist and Mac's waist, keeping us mostly upright, which is a good thing because stocky Stan is crowding us from the other side. We're essentially making an uncoordinated sandwich of bodies.

In response to our collective yelp, the new swinger peers around the side of the large door. "Fuck," they say on an exhale, and I immediately groan. I know it's Raff from that one expletive.

"Wow! It's crowded in here," a nasally feminine voice declares.

When Mac and I untangle from Guy, I realize that Raff is being followed into the bar by two painfully preppy-looking girls.

I say girls, but to be clear, they are in their early twenties. It just feels wrong to call someone wearing an oversized pink headband a woman. I recognize the nasally one immediately. Nora started at Princess a few days after me. She's ambitious, driven, and totally impatient— the perfect embodiment of a recent culinary school grad.

Behind her stands another girl, who I later find out is named Shirin. Shirin is easily one of the most absurdly shy people that I've ever "met". I use the term loosely because no one introduces her. Shirin is face down on her phone from the moment they enter the bar, and she doesn't speak to any of us directly. She only whispers to Nora, who then makes declarations to the group as though she's a brand spokesperson. "We love this song," she informs us when Seven Nation Army comes on.

I'm super confused as to why Guy and Raff are out with Nora and Shirin. I'm even more puzzled when they have suddenly joined our group. Guy suggests we move to one of the larger tables in the bar's back room.

Nat has decided to teach Shirin how to play pool. Busty and pear-shaped, Shirin is totally Nat's type physically. "I'm going to get her to talk," she'd whispered mischievously to Lex as they slipped out of the booth.

Lex needs to get away from leering Liam, so she happily tags along. However, Shirin won't play unless Nora is standing right next to her. And Nora is desperate to continue to talk Raff's ear off about some ideas she has for the restaurant. So now a crowd has formed around the pool table.

Huh. So that's Raff's type now. Well, whatever. I'm not jealous. Especially since Nat informed me that Raff has somewhat of a reputation for being a bit of a fuckboy now. To be clear, I didn't ask about Raff. He's just someone that, over the years, my family gave me periodic updates about. Like I'd care.

Nora reminds me of the Kit Kittredge American Girl Doll, complete with tiny front teeth. Full of initiative and the optimism of youth, she seems a little too high-maintenance for someone as noncommittal as Raff. Fuck he used to call me every evening to check his start time for the next morning at the bakery. I stupidly flattered myself by thinking it was just an excuse to talk to me on the phone late into the night. I now suspect that it was because he hated to commit, even the weekly schedule to memory.

It turns out that Raff and Guy had randomly run into Nora and her silent companion two bars ago. Unfortunately, Nora didn't get the hint that they were trying to shake her when they kept changing locations. In a final attempt to ditch them, they ended up here. The Tide Water seemed like the perfect place to scare off the eager escort.

Stan and Liam are still lurking around. They've been pushed to the outskirts of conversation since Guy and Raff arrived. Stan kept trying to regain Mac's attention. When his continued negging stopped working, he decided to give her hair a playful tug. A gesture that was swiftly met with Guy silently placing an oversized palm on the short man's shoulder.

Guy and Mac are now at the bar alone playing a game that they lovingly call "Boob Hunt." That's not the real name of the game, of course, but the oversized touch screen video console doesn't display any official title. It's an erotic take on the "spot the difference" game. Two near-identical soft-core pornographic photos from the 1990s are displayed side by side. Players must race to find all the differences before the timer goes off. It's kind of like a disgusting version of Highlights magazine. Guy and Mac are weirdly proficient at this game and hold the second-highest score.

With everyone distracted by pool or boobs, Van and I sit alone. She slides over to me, slipping her hand into mine. Her elegant thumb softly rubs the stick-and-poke tattoos on my fingers. "Are you ok?" she asks. I take a long sip of my fresh vodka cran.

Van isn't supposed to be here right now. Cary lives closer to San Francisco for work. She was planning to stay over at his place tonight after the fitting. Between work and wedding prep, they get very little time together. Nat had actually agreed to cover her yoga classes all morning so that Van could spend the day with Cary. However, after my abrupt removal from the schedule, she agreed to come home so that she could cover tomorrow. I take another sip, ignoring the sour feeling in my stomach.

"They'll come around," she says.

"Like I give a shit," I say tersely.

She looks taken aback, but then nods. "So then what do you want from them?" she asks. I open my mouth to say something, but quickly change my mind. I take another long sip. "It's ok to be upset," she says, realizing that I'm not formulating a reply. I've just simply stopped responding.

"Sorry, Mama," I say finally. "I ruined everything again."

Van slides her arm around my shoulders and puts her head on top of mine. "You could never," she says. Ha. If there's one thing I do, it's mess things up. Time and time again. I just didn't think it would be this soon. I hate that Van has to take care of me right now. She's the best of us. Perfect in every way. I'm glad that she's getting her happy ending, though. I'm just sorry that she has to deal with me to obtain it.

I go rigid at her gentle kindness. Kindness that I definitely don't deserve. My stomach feels overwhelmingly tight. My skin is on fire. I need to take less from her. I slip out of Van's grasp and stand. She looks at me with concern, moving to rise, but I put my arms up, easing her back down. "All good. Just need to use the bathroom," I lie, feeling the saliva pooling in my mouth as I stumble away.

The lighting in The Tide Water is low and tinted a hellish red. Old-school Venetian glass candles are on every table. We have a collection of them in the yard of the blue house—our favorite item to steal when the impulse strikes us. The flickering wicks cause a slight movement in my periphery that gives the bar a spinning feeling. My eyes dart around to the multiple vintage velvet portraits of naked buxom women that line the walls. On a hot day, they seemingly weep nicotine tears of condensation. Their eyes follow my crooked line aimed at my destination.

I knock into someone as I push my way toward the long, narrow hallway that leads to the disgusting bathrooms. There are only half-height swinging saloon doors that close off the men's and women's restrooms from the hallway. You can see straight into the stalls. Basically, if you have to pee, everyone will know. Mercifully, both women's toilets are empty. I rush inside and kick open the stall as the momentum of my vomit immediately doubles me over.

I feel a hand quickly gather up my hair as I retch. In the chaos, I basically had to choose between holding my dress up or holding my hair back. I'm grateful for the assistance because, in my stupor, I chose the dress. Bless you, Van, you beautiful angel. She must have followed me.

When I've finally caught my breath, stomach empty, I spit a few times for good measure. God, this is humiliating. Van's hand is still holding my hair. "Thanks, Mama," I mumble. My eyes are watery and my nose stings. I sniff a few times to clear it. It's then that I realize what I'm smelling... Barbasol shaving cream and citrus. Van isn't the one holding my hair. It's fucking Raff.

Chapter 7

RAFF

Ashley's dark eyes are wild when she stands. It's clear that I've surprised her. Our bodies are close. She stumbles backward into the graffiti-covered wall of the stall.

Her cheeks are rosy. Her lips are damp and pillowy. I'm suddenly aware that I'm still fisting her hair as she jerks her head back, gasping. "Easy," I say, quickly releasing her. My hands instinctively drop to her shoulders in an attempt to steady her.

I haven't touched Ash in over ten years. When my hands easily encompass her biceps, I'm instantly reminded that despite how tough and resilient she makes herself appear, Ashley Morgan Lobo is actually tiny and delicate. Her bare skin is glacial. I can feel goose flesh under my palms. She wriggles in my grasp, but I hold tight.

"You good?" I ask, craning my head down to get a better look at her. The lighting in here is shit. Everything is cast in shadows.

"Totally. Just saw your dumb mustache and I hurled," she says with a defiant smirk.

I laugh despite myself.

"What, Rat?" she huffs.

For the first time, my shoulders don't jump up in response. "I knew you hated me," I say, amused smile spreading across my face. Honestly, what a fucking relief. The idea that I could be nothing to her was driving me nuts.

"Whatever," she says, breaking free from my grasp and pushing out towards the sink. She twists the faucet on. I watch her through the mirror as she washes her hands. Her outfit is wild.

A black dress that nearly drags on the ground with a totally open, low-cut back. The material pools downward as she leans over the sink. I can clearly see a tattoo of a flapper with sad eye makeup on her ribs. Shit. She has tons of ink now. When I knew Ash, she was all baby fat and virginal tan skin. That seems like a lifetime ago.

"Can I help you?" she questions pointedly, catching me staring.

"Why aren't you like this all the time?" I ask.

Ash rolls her eyes. "Like what?" she says, leaning her mouth down to the running water.

"A bitch," I say, crossing my arms.

She makes a little gagging sound. I watch the wayward droplets stream down her chin and neck. She swishes the water back and forth before spitting into the basin. "Maybe

I just don't want to give you the satisfaction," she says, turning towards me.

"Satisfaction," I echo.

She feels around the empty paper towel dispenser. Ash purses her lips as she shakes her wet hands. "You would love it if I were a bitch, so that you'd feel justified in being an—"

I cut her off before she can finish.

"I'm not always an ass," I say, extending the front of my T-shirt towards her.

She scoffs, but I do clock when her eyes dip slightly to the exposed skin on my stomach. Is she checking me out?

"An ass is an ass is an ass is an ass," she repeats, ignoring my offer. Ashley has instead decided to windmill her arms as she continues to chant. I laugh again with a slight shrug. This fucking chick.

"You didn't always feel that way," I say. Letting her hands fall to her sides, she stares at me. That blank expression she wears settling back on her face.

"Careful, Rat. You're gonna make me barf again."

This would be a sick burn, but she stumbles as she turns toward the door. I'm close enough to catch her.

"Come on," I say, pulling her by the elbows.

"There you are," Nora scolds when I get back to the table. She's practically tapping her fucking toe at me. The two creepy dudes are nowhere to be found. However, none of those damn bread girls are either. Shit.

"That Ash's bag," I ask, pointing at a discarded black purse.

The quiet girl nods. "Is she ok?" Nora questions as I pull the bag over my shoulder.

"I'm taking her home." I'm already leaving before any of them can interject.

Mac should be dealing with this, but she's probably off with Guy right now. Fuck even he would honestly be better suited to handle this. I pull out my phone and call him. No answer. Something tells me he has his hands full, too.

I find Ash propped up on the barstool where I had left her. She's actively ignoring the ice water that the surly bartender has placed in front of her. "Drink," I command, dropping my head low to her ear.

"Who are you, my fucking dad?" The defiant smirk is back as she pretends to tip the glass over. However, she's drunk. So, she actually pushes it onto her lap.

Before the string of expletives leaves the bartender's mouth, I've already scooped Ashley up and over my shoulder. In two steps, I'm pushing out onto Jupiter Street. For a Monday night, it's pretty crowded. Summer tourists saunter between bars with retro neon-lit signs. Locals in flip-flops, flannels, and flat-billed hats smoke cigs and laugh loudly. The break of high tide crashes on the rocks across the street. It's too dark to see the water, but the sound is an unmistakable drone underscoring the activity all around us. This is a Santa Luna summer.

I cross to the empty side of the street toward the beach and set Ashley down onto the seawall. "Can you make it to the blue house?" I ask. The Victorian that they all live in isn't more than a fifteen-minute walk from The Tide Water. Her mom can put her to bed.

Her bottom lip wobbles. I instinctively take a step back. I think that she's about to puke again, but then I realize it's her teeth chattering. Shit. I take off my denim jacket and slip it over her shoulders. Then ask the question again.

"I'm fine," she says.

I watch her attempt to slide off the five-foot seawall. It's awkward and frankly looks painful. Santa Luna City Council decided to line the seawalls with sharp stones that jet out. The intention is to keep kids from doing skateboarding tricks and prevent the unhoused from setting up camp. Right now, I feel like I'm watching medieval torture as her exposed legs scrape against the jagged surface.

I pick her up again. This time, in a clumsy bear hug. Our fronts awkwardly pressed together as she kicks and thrashes.

"Put me down, Rat," she demands.

There's that fucking nickname again. My grip tightens. "I'm trying to be nice, you brat." She's light, but it's too uncomfortable to be holding her while she's fighting me. Plus, I can feel people staring at us. So, I place her down gently.

"I don't need you to be nice to me, you ass," she bites out.

"I'm not an ass," I say.

She narrows her eyes at me. "Fine."

I fucking hate that word.

I run my hands through my hair. She sways for a moment. I should leave her outside. Call Guy to get one of her sisters to take her home. Just as I'm about to pull out my phone again, she whispers, "Jupiter and twelfth."

"You've proven your point," Ash says. I follow her into the third-floor walk-up. Her apartment is in a shitty Edwardian with a bead store on the ground floor. It's only four blocks from the bar. She zig-zagged her way straight into the bushes a few times as we walked. So, I had to put my arm around her shoulders to guide her.

I shut the door behind me as she kicks off her shoes and shrugs out of my jacket. My eyes dart around the bizarre space. There's a tiny kitchenette mere feet from a freestanding clawfoot tub and a toilet inside a narrow closet. Her clothes are hung on a rolling garment rack. Shoes were haphazardly discarded in a pile nearby. My eyes lock on a few books stacked up next to an old armchair. However, I don't see a bed.

"You got me home safe. Congrats. Now leave."

I ignore her as I open the fridge. "Do you sleep on the floor?" I ask, peering inside. Interesting, I think, as something in the crisper catches my eye. Then my gaze turns to the counter, where I find a sourdough loaf proving in a basket.

"Rat. Get out," she groans, drawing out her vowels.

"That's very Japanese of you," I continue as I scan the scarce items on the open wire rack that serves as her pantry. Oils, spices, different varieties of flour and sugar, and random cookware sit on a few shelves. She didn't have much in her fridge either. Shit, after seeing the state of this apartment, I'm worried that we're not paying her enough. Then I notice a stockpile of beurre de tourage in her freezer. Of course, Ash would have stacks of fancy butter shaped and ready for lamination on hand. Her life is baking. Or at least it used to be back when I knew her all those years ago.

"I have a bed," Ash says.

"Where?" I ask just as I turn to see her pulling an antique Murphy bed out of the wall.

The rusty metal frame sticks halfway down, and I rush over to help her pull it free. Our hands brush, and she jerks back. I like how flustered she is by me right now. It's a very welcome change from the past few months. “You’re welcome,” I say smugly as I turn back to the stove.

I hear her mutter something unintelligible as she flops into the armchair. She’s so different than before. More confident, maybe? Probably just the distance from her family. They are so enmeshed. Even now, except for Ash, all of them still live in the blue house with their mothers.

I smile, remembering what it was like to be young with her. Neither of us having our own place. Fuck or a car for that matter. We’d have to sneak around on the bus. Usually hooking up when my mom was at work because her humongous family gave very few opportunities for privacy. I remember getting really good at contorting our bodies to fit on my twin mattress. But that was a long time ago.

“So out on your own, huh?” I ask, setting a water on the stack of books next to her.

Ash wordlessly snatches the cup, glaring at me. I now understand why she enjoyed being so nice to me when I was acting like a shithead toward her. It’s pretty fun.

I set about my work, hearing very little protest from Ashley. I momentarily think that she might have fallen asleep. She’s gone totally silent. When I turn, I’m surprised to see that she’s naked. Well, naked-ish, but fuck. She’s in nothing but black panties. After catching a glimpse of her hard nipples on the brisk walk, I’d guessed that she wasn’t wearing a bra earlier. Now I no longer have to wonder what was underneath. Her lithe body is on full display, dress discarded on the floor. Her back is turned to me as she crouches down to rummage through a heap of laundry near the bay window. It's both grotesque and captivating.

I look back at the pan, ignoring the sight of her golden skin. When I hear movement again behind me, I turn off the burner and summon a casual tone. "Why do you have Princess dough?"

"How do you know it's Princess dough?" Ash replies. She's in a well-worn oversized Wings tee and tiny black sleep shorts. Slender tan legs on display.

My stomach tightens as I glance at that pair of panties now discarded on top of her laundry pile. I give her a look as I hand her the plate. "It's totally over-proofed," I say. She rolls her dumb eyes, and it's then that I feel it again. That gnawing urge I haven't felt in years. I bite the inside of my cheek.

"Pizza bagels," she replies with an exhale.

"You're making bagels with my dough," I ask. Ash nods, staring at the quesadilla. Oaxaca cheese, tortillas, and salsa verde were pretty much the only food she had in her fridge that wasn't in various stages of the baking process. "You gotta eat something greasy after a night of drinking. Those are the rules," I say.

Her nostrils flare, but she takes a bite. "There. Happy now, butthead," she asks, extending the plate back to me.

An urge twitches somewhere deep.

"Empty plates make me happy, brat." I go to sit on the bed, but it makes a god-awful creaking noise that has me standing immediately. Ashley laughs, and my head jerks. I'm surprised to hear it. I don't think I've heard her laugh in years. It's like seeing a ghost.

"Thank you," she says begrudgingly. We stare at each other. Her: in the oversized, worn leather armchair. Me: standing over her. The hum of the fridge, the whooshing of the ceiling fan, and the distant sounds of the street below.

For a moment, I consider asking her why she was so drunk tonight. Why is she not at the blue house? Why would she, of all people, want to work with me? I consider talking to her like we used to talk all those years ago. No bullshit. I want to say a million things. But I don't.

"Go to sleep," I say. I grab my jacket. I walk to the door. I do not turn around or wait for a reply. I walk down the three flights of stairs, cut across Twelfth to Mars, and up into the residential neighborhoods toward home.

The air is cool. Moths hover around streetlamps. Dogs bark inside dark houses. Shadows dance in the headlights of passing cars, same shit as always, only different now. I'm suddenly hungry again.

Chapter 8

ASH

"What the hell is going on?" Laurel asks as I help her refill the lowboys behind the bar. I've been working at Princess Pizzarina for over two months. At this point, my prep is a breeze. Ever since my spectacular humiliation at The Tide Water last week, I've been making myself very helpful in an effort to avoid any unnecessary interaction with Raff.

"Did you guys fuck," she says, causing me to nearly drop a Cambro full of limes.

"No." My face is neutral. I don't want her to pry. Raff's babysitting is something I'd rather take to the grave. I finish my task quickly, then straighten to leave. Laurel is hunched over the keg system, making sure all of her lines are working. Her wispy hair is curtaining her face in chaotic blonde frizz. She keeps going, oblivious to my intentions.

"Cuz you both seem weird now. Like, weirder than before."

All it took was one look at his crooked smile the next day, and I knew. "How'd you sleep last night?" he'd asked innocently.

"Great," I'd lied. Fuck. I was no longer in a position of power. He'd figured out the game.

So now instead of being in my face all the time, huffing and scoffing. Raff and I have become a pair of polite, courteous coworkers. Him: respectful and overtly sweet. Me: nodding and bowing in a genteel response. It's honestly like something out of a British comedy of manners.

"What do you mean, weirder?" I say.

Laurel laughs. "The Raff cycle is all out of whack. Like, before you got here, Raff would start totally cool with all the new cooks. Then he'd start messing around with them, especially the girls. You know what I mean..." she pauses for dramatic effect.

"Yeah. I get it," I say. She doesn't continue. I rub the space between my eyebrows. "He would hook up with them or whatever," I confirm begrudgingly. Satisfied, Laurel continues thoughtfully.

"Well, he wouldn't mess around with the guys like that. He'd be, like, bffs with them. And then one day bam!" She brings her hands down on the bar with a loud smack. "Like, a total Gordon Ramsay and shit."

Laurel has confirmed it. Raff's pattern is still a thing. I can't tell her that I'm already aware of it. That at one point, many eons ago, I was patient zero. I narrow my eyes.

"All I'm saying is that you're, like, different. He started all Kitchen Nightmares on you from day one, and now you're, like, what? Best friends."

She lilts the end of her statement into a question, which makes me bark a laugh.

"Raff and I will never ever be best friends," I say.

Laurel makes a skeptical 'hmm' sound as she tucks a wayward tendril behind her ear. "So then you guys fucked," she repeats.

"I'm going to help Nora," I say, slipping out from behind the bar.

Laurel waves a bar towel at me. "That wasn't a no!"

Unfortunately, when I get into the kitchen, Nora is setting up her mise en place and, of course, yapping Raff's ear off. I move to make a U-turn back out into the dining room, but Raff's hand juts out, catching me by the wrist. My body goes rigid as I fight the sudden jolt of electricity transferred by his touch.

"Where's my pizza bagel?" he asks.

My face suddenly flushes. I'd forgotten that I'd told him about my experiment. "In the garbage," I reply sharply.

That stupid crooked smile spreads across his face. I'm done with the manners. The pretense is over. If he wants a bitch, I'll give him one. There's no need to keep up the game if he's not going to play it the way I want. Besides, he's only going to find a way to inevitably push me out. So, I might as well be here on my own terms.

“There she is,” he muses. I roll my eyes, twisting out of his grasp.

“Did you make... bagels?” Nora interjects, confused.

I shake my head. “No. Couldn’t get the crust right.”

Raff leans back against the counter, thinking.

“Bake them here,” he says.

I wrinkle my forehead.

“If you bake them off in the pizza oven, the outside will get some char.”

I consider this for a moment.

“The inside should stay chewy,” he adds.

I stare at Raff blankly. “Nah. It was a dumb idea,” I say.

He scoffs.

“Why?” *Because I came up with it,* I think. I don’t say that. It’s a proven fact that no one wants to eat my food. He should know better than anyone else after our failed pop-up. My failed pop-up. He never actually showed.

“Try it,” he says as he walks past me. “Or don’t. Whatever.” He’s through the swinging doors before I can protest again.

“I wasn’t done,” Nora huffs. I try not to smile. That rat bastard. Raff just fucking used me as a momentary distraction to escape. Nora’s not a bad person. She’s just headstrong. But she ain’t making any friends either. Nora is constantly sharing her feedback and opinions. She’s totally oblivious to the environment. Kitchens are sometimes about vibes over skills. You have to be able to win the team over before you expect anything to improve.

Now that I’m exiled from the bakery and the blue house, I’ve had more time to focus on my work here. This place has momentum. Sure, it’s popular, but there’s a difference between a trendy restaurant and a local staple. Princess needs to make the gigantic leap from “sure, we could check it out,” to “you MUST go.”

To the untrained eye, Princess Pizzarina and Mother Wolf might seem to be on the same level. Mother Wolf has over four decades of loyal customers. In increments of Saturday mornings, I’ve seen cooing babies drooling on a hunk of Pain au chocolat grow into full-blown adults ordering black coffee. There is an entire community that has made the bakery part of their daily routine. Hell, one of our ROMEOs (retired older men eating out), Dave, has eaten breakfast at Mother Wolf every day for the last twenty-five years, barring a few trips to Portugal to visit his son.

We are embedded in people’s lives, from the mundane morning coffee run to once-in-a-lifetime moments like wedding cakes. They aren’t regulars but rather acolytes who strive to convert everyone to a devotee. They’re the ones who have made Mother Wolf synonymous with Santa

Luna. It's not a trip to our coastal mountain town without a stop at the bakery.

Princess is still finding its footing. It is a fun spot for the college kids, the *new* place in town. However, popularity won't guarantee that you'll be able to persevere. Minor inconveniences like rain, tourist traffic, or a new cooler offering in the area can totally topple any trendy spot. Princess is good, but I haven't seen an unwavering group of regulars yet.

To weather the storm, you have to consistently offer undeniably great food and service that keeps people coming back time and time again. With years of bar and restaurant experience between them, Raff and Guy know this. Which is why, I suspect, they shoulder so much of the burden to run this place. They haven't found the crew that can keep the ship on course without them constantly steering. They're white-knuckling the popularity and praying they don't smash into the rocks. If they don't figure it out quickly, they're going to lose what they've already built.

Great restaurants capture the magic. There's this spell that's cast in certain restaurants. Something that they can't teach you in culinary school. You have to experience it. It's the anticipation after you order. That sudden uproar of laughter that explodes over the din of conversation. The urge to keep talking despite empty plates. It's about feeling that your meal is totally intimate, even while you're cocooned in a room full of other people. That moment when the table decides to get just one more round. Princess has that intangible energy that's going to cement it in the bedrock of Santa Luna. That is, *if* they can sustain the vitality.

Maybe it's because I've been getting more sleep now that I'm not at the bakery, but I think the kitchen crew is starting to gel. Chuy and Miguel have been able to laugh and joke in front of Raff. The servers are no longer scurrying out from underfoot whenever he's in the back of house. Hell, I think I even saw Guy take a lunch break for the first time since I started working here.

Tonight confirms it. It's a Tuesday. Typically, a mellow night in most restaurants... but much to Raff and Guy's credit, Princess Pizzarina isn't typical. On Tuesdays, the bar sells half-price PBRs and their friend Marco deejays. A former skater with a bushy beard and a total dad bod. He has some lame alias, Dj Stop-Sign. I think he earned the nickname because he got hit by a car while j-walking when they were all teenagers. He plays funk and soul music. It draws a pretty decent crowd.

Tonight, Guy and Laurel are behind the bar, Raff is in the dining room at the wood-burning oven, while Nora and I are on the line in the back kitchen. It's only seven, but we're already slammed. It's the week of the Lumberjack Log Jam. The annual surf contest has brought in a fair number of tourists, in addition to those looking to drink and dance.

Chuy and Miguel are typically the two who hold it down. The ebb and flow of kitchen traffic never throws them. However, between Chuy's niece's quinceañera in San Antonio and Miguel having a stomach bug, they're both off tonight. I'm expediting in the back for the first time. Nora is keeping up. We're working in sync.

This is something that I can easily do at Mother Wolf. My family and I have an unspoken rhythm. I've practiced the mechanics of working in that kitchen to the point of deep muscle memory. After I left Santa Luna, I'd found my way into restaurants all over the country. I'd get the repetition down and enter into the unique flow state of each new environment. Tonight, I've entered mine here.

The kitchen is alive. Tickets come in, orders go out. The minute a dish hits the expediting window, a server is there to deliver it. Glassware and peg racks go flying through the conveyor belt at lightning speed. Our dishwasher, Joey, is clearing bus tubs as soon as they hit the station. This place is sentient.

At one point, I look up to see Mac run by. She has several full liquor bottles in her arms. "Daddy," I call after her, but she's through the swinging doors without so much as a backward glance. The second time, I realize she is also wearing a Princess Pizzarina crew neck. I guess my sister is a barback tonight.

There's a moment when I have to bring Raff more dough. I step out into the dining room, and it hits me. This is it: the music, the energy, the experience. Princess Pizzarina is in her element tonight.

In the center of it all, I catch sight of Raff. He's haloed in golden light, radiating the same energy that the dining room is emitting. Long and lean with a muscular build, he looks like a mythical creature. Something you'd happen across in the woods, bathing in a stream, and playing a pan flute.

"You good, Rat," I say as I approach with dough boxes in hand. To his credit, he doesn't flinch when I call him that anymore. He's gulping ice water from a deli container. The thick condensation forms large droplets that race down his hand and wrist. My eyes follow the movement. He's bracing himself on the prep station. My gaze pauses on the pulse of the muscles, his toned forearms on full display. I ignore the quick clench in my core at the sight.

It's scorching out here. My breathing feels shallow as I adjust to the temperature—the wood crackles. I'm immediately met with that char smell that permanently lingers on Raff. His crew neck is nearly soaked through. I do my best not to notice how the cotton clings to his shoulders and chest as I wait for him to take the stack from my hands.

"How is it back there?" he asks.

I nod. "Great."

He nods. "Great." His fingertips brush mine slightly as he accepts the dough boxes. His flesh is hot. His face is flushed. I turn to head back to the kitchen, but reflexively, my eyes dip once more. Shit.

Chapter 9

RAFF

The water is cold as shit. It stings my skin as I break the surface. My feet touch the bottom, and I shoot straight up, gasping. "Fuck," I yell, paddling toward the lapping edge. Everyone is cheering.

We just had a fucking sick night. We closed an hour later than usual, sold out of three menu items, and no one quit. This is a first for us. So naturally, I just jumped off the side of Guy's garage into the pool to celebrate.

"Glad you didn't break your neck," he says, hoisting me out.

Guy is laughing. Honest to God, enjoying himself for maybe the first time in five years. This is a fucking win. Guy and I have been through some shit together. We're practically brothers. Sure, he's the reliable one, and I'm the fuck up, but brothers nonetheless.

Princess Pizzarina has been a test. A strain on the tangled knot of our friendship. I'm the fucking asshole with too many problems to make shit work. I'm the one who's always ruining things. Guy's resentment was getting palpable. If shit didn't change, I know he was going to walk. So tonight, I'm celebrating this win. I'm enjoying my success before the other fucking shoe drops.

I do my best not to shiver. My crew is watching. I have to look cool. My jeans squish and cling, steam leeching off of the top of my head as I run toward the house.

"Do it naked next time," Laurel calls, and the crowd erupts in hollers. Minnie barks.

Somebody wolf whistles. I flip them off as I duck inside.

Violent Femmes thrash on the stereo for the empty sunken living room. I nearly slip on the avocado green tile as I dash through the kitchen toward the bedrooms. The music grows fainter as I make my way down the hall and into the Jack-and-Jill bathroom. My wet feet leave a cartoonish trail of prints down the shag carpet.

My jeans slap against the basin of the acrylic powder blue tub with a satisfying thwack as I discard my wet clothes. I can hear voices. At first, I think it's the sound of everyone filtering back inside. But these are not the sounds of merriment. It's serious and whispered.

I wrap a towel around my waist and take a few steps toward the adjoining door. Inside Guy's room, I can hear them.

"After the wedding," one says.

"That's a horrible idea," the other replies. I know it's Mac and Ash. I shouldn't be listening, but I can't stop.

"No. They can't fucking treat you like this," Mac continues.

I hear Ash sigh. "You can't all quit."

"Fucking watch us. They're never going to change. If they can't accept that we're a part of the bakery, then we won't be." Mac's voice is getting louder.

What the fuck is going on? This sounds like mutiny. Those bread girls are brutal with each other, sure, but they're also thick as fucking thieves. A regular pack of wild jackals. However, I thought I was the only one who could see it was a fucked-up situation over there.

When I worked with them right out of culinary school, the Lobo matriarchs were crazy strict with everyone, always micromanaging each tiny move. Especially when it came to Ashley, she couldn't sneeze without one of them jumping down her throat.

I remember it was that weird time of year, right before the weather turned warm. Endless stretches of rainy days would give way to a random pocket of sunshine. When we had one of these warm days, people would order the egg salad. It would always sell out fast. After reading the next day's weather report, Ashley had the brilliant idea to take the unsold milk bread from the day prior and make these Japanese-style egg salad sandos. Fucking delicious.

It was a perfect Saturday. The bakery is on the far end of Jupiter, just steps from the beach. Everyone was buying the sandos to take out into the brief moments of coveted sunshine. They were selling like crazy until her mom found out. The old bitch literally took the rack off the counter and dumped the remaining unsold few straight into the trash right in front of customers. Ashley didn't even blink. Just kept working like nothing had ever fucking happened.

"We're not even living there anymore," Mac goes on. I can hear her walking around Guy's room. Her stupid shoes are unmistakable. "I'm going to be staying here. Started training to work in the bar too." That's fucking news to me. Thanks, Guy.

I shouldn't be listening to this. I open the door to my room. Find a thermal and a pair of joggers. I think I've gotten away without them noticing, but the bathroom door swings wide behind me. I wheel around, managing to pull on my pants.

"Get out, perv," I say. I guess Mac living here is going to revert me back to my teenage self. I feel like I'm yelling at Eleni.

"Were you spying on us?" Mac asks, narrowing her eyes.

I can see through the open Jack-and-Jill doors. Ash sits on the edge of Guy's bed. As we lock eyes, I'm suddenly reminded that my shirt is thrown over my shoulder, my joggers down low on my hips, damp skin still on full display.

"Let's get a drink," Ash says, standing. Without any change in expression, she disappears out into the hall. Mac rolls her eyes and huffs before following her out.

"Close the fucking door behind you," I call after them. Yep. This is going to be exactly like living with my sister again.

When I venture out into the living room, towel wrapped around my hair and joint between my teeth, everyone has moved back inside. House parties always make me feel like I'm in high school again. People are grouped around talking, drinking, and ignoring the Deftones that one of the busboys has put on.

No sign of Ash. Not that I'm looking for her. Mac stands in the kitchen with Mikey and Jorge, two of our more seasoned servers. They're townies who only work at night so they can surf all day. They never close their mouths all the way, between syllabus and boast, dark poop head, tan lines year-round.

I catch Nora looking up from her drink. I immediately push my way through the crowd in the opposite direction. Guy and I make eye contact from across the room. He's on the couch with Laurel. Minnie is draped across his lap. Her plume of a tail fanning Laurel's chin. Guy and I nod at each other as I slip outside.

I step onto the lid of the hot tub, then pull myself up to the roof ledge, just in time, too. I hear the slider open below. I watch Nora take a few steps out onto the patio. Her bright pink Crocs are iridescent as she stomps back and forth a few times, scanning the yard. I hold my breath, hoping that she won't look up. Then someone inside calls her name. She begrudgingly returns to the party. Hell yeah. Tonight is my night.

Old Raff would definitely be downstairs screwing Nora right now. Not because she's interesting or attractive, which arguably she is all those things, but rather because it would be so easy. Simple as popping three-day-old Massaman Curry into the microwave and hitting start. I'd just have to show her the littlest bit of attention, listen to her talk, and compliment her until we'd inevitably sleep together. Then I'd hate myself. She'd want something that I really couldn't give. So, I'd get rid of her.

It's like eating leftover takeout because you feel like you should... not because you're actually hungry. Gorge yourself on too much mediocre food, and you'll end up tossing it in the trash and loathing yourself afterward. It's been like this for years. I don't crave any of these women. I can't think of the last time I really, truly desired someone. That's not true. I'm just too much of an asshole to admit it.

Either way, new Raff has just successfully evaded Nora. Suck on that, Guy. I can be the responsible one for a change. I chuckle to myself as I lower my legs down over the gutter, letting my feet dangle. I fish around my pockets for a lighter. "Fuck," I shrug. Ok maybe tonight isn't my night.

"Need a light," a voice asks in the dark. I look down but see no one below. Then I almost leap off the edge when I hear scratching sounds behind me.

"What the fuck," I say. I scramble to free my hands from my pockets to stop my fall.

Ashley comes into view as she shimmies down the slope of the roof. "Did I scare you," she asks. It's dark up here, but I can make out her defiant smile.

"Are you drunk?" I ask. She shrugs in reply to my question, but I notice the beer bottle pinched between her thumb and index finger.

"I'm about to be high," Ash says, producing a Bic from her jacket pocket. She thwicks the flint. Her dark eyes sparkle in the dance of the tiny flame.

"Who said I was going to share?" I say.

She pulls the lighter back, but I snatch it from her.

I guess I shouldn't be surprised that Ash knows about my hiding spot. In high school, we'd climb on the roof to duck the cops when they'd inevitably come to break up our parties. Sometimes, even jumping across the gap onto Mr. Chen's house next door, lying flat on the other side of the peak. Totally unseen by the roaming flashlights below. I can't remember her being in attendance back then, but then again, there's a lot about that time in my life that I don't remember.

"Cool hat," she says, lifting her eyebrows toward the towel turbaned around my head.

"Oh, this old thing," I reply with mock humility. I think I catch the approximation of a smile. I inhale deeply, bringing the flame to the tip of the joint. Then, after a long exhale, when I'm sure it's cherry, I hand it to Ash. We don't speak. Just pass the joint back and forth, watching shadows from the party below stretch across the concrete patio. I pick up her nearly empty bottle, lifting it to my lips.

"Hey," she croaks on a throaty exhale, "waterfall that shit."

I roll my eyes. "We're sharing a joint. It's a little late to be worried about an indirect kiss," I say. And then for the first time she starts to laugh. A sudden burst of guffaws. I know she's high, which makes me laugh. I take another sip of her beer.

"Seriously though, get your own," she says, grabbing for the bottle.

"Come on, we're friends," I say.

She scoffs an audible 'ha-ha' sound, passing back the joint.

"Or friendly, I guess," I add, accepting it between my fingers.

We sit in silence for a pregnant pause. We are both contemplating this statement. Ashley asks, "Are we?"

Just as I'm saying, "We could be." We look at each other awkwardly. We both go to reply, but are interrupted. The rhythmic groan of Biggie Smalls, followed by a collective scream, erupts from beneath.

We both laugh. Her gaze darts away quickly, but I continue to watch her. Her cheeks have a blush from either the cool night air or the alcohol. The refracted pool lights give Ash's glassy, dark eyes a neon-blue tint. She's wearing a vintage leather jacket that I know she's had for years. In the dark, she looks really young. She's only two years younger than me, but right now she looks eighteen again. Ah, fuck it. "What's the deal?" I ask.

She leans back on her hands, staring up at the night sky. Out here, where the mountains meet the ocean, when the dense fog breaks, there's clear visibility.

"Nothing. Everything is groovy, baby," she replies flatly.

I shake my head. "No bullshit, man."

"So you *were* listening," she purrs. I take off the towel, tossing it down on the roof behind us, and lie all the way back.

"You guys were really fucking loud."

She looks down at me, but I keep my gaze fixed on the stars. "The usual shit," she sighs. I nod.

The joint has gone out. I don't feel like relighting it. I slip the roach into my pocket. "My dad's an asshole too," I start.

"Huh. I didn't realize it was hereditary," she replies.

I give her an overt fake laugh like the one she demonstrated earlier. "What I'm telling you is that I get it, you fucking brat."

She exhales as she leans back, laying her head on the damp towel next to mine.

"It sucks," I say.

"Yeah." She bites her bottom lip, thinking.

"So what's your deal?" she says.

I laugh. "I don't have a deal," I reply.

"No bullshit, man," she mimics. This fucking girl. I like that she's being herself. But then I feel it, the gnawing.

As much as I am pained to admit it, tonight was a success because Guy is right about Ashley. Not just that her being here would stop me from my usual bullshit. Don't shit where you eat and all that, sure, but it all worked because Ash is a beast on the line. I see her time away has built up her culinary skills beyond pastry. She can keep up with me. The crew fucking loves her. Hell, at this point, she can probably run that kitchen better than I can. Tonight was good because we didn't have to do anything other than be ourselves. I can't fuck it all up. I have to ignore the gnaw.

"You hungry?" I ask, rolling to look at her. She turns her head. Our faces are inches apart. She studies me for a moment. Dark eyes scanning my face. My breath catches when her gaze lingers on my lips. Fuck.

Quickly, her eyes flick up to mine. "Starving."

Chapter 10

ASH

Last night got hazy after Mikey and Laurel went on a beer run. There's a gas station at the end of the block, which we all lovingly refer to as Lefty's. It's not officially called Lefty's. It got that moniker because the guy who works the counter only has one hand.

Raff and I somehow convinced Laurel and Mikey to bring us It's-its. We'd raided the fridge when we came back inside. Raff made something he called "potato chip nachos," which basically consisted of a sheet pan full of kettle chips covered in melted Kerry Gold sharp cheddar cheese, sour cream, green onions, and pickled jalapeños. It was fucking delicious.

I remember eating alternating bites of the nachos and thinly sliced green apples dipped in a mixture of peanut butter and marshmallow fluff. After our smorgasbord, we felt that we needed dessert. Hence, our begging like children for the classic Bay Area frozen treat. I have a vague memory of dropping my half-eaten ice cream sandwich into the hot tub. Apparently, I wanted to go for a swim. I do not remember that it was naked with Marco the deejay and one of the hostesses named Torrey.

"You were playing mermaids while Stop-Sign was sucking face with that teenager," Mac informs me in the morning. I wake up with a jolt. My body is still adjusting to life without the bakery. I'm panicked for a moment as I get my bearings. Mac and I are under the scratchiest quilted floral bedspread that reeks of cigarettes.

It's still early, but neither of us can go back to sleep. We lay in bed talking in whispers. The first morning light peaks through the polyester drapes. It reminded me of when we were little. Mac, Van, and I would always go down into Abuelita's room. She'd let us watch cartoons on her small rabbit ear TV. Turning the dial on the brown plastic face was so satisfying. We'd always fight over who got to change the channels while one adjusted the antenna and the other watched the screen for the picture clarity.

Mac lent me some clothes. We both shower in the en suite, then make our way to the kitchen. The house is silent. The big white dog lying in an oversized bed peeks up at us lazily. She thumps her tail against the wall as Mac bends down to pet her. Mac instructs me on where to find things to make coffee. I set about starting a pot while she scoops a measuring cupful of kibble from a large plastic tub. The most pleasurable waterfall of pings breaks the early morning silence as Mac pours the dog food into a metal dish by the back door.

"It's only eight," Mac says, looking at her phone.

"You wanna lie back down?" I ask.

Mac shakes her head. "I want to do something I can't normally do on a Wednesday morning," she says wistfully. Typically, we would both be working. A lifetime of running a family bakery means that we often had to miss out on mundane morning activities.

"What about a yoga class? I think Nat's teaching today," Mac says.

I shake my head. "I'm too hungover to smell other people's feet," I reply. We survey the mess left over from last night. I grab the world's dingiest sponge and turn on the faucet. Mac pulls out a garbage bag from the roll under the sink. We both set about cleaning up. The sound of sputtering drips of brewing coffee and crunching kibble score our work.

By the time she's cleared the living room, and I've washed all the dishes, the coffee maker is beeping. The dog does an energetic little hop between her front paws when Guy shuffles in.

"Morning," he says on a yawn. He has serious bedhead. "Why are you two up so early?" he asks. He peers around suspiciously. "And cleaning?"

Mac pours him a cup of coffee, and he joins me at the retro dinette, muttering his thanks.

"What would you usually do on a Wednesday morning?" Mac asks, slipping into one of the vinyl chairs. The uneven table wobbles, and we all brace our mugs as coffee sloshes.

"Go surfing," Guy says.

Mac and I exchange a look. Guy doesn't notice. He's gazing down at the dog. She's laid her head on his knee while he scratches behind her ear.

"There's a farmers market on Bayshore right by a good surf spot," Guy adds. Mac smiles at me wickedly. She's decided.

Thirty minutes later, we're in the water. We stopped by my place on the way. Mac's boobs are huge. There's no way I could borrow one of her bathing suits. I also declined Guy's offer to swing by his friend Ryan's place to get his girlfriend's wetsuit. That's just too intimate.

Guy drives a little further south than his usual spot. He wants to get us into some beach breaks. So, he takes us to a place the locals call Ankle Biters, because that's where little kids typically learn to surf. The waves are smaller and better for beginners. His usual place, Shark-Bait, is a reef break and can be more unforgiving. Personally, I don't want to be smashed into any coral or rock when I inevitably eat shit. And eat shit, I certainly do.

Mac and I take turns using an ancient 9-foot-long board. Honestly, we're so little that at a certain point, I consider trying to paddle in tandem on the board with Mac rather than wait in the shallows with the dog for my next ride. Guy's a good teacher, but Mac and I are more of the indoor-cat variety. We both get up no problem. Thanks to all the yoga that Van and Nat force us to practice. It's the damn Bennys that are causing us to fall.

The Lumberjack Log Jam is a few days away. It always draws a bunch of kooks who decide that they'd like to try their hand at surfing. No sooner does one of us pop up than a tourist on a rented foam top drops in from above. At first, it's funny. Guy has to yell instructions from the line-up behind the break while the one standing in the shallows uses hand signals to direct the other through oncoming wave traffic.

When a kid on a boogie board kicks Mac in the face with a hard plastic swim fin, we call it a day. We slide the boards back into the bed of Guy's truck and clumsily change under towels. My long hair is tied up in a messy bun, droplets of saltwater falling onto my secondhand t-shirt that reads "Free Winona."

We walk toward the farmer's market. The marine layer has burned off, and the sun is warming our skin. Mac insists that we all slather our faces with sunscreen as we wait in line for overpriced, ethically sourced, painfully acidic coffee. "Classic Daddy," I say, which makes Guy laugh gleefully. She side eyes me as she produces a bottle from her purse and proceeds to squeeze oversized globs into each of our palms. She even rubs some of the excess onto the tip of the dog's pink nose.

Guy's phone rings. Mac holds the dog's leash while he steps out of line to answer it. By the time the barista hands us our criminally small cups of americano, Guy rejoins us with Raff in tow.

"Where's mine?" Raff asks.

Mac and I both reply simultaneously with some version of "get your own." We step aside as the barista obliges him with a tiny cup after he flashes her one of his stupidly attractive smiles.

Teensy cups in hand, we wander the stalls. Summer in Northern California is an incredible time for produce. We sample sliced citrus and fresh-picked berries, bursting with juice. There are all manner of tree nuts and crisp early-season apples. Big beautiful bushels of greens, red blushes of beets, and deep blue tubers. Mac disappears into a crowd and returns with a handful of honey sticks. We happily drink down the sticky-sweet gold.

The best of all is the stone fruit. Peaches, plums, nectarines, and apricots. It's the perfect time to gorge oneself on this precious crop. As we wait for Guy and Mac to buy kettle corn, Raff and I stand in the shade with the dog. He hands me a peach. It's so fresh that there are still leaves on the stem. I bring the fragrant body to my nose and inhale deeply. Feel the fuzz slide across my lips before sinking my teeth into its supple flesh.

An explosion of nectar fills my mouth as I bite into it. Juice dribbles down my chin, and I do my best to suck up the moisture. I close my eyes and chew. An exhale of a moan escaping. I let my senses indulge in the married experience of the light pollen smell and the deep peach flavor. It's so ripe. I desperately try to lick up the sugary fluid that races down my arm. An involuntary obscene whimper leaves my lips as I lap at my syrupy flesh. It's then that I feel it. Raff's eyes are on me. An expression of intense hunger as he watches me attempt to catch the sticky mess. I swallow hard.

“Do you want some, Rat?” I ask. I do my best to sound innocent as I extend the dripping fruit toward him.

He hesitates for a moment. Then, never taking his eyes off of me, he grips my wrist in his long fingers and brings the outstretched peach to his mouth. Slowly, he lowers his teeth to the tender cheek and bites down hard. With a sucking sound that makes my knees wobble, he takes in a mouthful of flesh. We hold eye contact as he straightens and chews. His lips glisten.

I'm instantly hit with a tingling sensation in the pit of my stomach. A feeling that I have not had in nearly a decade. I lick my lips as I watch him. My breathing deepens. He gently releases my wrist and brings the back of his hand up to wipe his mouth.

“Delicious,” he smiles wickedly. There's something so lewd about the way that he's said it that I can't help but laugh.

“Shit. Is it on my face?” he asks.

I shake my head and take another wet bite. My chest is heaving as I catch my breath. I know that my cheeks are red. We both look around the market. “Is it always this crowded?” I question.

“Nah. It's the Log Jam,” he replies.

My eyes roam around the horde and Raff adds, “it'll be crazier on the weekend.”

"Too bad you can't sell at the Jam," I say. I don't know why I said it out loud. I guess I'm getting more comfortable being around him again. That or I'm still fucking high from last night.

"That's a great idea," Mac says as she rejoins us.

"What is?" Guy says through a mouthful of kettle corn.

"You guys should do a pop-up at the surf thing this weekend," she insists. I immediately start to walk back my idea. But much to my surprise, Guy and Raff are agreeing with Mac.

"It's in three days. There's no way we could pull it together in time," I say. They're all immediately talking over each other, planning out how to make it all work.

"I can get us added to Silverstein's booth, no extra paperwork. Plus, we have all of our catering gear," Guy starts.

"And I can take pictures to put on your socials," Mac continues.

"We could make a menu with ingredients we already have on hand, so we don't have to order anything extra," Raff is saying.

"What the fuck is happening?" I ask. They all turn to look at me.

"We're doing a pop-up," Guy says.

"Good idea," Mac adds. Oh fuck. My stomach starts to sink. I never have good ideas. Especially not when it comes to pop-ups.

Chapter 11

RAFF

I didn't intend to see her this morning. In fact, far from it. Last night, I needed to make myself scarce after I'd watched Ashley meticulously bite around the chocolate-coated perimeter of her It's-It and then lasciviously drag her tongue through the ice cream circumference. My dick immediately jumped as I heard her tiny moans with each lick and lap.

No. Guy is right. I will not fuck this up again. No more hook-ups at work. I need to find a girl that I like and fucking date her. The end. Now if only my cock could get the message.

I'm still painfully celibate, and if I don't have sex soon, I might seriously combust. I feel like a cartoon wolf, panting and slobbering at a sexy dame. Which is why I went to hide in my room mid-ice cream sandwich. Only Jorge and Laurel were hooking up on my bed. Dear God, is everyone but me having sex right now?

I went back into the living room, hoping she was done with her explicit display. Unfortunately, when I returned, I was greeted by the sight of Ashley's perfect tits. Literally fucking perfect. They jiggled and bounced as she attempted to shimmy out of her skintight ribcage Levi's. Her jacket, shoes, shirt, and bra had already been discarded along a trail leading toward the slider. Fuck me.

I immediately turned back around and marched straight into the empty garage. I did clumsy barefoot kickflips on my skateboard for what felt like hours. I stomped on Guy's bass drum pedal every time I remembered ripe teardrops of forbidden fruit. Chanting my mantra *I will not fuck this up,* until I saw the last guest stumble down the driveway toward an Uber. When the coast was clear, I lay down on the couch in an attempt to sleep. My mind would not calm down. Also, Minnie kept trying to sleep on my legs, which was fucking painful considering my bluebells and that she's huge.

Around four, I went back to my room, stripped the sheets, and just face-planted onto the bare mattress for a few hours of tossing and turning. Ashley's tits... round and supple and fully fucking exposed to the cool night air. I went into work as soon as I felt safe to drive. My head fucking spinning. I shouldn't fuck this up again. Right?

I'm just horny. That's all it is. There's no reason why I can't just fuck someone who isn't Ash. She isn't the source of my sexual hyper fixation. It has to be that I just haven't gotten laid. What I need is a good old-fashioned hookup. A random night of fun with a random person that I'll never see again. That could satisfy my hunger. That would be... fine. There's no way that could fuck things up. It would be for the best, honestly. We can't lose Ashley.

Yes. There are so many reasons why you cannot have sex with her. For one, Ash is good at her job. Shit, probably the best we've ever had. Second, she doesn't want anything from me. Tara, Shelby, Olivia, and all the rest always made me feel like they wanted me to be something that I can't fucking be. Ashley already knows that I'm a disappointment. In fact, she's intimately familiar with my shortcomings. I've screwed her over, and yet here she is despite that. I can't fuck that up.

I prepped the dough for tonight. The entire time that I was pouring 00 flour into the industrial mixer, one thought kept circling over and over in my brain. Turning around with each spin of the mixing paddle. A thought that had the gnawing hunger spiking. What if I don't actually fuck it up this time? What if it all works out?

I needed to talk to Guy. I called him as soon as I'd left Princess. Unfortunately, when I'd dashed down the hill toward Ankle Bitters, I didn't realize he'd be with Ash and Mac. Usually, they worked in the mornings at Mother Wolf. Then it came back to me, their conversation in Guy's bedroom.

I cannot fuck this up for Ash. She probably can't go back to Mother Wolf again. I am the captain of this crew of misfits. Ashley should have a place here. I can't disappoint her, no matter how badly I feel that gnawing hunger.

My throat became tight when I saw her this morning. Oversized sunglasses and messy salt-cured hair. Her tan skin was glowing on the patch of exposed shoulder where her cut T-shirt had slipped down. Then I saw her eat that fucking peach...

Literally nothing scares me. I've seen and experienced things that would curl your hair. I never pause or blink, just act. However, there's something about the way that I desire this woman. A screaming, retching, clawing hunger that I'm not sure can ever be satiated by anything other than having her. I need to consume her. It's totally fucked. I feel off kilter.

In the overhead light of the kitchen, Ashley's golden skin looks green under the blue hue of the fluorescence. Her almond-shaped dark eyes, upturned nose, and heart-shaped lips give her a regal quality. Her hair is stacked high on the crown of her head. Surrounded by the metal prep stations, she looks like an alien queen.

"What, Rat?" she asks harshly.

Fuck. I've been staring at her again.

After the beach, Mac and Guy headed out to start organizing all the logistics. While Ash and I went into Princess to work on recipe testing and menu planning. We've decided on two of our best-selling pizzas that we can easily make in the portable ovens, and meatball subs that we can make to order. When I began to bemoan how long it would take to make enough individual crusty Italian sandwich rolls, Ash's eyes lit up. She bit her bottom lip, the apples of her cheeks rounding in anticipation. Shit. This girl was seriously elated at the prospect of making bread.

About an hour into our work, Guy texted me that Silverstein had come through. We had secured a booth. Jeremy Silverstein is the heir to a popular Northern California winery and owns Santa Luna Brewing Company. Through his family's connections, Jeremy was able to turn his "little hobby," as his father called it, from a craft beer supplier to a local favorite. He's been chasing Guy and me to open a Princess Pizzarina location at a new brewery he's building higher up the mountain. Guy's dream is to get into microbrewing, and Silverstein is chomping at the bit to make it happen.

Jeremy is a very pleasant sort with a low, gravelly voice, unruly curls, and the habit of agreeing effusively during most conversations. He's a real mensch wrapped up in a Santa Luna casing. The tiny Jewish human embodiment of a "Shaka, brah." Perhaps it's because he's so short, standing barely over five feet six, but Jeremy is obsessed with Guy, who stands a full foot taller than him. Needless to say, Silverstein almost wept with joy when Guy called him this morning about us doing a pop-up as a part of the beer garden that SLBC will be hosting at the Jam this weekend.

On Thursday, Ash arrives early. We're getting our test bread baked while we prep for opening. "Just fucking do it," I'd told her. She begrudgingly agreed to fire off some of those pizza bagels she'd been messing around with. I helped her shape them while our testers were proving.

We work in a comfortable silence. Just the sound of Machine Gun by the Commodores on the speakers. Ash hums while she works. I'd never noticed before because I'm usually in front of house. Her tone is low and chesty. I fight the urge to look at her. I just want to watch her while she stands at the burner, boiling her bagels.

She's just slid them into the pizza oven out front when the back doors open.

"Hey," I call. I assume it's Guy coming to do the admin for next week. I don't even look up from my prep.

"Hey," a chorus of feminine voices singsongs back. I spin around to find a parade of Lobo women carrying boxes.

They immediately start to unload their cargo all around me. My eyes dart up to meet Guy, who's following Mac into the kitchen.

"What the hell," I say, gaze wild.

"We're taking over," the one with pink hair asserts as she lays out a few cake rounds.

Guy shrugs. "They're borrowing our kitchen."

Immediately, they're all invading my space. Pinky is changing the music. The tall Lobo is helping the not Lobo unload pipping bags. All while Mac is directing traffic. Before I can even repeat my question, they've taken over, pushing me into a corner of the kitchen.

Ash returns through the swinging doors. All of the Lobos yell in unison, "Hey, girl, hey." Ash's brow furrows. "What the fuck are you guys doing here?"

Feeling ignored, I also chime in. "That's what I want to know."

As Ash sets down the tray of bagels, her family descends. They all begin tearing into and consuming the piping-hot dough.

"We had some cake orders that needed to go out," one starts.

"Obvi. We can't work at the bakery," another chimes in.

Exhaling steam mid scolding mouthful, Mac says, "These are fucking good. Is this for the Jam?"

They're overwhelming. My eyes dart to Ash, who's just leaning against the prep station on her elbows. She's taking in the scene thoughtfully as they continue to assault her with questions and suggestions. I walk over and take one of her bagels.

My theory was right. I give the exterior a testing squeeze that crunches delightfully under my fingers. Firing them in the wood-burning oven has given the crust a bubbly char that is synonymous with our signature pizzas. She boiled them in water sweetened with malted syrup. So when I tear it open, I'm greeted by a steaming, fluffy crumb that boasts even gluten bubbles. I slide a torn section into my mouth. Satisfyingly crisp on the outside and pillowy soft chewiness on the inside. An amused chuckle escapes me as I chew. These are perfect pizza bagels.

"Breakfast sandwiches," I muse through the cacophony of chatter.

Ashley's piercing dark eyes slice to mine.

"We're focused on selling during the afternoon events. But the surfers and spectators get there at, like, eight. They'll want to eat," I say.

Ashley starts to open her mouth in protest, but Mac is already butting in. "That's a great idea. You can maximize your revenue potential."

Guy is smiling from the office door, his arms folded over his broad chest. "I like the sound of that."

We all look to Ashley. She has a sudden look of panic in her eyes. It only lasts momentarily, but then it's replaced with her usual stoic expression. "Sure," she relents on an exhale.

I keep my gaze fixed on her. Wondering if I'll be able to catch that expression again. I don't turn away even after all the Lobos go about their work.

Ash can feel my eyes on her. She looks at me. "You sure about this?" she asks.

I give her a nod. "It's a good idea," I say.

Her mouth presses into a tight line.

I have the urge to reach out to her. Instead, I watch as she turns to the colorful one and picks up one of her pink locks.

"New color already," she asks.

Pinky nods effusively as she pipes an icing dam on a layer of cake sponge. "And are you guys making dessert?" Pinky asks, then spoons raspberry compote into the filling dam.

"Yeah, you totally need something sweet for all the kids," the tall one adds.

"I don't do dessert," I reply, crossing my arms.

They all bust up into cackles of laughter.

"What," I huff.

"Oh, we fucking remember," Ash replies.

Of course, she's alluding to when I very briefly worked at Mother Wolf. I hated having to make any of the desserts. I'd often ask Ashley to repeatedly show me how to execute a recipe until the task was complete. Yes, I was an asshole even back then. But I'd repay the favor by kindly making any savory items that were on her prep list.

She's smiling at me. Her nose scrunches and her eyes narrow when she's truly happy. I feel like I'm looking at eighteen-year-old Ash again. I remember a time when, after a shift at Mother Wolf, we'd tried to go through the McDonald's Drive Thru on my bicycle. I pedaled while Ash was balanced in the U-shaped dip of the handlebars. When the employees wouldn't answer the intercom, we started to scream about having a "Mac attack," and they needed to call the ambulance immediately. They actually called the cops instead.

We ended up going to my mom's empty apartment. The only food we could find was an oversized lion's mane mushroom that I'd bought to expand my mother's horizons. So, we battered it up and made nuggets with garlic mayo. We ate them in front of the TV, watching reruns of The Price Is Right. They were better than any fucking Chicken McNugget we could have bought.

Again, I have the urge to reach out to her. However, this is a very different type of urge than before. Her face has relaxed into a pensive expression as she rolls her bottom lip between her teeth. I feel a hunger pain. I take another bite of the bagel. I shouldn't fuck this up.

"We could make something ahead of time. It's going to be hot, so maybe something cold," she says thoughtfully.

I think for a moment. She's right. On the day when we're firing pizzas and making sandwiches to order, we need something easy. "What about panna cotta?" I ask.

She smiles. "Yeah, we could make two types. Maybe something like a caramel and pretzel?" I nod. It sounds fucking delicious. "And something seasonal," she continues.

A wicked smile crosses my lips. "Peach," I say as our eyes meet. Her full lips slowly spread, the apples of her cheeks rounding. There is a mischievous look in her eyes.

My fucking dick strains as she wets her lips and says, "My favorite."

Chapter 12

ASH

My teeth chatter and my hands shake. The sun is just starting to break the marine layer, but the temperature remains in the fifties. Thank God for the portable Ooni ovens. Raff lit one to toast the bagels, but more importantly, to keep us warm. Even with the heat, I still feel shaky about today.

I haven't been sleeping well since Mac told me their plan. I know that Cita and Lulu must have hit the roof when they all gave notice. They're working limited shifts to make sure the entire bakery doesn't come crashing down. After Van's wedding, only the Lobo matriarchs will remain at Mother Wolf, the end of our family legacy.

Mac told me that Cita and Lulu have been alternating between giving them the cold shoulder and barraging them with nasty voicemails. My phone has yet to ring. That's fine. It was easy for Cita and Lulu to cut me loose. It's always been that way. Ashley is the bad one. Ashley can't do anything right. Why would you do that, Ashley?

I remember one time, after Abuelita died, I got to go with them to the wholesale restaurant supply depot. I was home sick from first grade. Despite my fever, I was so excited. My dream was to be a baker just like them. So, I couldn't believe my luck when I got to spend the entire day alone with my idols. I desperately wanted them to be impressed.

I thought that if I was good and helpful, they might even buy me a treat. I wanted a thick apron just like the ones they used in the bakery. Not the thin cotton ones they had us wear, but the real deal. So, I bent over backward to make myself perfect. I carried their purses, pushed the cart, organized their shopping list, listened intently to Lulu's conspiracy theories about George W. Bush, and laughed at all of Cita's jokes, anything I could do to be what they needed.

It was a long day. Cita kept stopping to talk with the employees. While Lulu would follow every random sparkly thing that caught her eye. A lot of my time was spent trying to stay together. I'd push the oversized cart up and down the wide aisles, attempting to keep up with them both. My muscles were screaming from the exertion, firing explosive pains up and down my tiny legs.

We'd been in the store for what felt like hours. I was still pretty young, maybe six or seven. I'd been on my feet in the cold warehouse without any food or water. I was sweating through my Snoopy pajamas and puffer coat despite the freezing temperature. My teeth chattered, and my hands shook, but I kept pushing. I am unbreakable.

Finally, we lined up at the register. My hair was damp and sticking to my forehead, my breath heavy, but I had done it. I was perfect. My treat was imminent. I scanned the cart. No apron. That was fine. I'd probably need to build my way up to that anyway. My eyes continued to search the wire basket. Nothing overt that would scream validation inside. I spied packs of gum and novelty candy for sale at the counter. A pittance compared to how hungry I was, but surely, they would allow it. I'd been good, right?

I stretched out a quivering finger toward a box of pink Nerds. I turned to my mom, eyebrows pulled upwards, and a slight pout to my bottom lip. Cita exhaled sharply. "Seriously," she said in an exasperated tone.

Lulu leaned forward, plucking the box in question off the rack. She brought it up inches away from her hazel eyes and squinted at the back. "That's a ton of sugar," she tutted.

I nervously glanced at the bald man who was ringing us up.

He looked down at me through smudged coke-bottle lenses and shrugged as if to say, "You're on your own, kid."

I turned back to my mother, who had a displeased expression.

"You kids are always begging for shit. We're not made of money."

I nodded solemnly. Since my father had died two years earlier and then Abuelita a couple of months later, money was tight.

Cita handed the bald man her credit card as she extended the car keys toward me. "Go wait in the van," she said in an all too familiar tone. On shaky legs, I made my way out to the car. My limbs felt heavy from all the exertion. My clothes were damp. I could feel my mouth pooling with drool, probably because I was so hungry. When Cita and Lulu finally emerged, I jumped out to help them load bags into the back. The sudden movement made me see spots, but I blinked them back. I caught sight of my reflection in the bumper. I looked white.

The entire ride home, I'd felt my ears ringing as Lulu and Cita gossiped about a woman from Oregon, whom they'd hired to help out part-time. I just leaned my head against the window and kept swallowing back the saliva. As we exited the freeway, I started to feel an anxiety building in my stomach. I gulped it down. My gut was fizzing with each rumbling turn of the van. Right as we were rounding the corner to our street, I couldn't keep it in anymore. I opened my mouth to call out for help, but it was too late. I attempted to bring my hands up to catch it all, but the vomit was more than my six-year-old palms could hold.

Cita was furious. They made me clean up the interior as much as I could. Then, they sent me upstairs to the room I shared with Lex. I fell asleep shaking and clutching an oversized mixing bowl that Lulu had brought me after the van had been emptied and hosed out. I was exhausted but still uneasy. Despite my best efforts, I had broken. I wouldn't make the mistake of being sick again.

When my eyes opened, it was dark. I could hear everyone downstairs. The lingering smell of Lulu's jackfruit tacos hung in the air. I carefully made my way into the living room. There I saw Mac, Lex, and Van all sitting on the oversized couch. The rhythmic percussion of the box of Nerds being dumped into each of their palms and then passed to the next. The Nanny was playing on the television in front of them. I took a few steps forward. "Can I have some?" I asked, hand outstretched.

The sound of rustling as Cita flicked down the magazine she was looking at in one of the nearby armchairs. Suzy, the elderly papillon, perched in her lap. "No," she said resolutely. "You're sick. You can't have any."

I gazed at my sisters and cousin, all unsure of how to proceed. My eyes welled, but I knew what would happen if I cried. So, I tucked my bottom lip between my teeth and slid onto the couch next to them. I silently watched The Nanny as Cita recounted in detail how difficult and inconvenient it had been to spend the rest of the afternoon cleaning the van.

I am not surprised that they haven't reached out. I'm sure they view this all as an annoying inconvenience. It's always been this way. When I left five years ago, it was the same. I will always be too much for them to deal with and never enough for them to love.

I don't like that my sisters and cousin are getting involved. Sure, they have their problems with Cita and Lulu, but it's nothing like mine. It gives me that fizzy feeling in my stomach. It's hard to ignore.

Last night it was pervasive. I stayed up just staring out the bay window. I watched the empty street, thinking. I like working at Princess Pizzarina. The food is great. The people are amazing. Fuck, I even kinda sorta like working for Raff. But one question has been swirling around in my mind. Why does he trust me?

Raff has been weird since we got high on the roof last week. I guess we're friends, but he has this sense of confidence in me that is unsettling. Not just because a few weeks ago he was screaming in my face, but because it's too easy. I have to be careful. Raff seems to think that I know what I'm doing. If history has taught me anything, it's that Ashley is always wrong.

"You good?" Raff asks, bumping my shoulder with his. Shit. I've been zoning out.

I nod, feeling heat radiate at the point of contact. The first wave of customers has been steady. To my utter shock, we're nearly sold out of breakfast sandwiches. We kept it really simple. Two classic varieties. Either a bacon, egg, and cheese or an avocado, egg, and cheese.

Last night, the entire crew rallied around Raff and I. We bumped disco music as everyone worked elbow to elbow. Space was limited with regular dinner service. Plus, the influx of visitors for the Log Jam had everyone hustling to keep up with the orders.

The energy was palpable, and somehow the chaos just made us push harder. Lex and Nat made the panna cotta. Chuy, Miguel, and Nora helped with the extra prep and also ran the kitchen. All the while, the servers would pop back periodically to cheer us on. Mac and Guy were loading supplies and packing out Guy's truck until late into the night.

Even with all of their help, Raff and I were scrambling to get everything ready for today. The entire time, Raff seemed ecstatic. He didn't have to yell or intimidate. Everyone was just following orders and actually having fun. Despite the lack of sleep, Raff has carried that excitement into today.

The line for our booth has been long. People have been ordering bagels and then hitting up the overpriced coffee cart a few booths down. "Yo," Raff calls over the line at Mikey, who is headed toward the beach with his board.

He throws Raff two fingers and a nod as he yells back, "Save me one, chef!" There aren't many left, but Guy slips one of the B.E.C.s under the folding table we're using as a counter.

Guy is running the cashbox and expediting. Mac is amongst the crowd. She keeps the everyone in line as she gets people's orders and runs the tickets back to Raff and I. She's also brought her camera. Every so often, she stops to snap photos of everything, alternating between the Canon around her neck and her iPhone. She's been hounding Guy to post more on the Princess social media pages. So today she's capturing content.

Just as the surf heats are getting underway and we've sold the last few bagels, Van arrives with Cary in tow. They're each carrying a humongous flower arrangement. Van is obsessed with gardening. She's been growing her own bridal florals for their wedding. I guess the harvest is going well. She places the vases bursting with poppies, marigolds, clarkia, aster, prairie smoke, sunflowers, and dahlias on either end of our folding table.

"Sorry, we're late," she says apologetically. Since she's not staying at the blue house, she's been commuting back and forth from Cary's townhome.

"It's fine, babe," Cary says with a laugh. He places a meaty arm around her shoulders. "It's not like they were waiting for the flowers."

Mac's eyes narrow on Cary. She opens her mouth but is quickly cut off.

"These are beautiful, Van," Guy declares.

A smug smile spreads across Cary's face as he leans over the table to shake Guy's hand a little too hard. "Good to see you again, man," Cary says with a possessive air.

Guy and Cary are almost the same height. They dress similarly in the unofficial Northern California surfer uniform; Pendleton and a flat bill. However, between the two of them, Guy is the only one who actually surfs. His clothes are lived in and functional, while Cary's are expensive and performative. With the exception of today, I have never seen Cary anywhere near the beach. Maybe that's why he's being such a dick to Guy. He feels threatened. Like Guy's challenging the carefully calculated image that Cary's trying to project of himself.

Guy nods. "You guys hungry?"

Just as Van is saying "yes," Cary shakes his head with a snort.

"Nah, trying to watch the macros before the big day." He gives his nearly flat stomach a pat with one hand as he tightens his grip on Van with the other. Raff and I turn back to the portable flattop, biting our bottom lips in an attempt to try not to laugh. However, when I catch Raff's expression in the corner of my eye, I can't help the chortle that escapes me.

"Am I gonna have to fight this guy?" Raff whispers.

I shake my head. "No. I think Mac's going to do it," I hiss back.

We both glance over our shoulders at Mac, who has her arms firmly crossed over her chest and a deep frown on her face. We both burst out in uncontrollable peels of laughter. Raff makes a quick scrambled egg and slides it on top of our last bagel with avocado and cheese.

"Here," he says with a nod, "for the tall one."

I shake my head and accept the plate from him. "You've known us for years. How do you not remember our names?" I ask.

His amber gaze lifts to mine. "I know your name," he says with a cocky smile that sends an excited shiver through me.

Then I immediately hate myself. Raff has always been able to get under my skin. I don't know how to stop it, and these cracks are only getting deeper.

"Here, Mama," I say, handing the foil-wrapped sandwich off to Van.

"Enjoy, Vanessa Lobo. Prettiest girl in our graduating class," Raff says sweetly.

I shake my head at the way he overly accentuates the pronunciation of her name. She accepts it eagerly before being dragged off by Cary, who shoots Raff a glare over his shoulder.

"You're annoying," I say to him as I roll my eyes at his stupid, proud grin.

The competition rages on. We reset for the afternoon as we hear the periodic roar of spectators. Guy and Mac head back to the restaurant to pick up the coolers full of panna cotta and dough. Sometime between the youth and adult heats, a band starts to play Willie Nelson and Waylon Jennings covers.

Children and old people sway and hop to the music. Raff cheers on an enthusiastic toddler who is head-banging to the classic country music. He raises his complimentary beer that someone has handed each of us.

"Keep on rocking, little dude," he calls out. I laugh and again despise myself for it.

The smell of churros and grilled meat fills the air. The beer garden opens, and people wander up from the cliffs overlooking the competition to the long picnic tables that populate the area cordoned off by the heavy orange plastic festival fencing.

My nerves don't have time to take over. We're busy. As the competition wraps up for the afternoon, a huge line has formed at our booth. Sure, there are other food stalls; the fire station is barbecuing burgers, the women's auxiliary is selling baked goods, and of course, there are tacos. But the longest line by far is for Princess Pizzarina.

Thank God, Raff, and I have figured out our shit in the kitchen. We're firing on all cylinders. Effortlessly working in tandem as we crank out orders. Guy and Mac's system from this morning is working flawlessly.

At one point, Nora and her shy friend Shirin stop by. We put them to work running empty Cambros and coolers back to Guy's truck. Or at least Nora helps. Shirin has caught the eye of Jeremy Silverstein, the enthusiastic beer guy. He's been talking her ear off about a Persian-inspired lager he's been working on. Shirin has been smiling politely behind oversized heart-shaped Chloe sunglasses.

We sell out before three. "Come down to the restaurant and keep the party going," Mac yells to the crowd.

Raff turns to me, one side of his mouth lifting into a lopsided grin. "You ready to do it all over again tomorrow?" he asks.

I sigh, but fix my face into a smile. Today went well, but tomorrow is another opportunity to fuck it all up.

I can't exhale until Guy and Mac drive off with the last of our stuff. I'm hit with a huge wave of exhaustion. I tip my head back and close my eyes. Through my eyelids, the sun scalds orange orbs into my retina, but it's helping me wake up. I let the sunshine warm my face and just try to breathe. I know that we need to go prep for tomorrow. Probably double it based on today. Plus, Raff has to check on the kitchen. Miguel, Chuy, and Nora have been running Princess on their own today. Raff and I will swap in to help in about an hour.

The schedule is cycling through my brain when I feel a slight tug on my sleeve. I peek open a lid and gaze down. Raff has my shirt pinched between his long forefinger and thumb. "You rang," I say flatly, letting my head loll to the side. Little spots dance across my vision as I squint at him.

"Wanna get something to eat?" he asks.

My eyebrow lifts skeptically. "With you?" I don't mean the question to be so harsh, but we haven't willingly hung out alone together.

"Yes, you brat. Unless you have something better to do for the next hour," he says.

I weigh my options as Raff slings his backpack over his shoulder. My original plan was to take the bus back to Princess and then sleep in my car before heading into work. I know that's what I should do, but there's something about the way Raff looks over his shoulder and grins that has me following him.

Chapter 13

RAFF

Tacos taste better on the beach. Ash knows the family that runs the taco stand. So they loaded us up with carne asada, pollo, and carnitas tacos. Foil-wrapped platos and Mexican Cokes in hand, we descended the wooden staircase that zigzags down to the beach and found a spot just past the cliff face. Shoes kicked off, we sit with our toes buried in the sand, paper plates balanced on our knees as we eat.

I notice that her eyes keep falling to my forearms. Despite being twenty when I last worked with Ash, I felt like I was still coming out of puberty. I was gangly and scrawny. Just a punk kid who didn't have any awareness of his body. I'm still pretty lean, but years of manual labor in kitchens and surfing have given me some muscles. I narrow my eyes and smile at her. "Are you checking me out?" I ask. I pull up my sleeve and flex.

Her eyebrows pull together. "I was looking at your tattoos, you conceited ass."

Damn. I wish she had been checking me out. Her cheeks flush red. Good. I like that she got flustered. "Here," I say, laying my bare arm in her lap.

She jerks at the sudden contact but doesn't push me away. Ash hesitates for a moment and then lets her index finger run up my flesh. I fight a shiver at the sensation of her touch. She uses her nail to trace the black lines of my American traditional mermaid. I've always had tattoos. Got my first when I was seventeen, but I've come a long way from the shitty snake on my ribs. Now my arms, chest, and back are totally covered.

When her finger reaches the hem of my sleeve, she stops. "Neat," she says flatly as she lets me go.

I want her to keep touching me. The gnawing hunger demands it. One tiny sip of contact is not nearly enough to satisfy its craving. I lean over, slipping my hand into hers and gently tug her arm into my lap. Again, she tenses slightly.

"Tit for tat," I say.

"Or tattoo, I guess," I add with a cheesy smile.

She huffs at my joke. "Fine, Rat."

When I feel her relax, I turn over her arm and study the smooth tan skin. She has a mix of American traditional and fine line just like me. It's only black ink as far as the eye can see. Flora and fauna are the main subjects. I let my fingertips brush up her inner arm. Goose flesh rises as I touch her, and she squirms.

"Are you ticklish?" I say wryly.

"Hell no!" She yanks her arm, but I hold tight. We lock eyes. "You better not," she warns.

"I would never," I gasp.

She holds my gaze, unconvinced.

"Scout's honor," I say, holding up three fingers in a salute.

"I doubt you were ever a Boy Scout."

I laugh. "You'd be surprised. I was quite the good boy before you met me." I peek up at her through my lashes.

She sighs and straightens her arm. "You were never a good boy," she throws back at me. "The first time I ever heard your name was when you were getting called into the middle school Principal's office for climbing over the dumpsters behind the gym and escaping."

I feign ignorance with a low hum as I overtly scrunch up my face and tap my temple. "You walked back into school soaking wet and wearing a pink romper," Ash adds.

"I had important business to attend to," I reply. I can't fight my smile as her mouth falls open.

She shakes her head. "I knew it. You're such a bullshitter," she says, tossing a fistful of sand with her free hand and attempting again to pull back her other arm.

I hold on. "Alright, you want to know," I ask.

She looks at me skeptically but nods.

"My sister. Some girls poured paint on her in art class. She couldn't get my mom in trouble at work again, so I jumped the fence, ran across the street to the elementary school, and swapped clothes with her."

Ashley is dumbfounded. Her heart-shaped lips part as she blinks at me.

"Surprised," I ask. She exhales slowly and then turns to look out at the ocean.

"Impressed," she answers.

I smirk.

"Who knew the Rat King had a heart of gold?" she says.

Ah shit. That's what they all used to call me, the old Raff in his prime. I'm about to tell her that I'm not the Rat King anymore. That I'm leaving it all behind, changing. But what's the point? Words are useless. You just gotta show people.

I watch her scoop up a handful of sand and let it pour out from between her fingers. I run my fingertips up her arm again, and she shivers.

"Seen enough," she asks, turning back to me.

I shake my head, giving her hand a slight squeeze. "Of you? I could never get enough," I say.

She stares at me for a long beat. Our breathing synchronized and deep. "What are you doing?" she asks.

I shrug. "Holding your hand."

She shakes her head slowly, dark almond eyes still locked on mine. Our breath is still flowing in time with each other. The sound of the waves setting our synced rhythm.

"That's not what I mean," she says softly.

My eyes dip and watch her tongue skim the curve of her bottom lip. "What do you mean then?" I ask.

Ash's expression returns to neutral. She pulls her arm back, and this time, despite myself, I let her go. I don't want to freak her out. She stares at the waves. A group of small, speckled brown and white birds scuttles in and out of the tide, unsure if they're chasing or being chased by the water.

"We should head back," she says, gathering up our trash.

I shouldn't have even done it in the first place. Fuck. Ashley's going to bolt. I don't fucking blame her. Guy's going to be pissed for sure. I don't move.

"Sorry," I say almost on a whisper.

She looks at me. "For what?" she asks.

"For wanting you so badly that it gives me a stomach ache. For needing to consume you," the gnawing screams.

I slowly shake my head. "I don't think I ever said it before. About, uh, Mother Wolf and how everything happened back then." Her mouth presses into a firm line, and her nostrils flare, but she doesn't give away any emotion. "It's fine."

I hate that word.

I want to grab her hand, to feel her, any part of her that I can get. "No, it wasn't," I say. "I should've just shown up."

She stands, letting sand rain down on me. "Seriously. You don't have to do this. I'm fine. It's all fine. Let's just drop it," she says. So, we do.

Chapter 14

ASH

"Oh my god, just shut up and get into the truck," Mac says. Today has been exhausting. Guy set the alarm, and we all rushed out the back door. Mac decided that I should just stay with them tonight to avoid driving while tired.

"I'll take the bus," I'd protested.

Then Mac went on a long tirade listing all the reasons why I should just go back with them. There was one important reason that she didn't have to say. We all knew what could happen when someone fell asleep while driving. I finally relented with an annoyed, "Daddy, chill!" So now I'm sandwiched in the back of the truck between Raff and Van.

The backseat of the truck cab is so tight that I'm plastered against Raff from hip to knee. I ignore the throbbing deep in my core. Try not to notice how nice the pressure feels against me and how it makes a pulsing ache grow between my legs. Shut up, stupid, horny Ashley.

I'm usually good at ignoring this type of feeling. I don't date, so if I want to have sex, it's usually casual or random. Admittedly, it's been a while. Not since before I moved back four months ago. Longer if I'm being honest, I just haven't met anyone new that I've found more interesting than cooking.

I do my best to focus on Mac as she describes Van's upcoming bachelorette party. It's a very short drive to Guy's house from Princess. I can do this. I readjust my positioning, scooting my butt a few millimeters away from Raff. But as soon as I do, he lets his knee fall wider, not letting the connection be broken. I glare at him.

"What," he says innocently.

There's vibrating to my other side. "Oh, sorry. Hang on," Van says and lifts her hips to access her pocket.

The movement forces me to lean toward Raff. I'm practically in his lap. Despite myself, I inhale his charred essence. I hate when he grins down at me after we straighten up.

"Did you just smell me," he asks on an amused whisper.

I'm mortified. "Ew," I say quickly. "Shut up, asshole."

Luckily, I'm drowned out by Van's phone call.

"Ok. Yeah, mami, I'll see you tomorrow," she says in a low tone. My heart sinks. I can hear Lulu on the other end. Lulu and Cita may be identical twins, but they differ in one major way. Van is Lulu's world. They're best friends. Lulu never goes one day without saying goodnight.

"No, I already told you, I'll be with Mac. Ok. I'll tell her. I love you. Night," she says and hangs up. Van's eyes quickly dart to me and then back down to her lap.

With a quiet apology, Van slips her phone back into her pocket. Again, I'm pushed toward Raff. This time, though, I feel his long fingers wrap around my biceps. He gently holds me for the briefest moment before helping me straighten. There's an awkward silence. I don't feel the need to fill it with anything other than longing. I want to be loved like how Lulu loves Van. I want to be inquired after. I want to be cared for by someone just once.

"We should get Thai," Guy says.

"Is it still open?" Mac replies, pulling out her phone.

I'm grateful for the unimportant conversation. My ears ring, and I swallow. Then I feel it; light pressure against my elbow. My eyes drop to see Raff's hand. It is resting on his thigh, but he's extended his pinky out. His long finger is gently pressing into me. Small but deliberate as if to say, "I'm here."

I opt for a shower while the others argue about where to get delivery at this time of night. When I emerge, they're all sitting in the living room. An old episode of The Simpsons is playing on the large TV. Guy, Mac, and Van are all occupying the modular retro sectional. The big white dog is stretched across them like a throw blanket. Raff, hair wet like mine, sits in a rounded velvet accent chair. So my only option is the leather chaise lounge. "This house is a trip," I say slipping onto a reclined position.

"Louise had fucking sick taste," Mac says as she lets her hands run along the dog's back. "You should see her closet." Van and I look at each other, eyes wide. Then our gaze darts back to Mac.

"I'm sorry, I don't think I heard you correctly," I say, rubbing my ear with my knuckle. "Did you just casually mention that Guy has a closet full of vintage clothing?"

Van and I don't have a lot in common. However, the one thing that we bond over is thrifting amazing clothing from the 1970s. Sure, I'm more Smoke On The Water while she's all Silver Springs, but we still get worked up at the prospect of premium vintage. I see Van ball up her fists as I feel myself lean forward.

Mac's brow furrows. "Hands off, you derelicts. That stuff belongs to Guy."

"We wouldn't steal it," Van starts as I'm saying, "can't we just try it on?"

Mac exhales sharply, "No."

But Van and I are both sticking out our bottom lips, eyes wide and eyebrows pinched as we make a sort of pathetic whimpering sound. This causes the dog, who has previously been lying like a limp noodle, to jerk upright and start to bark.

Guy's booming laugh echoes. "Aw let them have some fun," Guy says.

Van and I both jump up with a "Yay."

“Thank you, step-daddy,” Van says with a little clap, which only makes Guy laugh harder.

“Fine,” Mac huffs, but we don’t hear her. We’re running down the hallway toward the primary bedroom. We push open the closet doors, the mirrors rattling as they make contact with the jamb.

“It’s amazing,” Van says.

“I’m going to cry,” I whimper.

Turtlenecks, quilted jackets, bubble-sleeve dresses, denim skirts, jumpsuits, ditto jeans, disco tops, and yes, even a pair of hot pants stretched out before us. I wish I could say that we showed restraint, but that would be a lie.

We both started to feverishly pull garments off of hangers, comparing what we held to what the other was holding. Our eyes watered from the smell of nicotine, but we didn’t care.

“Dude, Mac is missing out on these shoes,” I say, holding up a particularly impressive pair of Famolares platform wedges.

Van nods before suddenly gasping. “Look,” she says, extending a slender finger.

“Kaftans,” I whisper.

Moments later, we’ve ripped off our clothing, nothing but smooth, drape-y chiffon between our bodies and the world. I twirl and let the fabric billow. Obviously, I'm a little too short for the garment. Guy's grandmother was probably closer to Van's five-nine rather than my five-six and a half.

"Wait," Van says, digging into the closet again. "This one was made for you."

Before I have a second to protest, off comes the Kaftan, and Van is pouring me into a black mini dress with long flared sleeves and a deep v that goes almost all the way down to my belly button.

"God damn, where was Guy's grandma wearing this?" I ask as I readjust my boobs in the mirror. Van and I look incredible.

"I need to take a picture," she says, then flings open the bedroom door to dash down the hallway.

I study my reflection in the mirror. This dress looks like it was made for me. It clings to and accentuates all of my curves. I hate looking at myself for too long. It feels indulgent. My eyes focus on how the shag carpet looks like alien grass between my tan toes. Movement behind me in the mirror catches my eye, and I reel around.

"What the fuck," I say on a gasp. Raff stands in the doorway. A kitchen towel over his shoulder. An odd expression on his face.

"Foods ready," he says slowly.

"Delivery," I ask dumbly because what the fuck am I supposed to say in this situation?

He shakes his head. "They canceled our order. So, I made something," he replies. He doesn't move to leave. We just kind of stare at each other.

"I'll change," I say, then stretch around to undo the zipper. Unfortunately the sleeves don't allow me to reach the back of the dress. "Sorry," I say. "The, um, zipper..." I don't even have to finish the sentence before he's coming towards me.

In a few swift steps, I feel Raff's hands at the nape of my neck. My pulse is thundering in my ears. The ache throbbing deep inside. I press my lips together, desperate to conceal my shameful need for him. Raff's long fingers curl gently around my clavicle, holding the fabric in place. The contact is so intense that I have to will myself to keep breathing.

His other hand guides the zipper lower. The cool air makes my skin tingle as the garment parts. Wider and wider, it slips open, loosening its hold on me and exposing my secrets to the world. I almost scream out as the contrast in temperature between Raff's warm breath on my neck and the drafty old house's atmosphere meets.

Finally, when the gliding stops at the base of my spine, I feel Raff's hand slip inside. He parts the fabric, and his warm, flat palm skims up my back. His rough skin gently brushes my soft flesh. My eyes fall shut as a ragged breath escapes me.

The sound of footsteps behind us has my eyes snapping open. As quickly as it happened, Raff's hand is gone. Van enters the room just as Raff is on his way out.

"Oh good, you're still in the dress," she says waggling her phone at me. She zips me up and then takes a few photos. "Why are you so flushed?" she asks after we've changed.

I just shrug. "I'm hungry," I reply.

Chapter 15

RAFF

I am going to combust. I glance at Guy across the dinette from me. He's talking to a very sleepy Mac. She's showing him pictures on her iPhone while drowsily attempting to eat spaghetti al pomodoro. This is the least intense I've ever seen her. I stare down at my bowl, willing myself not to turn my head.

Next to me come the most salacious sounds I've ever heard. Ash is eating my pasta. Her pillowy soft lips sucking and slurping strands of noodles. Little moans of pleasure escape her as she eats each mouthful of coils. Fuck. I tighten my grip on my cutlery.

Thank God she hasn't noticed what she's doing to me. Van is on her other side, swiping through photos that she took of the event. Pick up your fork and eat, I tell myself. My stomach is heavy. Even if I wanted to, I literally could not imagine eating right now. I am starving, but nothing I can cook will ever satiate this hunger. I can't stand up to leave either as all of the blood in my body is rushing towards my lap.

"You look sick," Guy says. My eyes snap up to him as I shake out of my Ashley induced trance.

"What," I mutter.

He holds up Mac's phone towards me. Thank fuck. He's not talking about my current expression. There on the screen is Ash and I in the middle of the chaos. We're both in focus, moving around each other as the rest of the action is nothing more than smears of light and color.

"Oh shit," Ashley says, leaning into me to get a better look.

I suddenly jerk back, toppling out of my chair onto the tile floor. Forks freeze midair as everyone stares at me.

"What the hell," Mac says as Guy is furrowing his eyebrows. "You ok, man?"

I jump up and snatch my bowl. "Totally. Just tired. Night," I say hastily as I rush off down the hall. I do not miss Guy's confused expression.

What the fuck am I doing? I'm so fucking fucked. The door shuts behind me with a snick as I toss the bowl on my dresser and faceplant into my mattress. I suck. The gnawing has been raging tonight, and I can't rein it in. I should not have touched Ashley's back like that, but damn, she looked so fucking good in that dress. I'm a fucking pervert.

I'd take a cold shower right now, but I already took one. Literally feeling her pressed against me in the car was enough to get me going earlier. I feel like a horny teenager. It only makes sense because I haven't gone this long without sex since I was one. Guy is going to kill me. He's going to kill me, and then he's going to blow up the fucking business. Of course, he is, because I fucking deserve that. I'm such a piece of shit. I've got to get control of this beast.

I roll off the side of my bed and do push-ups. I don't keep count. I just keep pressing my body weight up and down. Sweat beading on my forehead and arms, screaming, I keep going. I don't stop until there is no more desire. No more need inside. The sounds in the living room and the gnawing are both quiet.

I collapse down onto the carpet. Let myself just breathe, heavy and ragged. I didn't bother to turn on the overhead light, just exist in the warm glow of the old ornate lamp that Louise had on the dresser before I moved in. When it feels safe, I peel myself off the floor and stumble down the hallway.

The house is silent. The lights are off. Minnie isn't in her bed. I'm sure she's sprawled across Guy's feet. The pointy starburst wall clock in the kitchen reads two fifteen. I place my still-full bowl in the fridge. As I straighten up, my eyes adjusting from the incandescent refrigerator bulb, I notice a figure standing in the large archway that leads into the living room. I yelp and stumble back a few steps.

"Jumpy," Ash says with a little satisfied grin.

"Can you blame me? You're creeping around in the dark," I reply. I lean against the sink and catch my breath.

She's wearing a pair of borrowed shorts and an oversized T-shirt. I try to swallow down the lump in my throat as I catch the outline of her erect nipples.

"I was trying to sleep when you came blasting in here," she returns.

I exhale, raking my fingers through my hair. "There are too many Lobos in this house," I say and cross my arms. "Why are you haunting the living room?"

She exhales and turns back the way she came. "There wasn't enough room with Mama and Daddy in the bed. So, I'm on the couch," she says, pointing towards a discarded pillow and crumpled serape.

My skin prickles. "Slept on that couch many times. It's going to suck for your back," I say.

She nods. "That I can handle. It's how cold it is in here," she replies.

I shrug. "Come on," I say, crossing to the couch and grabbing her pillow. Guy is actually going to fucking kill me. Moments later, she's in my bedroom. Her eyes are darting around. She cautiously takes in the room as I chuck her pillow on my bed. "There," I say, extending my hand in invitation. She doesn't make any movement towards me.

"Where are you going to sleep?" she asks slowly. I point at the floor.

Her eyes move towards the bed. Then she exhales, raising her gaze to the ceiling. "Just fucking get in, Rat," she huffs.

I watch her climb from the foot to the top of the bed and tuck herself against the wall. She clutches the pillow to her chest. I hesitate for a moment.

“Are you sure?” I ask.

She bites her bottom lip thoughtfully before saying, “No.”

I turn off the lamp and then slide into the bed next to her. We lay there in silence. Two corpses unmoving. I know she’s not asleep, and there’s no way I can fall asleep with her so close to me.

“Why did you touch me earlier?” she whispers.

I stare up at the ceiling, unsure of what to say. I can’t tell her the truth, but I also can’t stop the words “because I needed to” from escaping my lips.

Then I hear it. A chortling snort from her side of the bed.

“What the fuck,” I hiss. Is this chick really laughing at me?

“You’re so fucking lame,” she says.

“What? Why,” I demand. I hear rustling next to me as she repositions herself and then poof! She’s smacked me directly in the face with her pillow.

I jerk upright, but not before another swing of the pillow collides with my cheek. “Stop,” I say grabbing her weapon before her next blow can land.

"You suck so much," she says.

I frown at her. "I'm sorry if I'm attracted to you," I say.

"Knowing you, Rat, it will pass. Just like last time," she says.

"Ouch. That was so mean. I can't handle these feelings I have for you." I place a hand over my chest, rubbing the tender center.

She takes that moment of distraction to wrench the pillow out of my grasp and bring it down hard on the top of my head. "You'll move on like you always do," she says. Is that what I always do? It hasn't felt like it.

I have no time to think as another muffled smack hits me in the neck and shoulder. The fabric slaps my ear and causes me to reel for a second. "Would you quit it already? I'm not going to fuck you over again," I say.

She scoffs.

"I'm serious. I have these overwhelming feelings," I start, but she's cutting me off.

"Just ignore your fucking feelings."

"Like you," I snap.

Her mouth falls open, and her pillow lowers. "You're an asshole," she says.

I exhale. "Yeah, I know. But that doesn't mean I don't also like you," I reply.

Frustrated, she flops back on the bed. "You can't like me," she says with a huff.

"Trust me, if I could just ignore these feelings, I would," I say.

"So like what, you want to fuck me?" she asks.

Now it's my turn to laugh. "Ok, blunt." I glance down at her, and she's curled around the pillow again. God damn, I want to be that pillow. "Sure, I guess. Amongst other things," I relent.

She peeks up at me. "I don't do relationships, you know that, right?"

I nod as I slowly lower down onto my side and meet her gaze. "Is that because of me? What I did," I ask.

She stares at me. Her face is fixed with an indeterminate expression, but I can tell she's agonizing over what to say next.

"Maybe," she replies finally. "But in all honesty, I think I'm just cursed."

I take her in. She's being vulnerable with me. I want to reciprocate but I'm not really sure where to start.

"Like by a witch," I ask.

She smiles. "A great-grandmother," she says on an exhale.

"Well, I'd offer to kill her and free you, but I think that time has already robbed us of that solution."

Her smile widens.

"You want to tell me about this curse? Maybe we can break it," I add.

Her expression turns sad as she rolls onto her back. Her gaze is fixed on the ceiling. "I'm unlovable," she says. My body acts on its own. Despite everything and knowing better, I cannot stop myself.

My arms wrap around her, and I pull her into me. Both of our hearts are thundering. I can feel her body stiffening, but I don't stop. I bring her as close as possible. The pillow squishing into the exposed flesh between us. I feel the sharp quills of the down feathers prickling into my torso and chest.

"That's not true," I say.

She starts to protest but I continue, "I'm going to prove you wrong. I haven't moved on."

I feel her soften in my hold. Her circulating breath has slowed. I do not let go. She's not fighting me anymore. I feel her wrap her arms around me, snaking my center. Her face presses into my chest, and I hear the sounds of a deep inhale. I smile. "Stop smelling me, weirdo," I say.

"Shut up, asshole," she murmurs into my chest. The sensation causes goose flesh to spread over me.

"You're such a fucking brat," I fire back.

She's immediately shushing me. Our arms and legs are entwined as I hold her close to my body. Nothing is settled, but neither is it uncertain. This is how we stay until the dark night sky gradients into the blue of early light. Both of us awake. We just waiting for tomorrow.

Chapter 16

ASH

I am confused. Raff and I don't sleep. We just basically wait until it's time to start the day. When we untangle from one another, we wordlessly get ready, make coffee, and wait for the others to get up. I feel both content and unsettled.

We stand at the back door staring out over the mountains behind Guy's house. The sun hasn't yet crested the peak. We stare at the pool water dancing with the morning breeze. "It's going to be cold as fuck," Raff says leaning into me. I shiver. Not from the prospect of the temperature but because of his proximity. My body is alive with electricity.

"How many?" I hear a voice say from behind me.

Raff and I both turn to see a freshly showered Van being followed by Mac, who's clutching a pair of Charlotte Stone mules.

"Not that many," Van sighs.

I move to them slowly as they enter the kitchen, finding mugs and pouring coffee.

"Only eight," Van says, looking down at her phone. Mac tips her head back on a deep sigh.

"What's this?" I ask. Mac is tutting as she lets her head loll. Van gives me a tight smile as she opens the fridge to find the milk.

"Her fiancé is blowing her up," Mac says.

"He just cares, is all," Van adds quickly.

I hear Raff shift awkwardly in the living room. Van is a major pushover, especially when it comes to Cary.

"Sure, *today* he does," Mac starts. "But what about when he's with his friends and goes totally radio silent?"

"What?" Raff barks from the living room.

Van's cheeks burn red as a smile spreads across Mac's face. Guy is shuffling in now with Minnie on his heels.

"That's disrespectful," Raff continues.

Guy makes a face as Mac pulls down another mug.

Van rushes to the living room with the dog, excitedly following her. "He's busy, and I didn't tell him that I was staying here," Van explains.

I peek around the corner to watch the exchange.

"Listen, you're a strong, independent woman," Raff declares.

From the other side of the wall, Mac is interjecting, "I know that's right."

Guy's booming laugh, a little rusty with sleep, follows.

Van has slid next to Raff on the couch. The big white dog is happily weaving between their legs. With her hair pulled into a long braid that falls over one shoulder, she looks like a Disney Princess, eyes wide and hopeful. It's a stark contrast to Raff, who I know hasn't slept or shaven in twenty-four hours, and with his hood pulled up looks like a total unkept dirtbag.

"You're a privilege. If he wants you, he has to take all of you. Not just when it's convenient for him," Raff says before taking a pointed slurp of his coffee.

"Yeah, and the Rat King would know. He's an expert in treating women like shit," Guy says with a laugh.

Mac joins him. Van is shaking her head, eyebrows furrowed and lips pursed.

Raff's eyes shoot to mine before he snaps back, "Fuck you. In the past, I might've. But not anymore."

This only makes Guy and Mac laugh harder.

Raff is up on his feet. He's in Guy's face now. "I'm serious, man." It's comical how little Guy makes Raff seem without even trying, but Raff doesn't back down. "It's just like we were talking about in the driveway," he growls out.

Guy puts his hands up, sensing Raff's temper. The dog is circling them with a few exhilarated sneezes, oblivious to the tense atmosphere. "So you found someone you want to date then," Guy asks with a questioning lift of his eyebrow.

Raff stares at him for a beat, jaw working. I swear I can literally see the steam releasing from his head. This dude and his temper. "Yeah, I did," Raff says, finally relenting.

My breath catches, and I instinctively take a step backward as a wide grin spreads across Guy's face.

"Well, congrats, man," Guy says, seizing the opportunity of Raff's proximity. In a split second, he's throwing his arms around Raff in a humongous bear hug. Feet lifting up off the ground, Guy is jostling Raff around like a rag doll.

Despite my thundering heart, I laugh. That felt too real. This entire situation is giving me a rising sense of unease, but watching Raff squirm in Guy's embrace is funny as hell. After Guy has danced Raff's struggling body around the house, the dog barking and nipping at Raff's swinging legs, we head out for the last day of the Jam.

We drop off Mac and Van at Mother Wolf. I sink my teeth into my bottom lip as we rumble up towards the back door. Van taps me on the knee as Guy lets the truck idle. "Love you mucho, babe," she says.

I let the corners of my mouth turn up slightly. "Ditto, Mama," I say back.

Mac has already slid out into the hazy early morning when Van slips her toros between the front seats of the cab.

"Thank you, boys," she says as she takes both of their chins in her hands and plants a little peck on each of their cheeks.

"Ew, gross! Don't kiss them," Mac calls through the open door, her warm breath curling in the cool air.

Guy rolls his eyes. "Have a good day, Daddy," Guy teases before Mac slams the door shut behind Van. She flips Guy the bird as she walks towards the bakery.

Guy doesn't pull away immediately. He waits until Mac unlocks the back door and they're inside. I release the breath I'm holding. I've already ducked down low, but I jerk lower when the back door swings wide. Cita pokes her head out. She's got her short hair tucked under her signature red bandana.

She peers at us over the rim of her glasses, which are resting in their familiar spot at the tip of her nose. Guy and Raff wave at her. She scowls at them, uncrossing one arm to shoo them away. Guy is pulling out towards Princess when Cita turns back to go inside.

I'm convinced that she hasn't seen me. Then she hastily squints back again as she extends her pointer finger in a jabbing motion, pursing her lips and shaking her head. It happens quickly, but it happens all the same. I know she saw me. I know that she was communicating her disapproval. "Traitor." That's what she'd called me once.

My eyes fall to my lap. I chew the inside of my cheek as I run my fingertips over the line of stitching on the leather seat. I will myself to keep breathing. This is not a big deal. I am unbreakable.

"Who's ready to kill it today?" Guy asks, easing the unspoken tension.

My eyes glance up, and I meet Raff's gaze in the rearview mirror. He's been watching me. Studying my reaction.

"We are," he says, holding my stare.

Except maybe we're not. Today is much busier than yesterday. Word has spread about the Princess Pizzarina booth.

"Ta-da," Lex said when she arrived to help us. She unfurls a homemade banner.

"Holy shit," Raff marvels.

"I can't believe you made this," Guy gushes.

Lex has managed to make an incredible sign that features what I can only describe as a Mexican folk art-influenced anime-style space princess. It's vivid, eye-catching, and totally reflects the offbeat fun of Princess Pizzarina.

Lex flashes them Korean finger hearts as they shower her in praise. "Just give me free pizza for life, and we're even, 'k?"

Guy is laughing as he shakes her hand. "Deal."

They barely have time to fasten the banner to our canopy tent before a massive line has formed. Despite only having two items on the menu this morning, we're totally in the weeds from the jump.

Mac and Guy's system is apparently a byproduct of their close relationship, because Guy struggles to recreate the magic with Lex. Despite her cutesy nature and bubbly personality, Lex lacks Mac's efficiency. She spends more time chatting up customers than sending back tickets. So, there's not enough lead time for us to get orders started by the time guests are paying with Guy.

The other issue is that Lex has never written a ticket for line cooks before. Inconsistent and hard to read, we're spending too much time trying to figure out what she's scrawled in baby blue sparkly gelly pen.

"Pinky, I can't read your bubble letters," Raff shouts.

"Sorry, Cap," Lex chirps back. Thank God she buttered them up with that sign, otherwise Raff would probably be chewing her out right now.

I nudge him with my shoulder. "You good?" I ask. I avoid calling him Rat. It doesn't seem right anymore. When he meets my gaze, his eyes soften, and he nods. "Don't worry, I got this," I say. I turn around to Guy. "Swap with her," I command.

Guy doesn't need me to explain. He's already moving out into the crowd. Cool. First hurdle down, I think, but I still can't shake my unease. Seeing Cita this morning kinda has me fucked up.

Things get smoother as the morning winds down. On the plus side, having a little cute weirdo like Lex running the cash box has somehow tripled our tips since yesterday. It also doesn't hurt that she's pulled her short pink hair into messy micro pigtails. She's crinkling her button nose as she talks to the last customers in line before we shut down to switch over to pizza service. Each of the college-aged dudes is practically climbing over one another to stand the closest to Lex.

"What's up, mother fuckers," I hear a raspy voice ask with an accompanying slap on my ass. I turn to see Nat in a skintight bralette and leggings set. Her face has a dewy glow, and, aside from her curtain bangs, her dark hair is pulled back into an effortlessly cool messy bun.

"Hey Chicky Baby," Nat calls over to Lex, who turns with a bright smile.

"Yo Dirty Dog," Lex returns with a little wink. These freaks are two peas in a fucking pod.

"Just finished class. Thought I'd come help," Nat says, turning back to me.

I'm only half paying attention as I'm pulling the last bagel out of the oven. "Thanks, babe," I start, but then wince. "Fuck," I hiss.

Raff is next to me before I've even finished the swear. "I got it," he says, taking over my station. I clutch the base of my thumb where it meets the edge of the oven. Nat pulls a water out of the cooler and pops the top. She slowly pours the liquid over my hand as I breathe through my nostrils. I shut my eyes and focus on the sound of the water splashing against the asphalt.

"Should I get another?" she asks, but I shake my head.

"That's gonna be a beaut," she says with a husky laugh as she pours the last of the water onto a clean towel and presses it over my burn.

"Nah. I got worse," I say.

Guy approaches with empty bins in hand. "Yo, Nat," he says.

Nat blows him a kiss. "What's up, Step-Daddy? Need an extra hand," she asks.

Guy's face flushes a bit.

"Careful, Guy, nicknames stick in this family," I say.

Guy takes Nat and Lex to Princess to swap out supplies, and Raff and I clean and reset for the afternoon. The throbbing in my hand hasn't dulled yet. Combined with the afternoon heat and the band that's just started their set, my head is starting to pound. I close my eyes and brace myself against a tent pole as the middle-aged rockers are strumming the first chords of Sublime's Wrong Way.

I feel an arm snake around my waist. "You need to sit," Raff says.

I exhale and shake my head.

"I'll be fine. I'm unbreakable," I say. My face flushes because I didn't mean to say that last part out loud.

"Shut up," he says as he walks me back to a camping chair behind the ovens.

"Seriously, Rat," I protest but he doesn't let me finish.

"Just take a break until Guy gets back, Turbo. I'm going to get you some ice from Silverstein."

It's not until he's walked off and I'm fully seated that I realize I haven't sat down since we got out of the car this morning. My muscles are screaming. All I can do is close my eyes and just let gravity push me down into the chair. I feel a shadow fall over my face.

"Ok, maybe I needed that," I say.

"Ashley?" A female voice asks. I crack my eye open and peer up at the person standing over me.

"Anita," I say a little surprised. "You're here?"

She nods and sucks her bottom lip. I bring my hands up to shield the sun from my eyes. It's then that I notice her long auburn hair is now cropped short in a pixie. Shit. This can only mean one thing.

"Portland was a total bust," she says.

I stagger to my feet. I have a feeling I know where this is headed.

"Tyler was such an ass. Anyway, I'm so glad I ran into you. I tried calling last night. Did you get my voicemail?"

My stomach bottoms out as I shake my head. My phone is charging in Guy's truck.

"Sorry to ask, but would Friday be too soon? I have a flight tomorrow morning, and I'm going to be driving back with all of my stuff."

My ears are ringing as I feel a cool sensation on my forearm. I glance down to see a cup of ice being pressed into me.

"Oh my gosh," Anita beams. "Raffael, right?" she coos with a flirtatious grin. Jesus girl, didn't you and Tyler just break up?

Raff nods curtly. I can tell by his expression that he's not interested in any small talk with Anita.

"Can you beat it? She's on the clock," Raff says.

Anita's jaw drops. What a fucking asshole, I think as the tiniest delighted smile spreads across my face. Anita is taken aback by Raff's blunt reply.

"Oh, uh, sure. Anyway, I'll message you about swapping keys. Thanks again for subletting," Anita says before wiggling her fingers at me and walking off towards the band that has now started their rendition of a Mighty Mighty Bosstones cover.

"Why are you standing up?" Raff asks.

"Call me crazy, but I don't like getting dumped sitting down," I reply.

Raff quirks an eyebrow at me as he cracks a water bottle and pours it into my cup. "Yeah, I remember," he says.

I swallow down a mouthful. "You never broke up with me. Remember? Just kinda turned evil."

He sighs as he sits down in the camping chair and pulls me down onto his lap. I make a strangled gasping noise. "Relax. No one's here," he says, his tone is commanding but calm.

He opens his palm to reveal two Advil tablets. "Employees don't sit in their bosses laps," I say attempting to wiggle out of his grasp.

"Are you trying to make me hard?" he grits out.

I jump up as I realize that in my attempt to break free, I'm basically grinding my ass on his crotch. Raff huffs as he straightens up, setting me back into the chair and lowering down to sit on the curb next to me.

"So why'd that girl break up with you?" Raff asks, placing the pills in my hand. I eye him as I toss the Advil into my mouth, taking a swig of water.

"She just wants her apartment back," I say.

Raff leans his head on my knee. I instinctively place my hand on his head. Shit. I shouldn't have done that. The gesture is only confirming that I'm reciprocating his feelings. I can feel his cheeks pulling upward in a smile.

"Shut up," I say.

He rubs his head into me. "You love me," he singsongs.

I rap my knuckles on the top of his crown.

"Ow," he moans, but we're both smiling.

I'm too tired to do anything else. He looks really small right now. I can't fight the urge to let my fingers run through his wavy dark hair. It's longer than it used to be, falling below his ears in a slight curl. He closes his eyes as we sit in silence, and I stroke Raff's head like a fucking dog.

"So where are you going to stay?" Raff asks.

I release a long, slow exhale. "I don't know yet."

There's a beat of quiet between us, nothing but the middle-aged dad band covering Reel Big Fish.

"You're not going to leave again," Raff questions in a low tone.

My fingers stop their raking. I hadn't considered it.

I've always been the one to leave. At a certain point, I realized that Cita would never be able to accept me for who I am. Invite me to join the club I so desperately wanted to be a part of. So I just sort of moved on. "See ya," Cita had said when I left to take a job at a popular bakery in San Francisco's Mission district. Except I didn't move on.

Despite relocating every time I got the urge. San Francisco, New York, Los Angeles... a new city when the opportunity arose. There was always something missing. A longing that I could never fill. I was always too afraid to admit what I wanted because I knew that it would never want me in return. However, the more I ran, the harder it became to deny. I wanted to be with my family.

"I don't know," I reply after a long moment. I guess that's the truth. I don't. I thought that this time around would be different. However, so far, it's shaping up to be exactly like the last. Hell, even Raff is pursuing me right now. I pull my hand back into my lap. My attention refocused on the condensation beading on the side of my red solo cup. The meds must be working because I can feel the throbbing in my hand starting to dull.

Raff bumps his head against my knee, the needy puppy craving the absence of my affection. "Stay with me," he says.

I look at him, momentarily forgetting we're talking about just housing.

"We can't lose you. You're a part of the crew," he says, wrapping an arm around the inside of my leg. Shit. Why'd he have to go and add that last part? Something seems to be catching in my throat.

I tip my water back, taking a long slug. "Nah. I'm replaceable," I say after I swallow.

Raff turns to look up at me, eyes locked on mine. "No. You're not."

I press my mouth closed. My nostrils flare a bit. My eyes feel overwhelmingly full, so I just close them. Lean back in the blue, slightly sandy camping chair and let the Northern California sun bake my face. Fuck. I am unbreakable.

Chapter 17

RAFF

I'm pathetic. I don't think I've ever had it this bad before. Except in talking to Ashley, I'm starting to realize that maybe I did have it this bad. For her all those years ago. A shivering current goes up my spine.

To be obsessed with someone, totally occupied by the mere thought of them, is uncomfortable. They control your every thought. The amount of power they have over you is unfair. I don't like feeling that vulnerable.

Back then, being too into Ash was terrifying. I remember one time we were talking about plans for the pop-up we were putting together. A total fuck you to her family business, but I'd stupidly convinced her it was a good idea.

We'd spent all night at my mom's apartment, tweaking recipes and just being with each other. Back then, we couldn't get enough. I remember having the overwhelming need to kiss her, not even fuck her. Just the unbearable urge to feel her mouth on mine, know unequivocally what her softest part felt like against me. Even if I didn't realize it at the time, that must have been the first moment that I loved her. Fuck. I hadn't even held her hand at that point. We were just pals.

My heart is beating like mad. I'm desperate for this tattooed goddess who sits above me on a Coleman Cooler Quad Camping Chair. I bring one of my arms around her leg, pulling it into me as I huddle close to her. I am her acolyte. I've come to worship at her feet. The thought that she might leave again is making me grip a little tighter now.

"Nah. I'm replaceable," she had said through a mouthful of water.

Except she's not. She never has been. I'm realizing that now. And fuck it, maybe I'm delirious with sleep deprivation, but if I'm really honest with myself, I've always been comparing everyone else to Ash. She is the standard both in the bedroom and the kitchen. I've been searching for her. This is fucking terrifying. My head is starting to reel as I realize I've been looking for what I already had and fucked up all those years ago.

"You guys look cozy," Guy says from behind us.

I release my death grip on Ash as she pushes to her feet. I immediately miss the contact of our bodies.

"That was fast," she mutters as she walks towards the truck.

Guy eyes me as he moves past. "Are we behaving ourselves?" he asks.

Fuck you, I think. I don't answer him. Just kinda slink off. I need to clear my head.

I push through the crowd. Past children eating funnel cake, panting dogs matted with sand, and elderly thalassophiles in their floppy hats, tie-dye, and hemp. My head is spinning. I need to talk to Guy. Explain everything to him. Get him to tell me to fuck off. That I'm being my usual self and to just get over it. All I've done is throw myself at Ashley and besides that little head pat she hasn't even acknowledged me. I'm losing my shit over someone who can't even make up their mind if they're coming or going. I want to get rid of this desperate need for her.

My blood is starting to boil. I'm mad. I want Ash, damn it. I want her to be able to stay with me. To keep cooking like we have and just be with her. I'm mad because every decision I've made has led me to this point. I can't be trusted to pursue her because I'll fuck everything up like I always do. I'm pissed that she probably won't consider me again because of everything I did when I was terrified of the overwhelming feelings I had for her. I fucking suck.

Despite trying to change I am still their Rat King, I think as I walk towards the bluffs. A large crowd has gathered to watch the final surf heats of the Jam. On the beach below surfers, groms, and specters are lining up for the annual, unofficial, and chaotic "soft-top circus" which closes out the Log Jam. Once a winner is crowned in the official contest, everyone takes over the water on soft-top surfboards, inflatable rafts, kiddie pools, and basically anything else that floats for a humongous party wave.

As I get closer to the edge, I feel the saltwater breeze lick my face in thick gusts. People huddle together as they get blasted, hair and loose clothing billowing. I stand apart from the revelry, alone in the ambiguity of my infatuation. I feel a sharp jab in my side.

"The Rat King himself," a gravelly voice says. My stomach sinks. Fuck.

"Hi Aggie," I say, turning. With a wide yellow smile and what looks to be fresh stitches on his chin, Andre Aguilera stands with his fleshy hands outstretched.

He tosses his arms around me in a brutish hug. "Qué huele, CB," Dre says in horrible Spanish as he pushes me away in a playful but hard shove.

I shrug my shoulders. "When'd you get back?" I ask.

Dre laughs like I've asked the stupidest question in the world.

He is literally the last person I want to see right now. But I guess the universe has a sick sense of humor as I now stand in front of the physical reminder of my shitty past that apparently, I can never escape. Doesn't matter how hard I try to change. He rubs his bottom lip with his thumb. A very bad sign that he's been thinking.

"How come you haven't come around?" Andre starts.

I suck my teeth. I don't want to placate this asshole's ego right now. "I've been fucking busy," I say.

A Cheshire smile spreads wide on Dre's face, immediately indicating that I've brought up exactly the topic he wants to discuss.

"That's right! Papa John," he says, rubbing his thick hands together. Time has accentuated Andre Aguilera's short and stocky stature. He probably could have been a varsity wrestler, but he didn't give a shit about anything in school. That's how we became friends. Or friendly, I guess. Everyone is an opportunity to Dre.

"Good to see you, man," I lie, turning back towards the booth, but Andre presses a fat thumb to my shoulder to stop me.

"Yo, so you know Chloe's been on me about paying child support," he starts, and my stomach immediately bottoms.

"I'm a cook, man. You know I can't float you," I say.

Andre is waving his hands. "Nah, Raff. It's not like that. I was thinking you could just hire me," Dre continues.

Andre is nuts if he thinks I'm going to give him a job. First, we became friends in detention. Both of us were helping ourselves to the science teacher's supply closet when the monitor on duty wasn't looking. Dumb dirtbag kid shit but something tells me that Andre still embodies the what's your's is mine mentality. Second, there's no way Guy would ever allow Andre anywhere near either of the Lobo sisters, especially after Mac got suspended for kicking him in the balls when he tried to feel her up during the flexibility portion of the Presidential physical fitness test in gym.

I blame it on how tired I am, but my initial response to his question is to laugh.

"What's funny," Dre says, his tone immediately switching from jovial to irate. "You think you're better than me, Rat?" He quickly starts to fist my shirt and my jaw tenses.

"Let go," I growl back. My hand slaps his fist away.

"Yo! Is this how you treat a friend? We're the same, you know that," Andre is saying, but I'm already seeing red.

I don't know who starts it but Andre and I are quickly grappling. He's pulling me by the shoulders as I'm grabbing his forearms. I just want to get him close so I can make contact. However, my tall lean frame versus his stubby center of gravity are unevenly matched and we're toppling to the ground. People yell and circle us immediately. We're rolling as we take turns pummeling each other in clumsy punches. I don't really want to hurt Dre. I just need the release.

Oh boy, do I fucking find it. I'm stronger than Dre, who's probably spent the majority of time post-high school chilling on his mom's couch, avoiding his responsibilities. Without even realizing it, I'm on top, raining down punches. All Andre can do is bring his thick arms up to block. It only lasts a minute or so before I feel big hands lifting me into the air.

"What the hell," Guy is roaring into my face.

I don't have time to react before I feel Andre on me again. He's striking my back and torso as Guy inadvertently holds me like a suspended punching bag.

"Fuck you, Aguilera," Guy says as soon as he recognizes my opponent. He's released me, dumped me into the dirt and ice plant, and is now lunging for Dre. Luckily, bystanders subdue Guy as Andre is able to make his escape. At least that's what I think happens. I can't see clearly as my eye is starting to swell shut.

It's pure chaos. People are holding Guy, who is about to take off after Dre. The knuckles on my left hand have totally opened and I'm applying pressure with my right. I feel a tiny tug on my elbow. I whip around to find Ash. As soon as we make eye contact, I feel the air finally refill my lungs. She wordlessly pulls me through the crowd. Without the ability to see, I'm totally helpless. I have to depend on her as she guides me back to the refuge of the camping chair.

Silverstein is immediately at my side. The dutiful charge nurse, he's waving around a first aid kit. "What do you need," he repeats several times in a business-like tone.

Guy is on my other side now, out of breath and hands on his hips. "Fucking Andre," Guy wheezes. He looks down at me, rage still sizzling in his eyes.

"What's wrong with you?" he snaps. It's so out of character that I feel Ash and Lex tense. "I thought you'd changed." That statement stings more than my face and knuckles.

"Sorry, man," I mumble as Silverstein wraps my hand.

Guy regains his composure and takes in the state of me. "Go home."

I start to protest, but as soon as I move my left hand, which is now mummied in gauze, I know he's right. Fuck. Of course, I fucked it all up again. Andre is right. We're the same. Scum.

"Hey, Raff. I'll drive you to the clinic. You're probably going to need stitches," Silverstein says. This is exactly like the last time. I've convinced her to take a chance and then I leave her high and dry.

I glance at Ash. She has her usual unreadable expression, but her eyebrows are fixed in a determined line.

"Go," Guy warns.

Ash gives me a little nod. She seems resolute. My pulse quickens as reality sets in. I've fucked it all up. How am I supposed to prove to this woman that I'm not going to ruin everything again, when I'm not even sure myself?

Chapter 18

ASH

There it is. The other shoe. That's all I can think as I watch Raff reluctantly climb into Silverstein's BMW. I'm already feeling overwhelmed, but today won't break me. I can handle this. I push my mom, the apartment, Raff, and all the other bullshit out of my mind and get to work.

Thank God Nat came to help. She's slipped a Princess Pizzarina crewneck on over her workout set. Probably more hygienic. She's taking orders while Lex helps me with cooking. I'm the only Lobo who went to culinary school, but we all grew up learning how to work in a bakery. By the time she left for college, my baby sister had more professional kitchen experience than some of my instructors.

The afternoon is clumsy and hectic, but we get through it. Several times I have to clench my teeth to will the mounting anxiety seeping into my thoughts back down into the dark depths of my psyche. The Advil wears off, and the pounding in my head and throbbing in my hand serve as a steady reminder of it all. A dull thump— Cita, thump— Anita, thump— Raff, and it all begins again. My brain is a tennis shoe in a dryer. This percussion of intrusive thoughts sets the pace for the work in front of me.

Guy keeps us going, and Nat is bringing the energy of a grizzled diner waitress to managing the line. She's sarcastic and a little dominating to the customers, especially the men, which apparently is exactly what this crowd needed. Today's clientele are drunker and more rowdy than yesterday. At one point, a man with a goatee wanders into the booth, waving a bill in front of my face. He tries to get me to break a ten, oblivious to the fact that I'm knuckles deep in dough. Guy grabs him by the collar and tosses him back into the throng of swaying and sunburnt revelers.

As the impossibly chaotic day trips into late afternoon, most of the families have gone home. The only people who remain are a troublesome group. A mix of barefoot locals and out of town weirdos. Guy decides we should pack up quick. Without Raff, we need to get back to the restaurant for opening. Guy has to step in when a group of men in Oakley's get handsy with Lex. The conflict starts to get heated as the men circle Guy. Silverstein, returned from the clinic, jumped in to ease tensions and offer them free beer.

We make it back to Princess Pizzarina right before opening. Nora is outside the loading dock, her face twisted in a worried pout, headband wringing in her grip.

"What's up?" Guy asks, sensing her panic.

Nora's eyes began to fill with tears. "I messed it up," she squeals.

In a few quick steps, Guy and I follow her inside.

In last night's efforts to sell more today, Raff and I decided to take dough prepped for Princess's usual service. Nora, in her eagerness, volunteered to come in this morning to make up the difference. Simple solution, right? Well... sure, unless you have a total novice out of culinary school, do the prep. Nora forgot to add the salt when she initially mixed the dough. Having realized her mistake, she added it after the fact. An error that made the dough tough and unusable.

Guy closes his eyes and exhales slowly. I know what he's feeling. Nora winces. I'm sure bracing herself to be destroyed by a verbal dressing down. However, Guy and Raff are polar opposites.

He reaches out a big hand and places it on Nora's shoulder. "It happens," he says calmly.

Guy is pulling out his phone. He sends a series of texts as he turns to me. "What should we do?" I'm a little startled that he'd think I was capable of fixing this. However, I don't argue. Right now, Guy needs help, and Raff is out.

Lips pressed closed I rub my tongue along the front of my teeth and then make a decision.

"Nora, start portioning anything that's salvageable from yesterday. Are Miguel and Chuy here," I ask.

Guy nods. "And Mac and Vanessa are on their way to help," he adds.

I bob my head, getting an idea. "I'll start prepping a small batch of dough that could maybe be ready in a few hours. How does everyone feel about going off menu?"

Chapter 19

RAFF

I push my way through the back door, and the kitchen is bumping. The clinic took way longer than I had expected. Thanks to the soft-top circus there were several gnarly surf injuries that took precedent over my stupid hand. It's nearly eight by the time I got all patched up and caught a Lyft back to the restaurant. After Silverstein dropped me off, I had ample time in the waiting room to really let the self-loathing kick in. With my hours of self-reflection and the help of some pain meds, I've come to a decision.

It's pure chaos back here. When the driver pulled past the front of the restaurant, there was a line around the block. A fucking line! For the first time since we opened people are queuing up to eat here. Sure, we've been busy but never this packed. I had been texting Guy all afternoon but no reply. It must be because we're so fucking slammed right now.

My eyes scan the kitchen for Ash. She's nowhere to be found. I'm immediately pulling on my apron and food-safe gloves, getting ready to help where I can. Chuy and Nora are working in back. Servers rush in and out of the swinging door. I crane my neck to see if I can spot Ash at the wood-burning oven out front. However, when I look out it's Miguel working the peel. My brow furrows. Where is she?

"Behind," Mac yells.

I turn to find Mac and Vanessa bringing trays of crusty Italian bread rolls out to a standing rack. What the fuck is going on? I step deeper into the kitchen to find Ash sliding dough into the oven. Her hair is tied up in a very messy ponytail, and sweat beads down the nape of her neck.

"You didn't have to come back," Guy says as he rushes past.

I turn to see him go by again, carrying a milk crate full of liquor bottles. I follow him out into the front of house.

"What's going on?" I ask.

"There was a hiccup. We had to improvise," he says, pushing through the crowd towards the bar.

As we pass one of the tables, I look down to see sandwiches. Impossibly crispy and flaky bread with what appears to be chili, honey, basil, mozzarella, and soppressata. These are the ingredients of one of our most popular signature pies. I see bread bursting with green garlic, mortadella, pesto, ricotta, and smoked mozzarella. I stop in my tracks. Guy doesn't have time to fill me in. He's ducking under the bar to help Laurel and Nat. Lex is calling out to-go orders as she helps our hostess, Torrey, manage the line of people clamoring to get inside. I can see through the large glass windows that Silverstein is outside walking up and down the crowd of people, handing out vouchers and free cans of Santa Luna Brewing Company's popular Super Moon Ale.

I survey the scene. This place is ruckus. More alive than I've ever seen it. The Photo Booth flashes, the pinball machines whiz, the Dead Kennedys thrash over the speakers. This is exactly who Princess Pizzarina was meant to be. The wind is finally blowing. Her sails are filled, and she's flying at full speed ahead. I spin on my heels and rush back into the kitchen. My heart is pounding as I stomp towards Ash.

My eyes are wide and crazed as I frantically ask, "What is all this?"

Her cheeks are flushed from the heat of the ovens. She grabs a discarded sample loaf, extending it to me. I take it in my hands and let my fingers crunch the outside crust as Ash fills me in on Nora's mistake. It crackles under my fingertips as I rip a hunk off and bring the bread to my mouth. It's slightly sour and delightfully chewy. I quirk an eyebrow.

"I used your biga to start it," she says timidly. We'd made it for the meatball subs that were inevitably too complicated for the pop-up.

I'm simultaneously nodding and shaking my head in this weird oval shape. Ash is leaning backward, protectively recoiling.

"I'm sorry. I know it isn't your menu," she is explaining.

I'm so overwhelmed by everything that my body takes over. My arms are around her, pulling her lithe frame into mine. My determined mouth is crashing into hers as a surprised gasp escapes her. She's tense at first, but as I embrace her, she melts into me slightly. I feel the softness of her shape against the hardness of mine, and I'm electric. I cannot let this woman go.

"Don't freak out," I hear Guy saying as he approaches from behind.

As soon as he rounds the corner towards the convection oven and takes us in, his tone shifts.

"What the fuck," he's barking now.

I return Ashley to her feet and catch Guy as he closes in on us.

"What are you?" he says, but I'm embracing him now and planting a big smooch on his lips.

"Are you high?" Guy asks, struggling out of my grasp.

Chuy pokes his head into the alcove. "You ok, boss?"

Guy is waving his hands. "Run, Chuy, or he'll get you next." Chuy bats his eyelashes at me before he turns back towards his station.

"You both are geniuses," I say, turning to the large stand mixer.

"Yeah, he's definitely high," Ashley says.

I spin back to them. “No, you’re both wonderful. Whatever you’ve done is working. Tell me how to help, Chef,” I say to Ash, putting my hands on my hips.

They exchange a look and Guy just shrugs. “Take it away, I gotta get back out there.”

My actions and intentions are clear now. I cannot change the past. Every decision I’ve made up to this point, good, bad, or whatever, has led me back to the same conclusion; Ashley Morgan Lobo. The mere thought of her terrified me before. I spent years running away, but like Kevin McCallister said, “I’m not afraid anymore.” I’m ready to show her that, despite everything, I’m never going to run away again. I have changed.

Chapter 20

ASH

Today was insane. I can't believe I made it through. I'm beyond exhausted as we all part ways in the parking lot. I want to go home and sleep until Tuesday. I wave off Van and Mac, who are going to Guy's again tonight. Pockets stuffed with tips, Lex and Nat left right after last call. Both of them are working at Mother Wolf tomorrow, so they needed to get to sleep.

"Are you sure," Mac says leaning out of the passenger window as Guy's truck idles.

I shake my head. I just want to sleep in my own bed... or what will be my bed for the next two days. I watch them drive away before I unlock Belinda and slide in.

Miguel throws me deuces as his maroon 2003 Buick Century pulls out of the parking lot. I'm the last one there. I turn the key in the ignition of the old Jeep. However, instead of the familiar gravelly whirl of the engine nothing happens. Fuck. I turn the key again, pumping my foot on the gas pedal as if that's going to miraculously do something to fix the problem. Again, nothing happens. "Fuck," I yell and let my head fall forward onto my steering wheel.

I hiss out an exhale willing the simmering emotions that threaten to slip loose back down. Not lifting my head, I feel around for my bag on the passenger seat. I quickly find my phone rattling around at the bottom. Unfortunately, it is fucking dead. I exhale sharply from my nose this time. Great.

It's nearly two by the time the bus lets me off on my block. Several times my head falls in bobs of exhaustion while I sat at the bus stop and then in the lull of the rumbling ten-minute ride. I sat close to the driver, terrified that in my state I'd miss my stop and have to spend the night waiting to take the loop around in the opposite direction to get home.

Yet I persevered. I made it back to what will be my last resting place. Ha. My key jams in the lock when I finally reach my front door. Fuck even the apartment is rejecting me. Yet another safe space that has revealed its true nature. I am unworthy.

I fling my bag, jacket, and shoes off as soon as the door closes behind me. I don't even bother turning on any additional lights. Unzip and peel off my ribcage Levi's, stumbling over the discarded jeans as I move towards the Murphy bed. I have one goal right now; sleep. I reach up and tug at the handle. The bed jerks down an inch then snags with a loud grind. The sudden stop in downward momentum almost yanks me up off my feet. "Come on," I groan attempting to wrench it free.

I brace the handle in both hands and pull down with all of my body weight. Nothing. My hand is throbbing again from the rubbing of the metal against my burn. I know that a headache is soon to follow. The bed remains steadfast, defiantly set at a 70-degree angle. There's a tapping now. At first, I think it's my head, but then I realize it's coming from my window.

I trudge forward, pressing my face against the glass then quickly jerk back as a pinecone smacks against the pane. I crane my neck to see outside. The shadow from the streetlamp makes it hard to see, but even with the long cast silhouette I know exactly who it is standing downstairs. Burn be damned I use all of my grip strength to hoist the heavy bay window open. "What," I huff down in a stage whisper.

"Buzz me up," he calls back.

"The door's open," I reply.

He pauses for a moment. "Really?" He blinks up at me.

I exhale sharply. Why are we having this conversation through the window? "Yes, the downstairs lock's busted," I say.

I see him scan up one side of the street and then down the other. "Should you really be yelling that out the window," Raff asks.

"Bye," I say as I let the heavy glass drop down to closed. I sink into the armchair, eyelids lowering.

I hear his footsteps on the stairs. I drag myself up to standing and unlock the front door. I wordlessly let him in, stumbling back into my chair. Raff locks the door behind him and surveys the scene; me pant less and exhausted. The bed unyielding. He sets down the items in his hands, crossing the room. "It's stuck," I say unable to even open my eyes. I hear the sound of tugging, grinding, and then the familiar thunk of the mattress falling into place. I peek up at him.

"Now it's un-stuck," he says.

"Thanks, Rat," I muster as I pull my Princess crewneck up and over my head. I chuck it in the general vicinity of my laundry pile. That will have to be tomorrow's problem. In my bralette and underwear, I crawl like an animal on my hands and knees the few feet from the chair to the bed.

"Why are you here," I say as I let myself fall face first into the pillow.

"I'm here to take care of you," he says.

I lift my head up, my brows furrowed. It's then that I notice what he's brought with him, a flat pack of moving boxes and a grocery bag.

"Can you take care of me tomorrow," I whine letting my head fall again.

He laughs softly. "Sure," he says.

With a robotic movement I slap my hand against the mattress next to me, summoning him inside. I don't have time to unpack any of this. It's dangerous to even entertain the idea in my current depleted state.

I hear the single light click off. The arduous sounds of Raff kicking off each shoe. Then the dip of the mattress as he starts to climb in.

"Wait," I say jerking my head up.

He freezes.

"I'm weird about kitchen clothes in the bed," I reply.

He nods, standing and unzipping his Dickies. I hear the swift sound of his sweater and shirt gliding over his head and plopping to the ground. I don't open my eyes, just wait until I feel his skin against mine. The sensation of his warm arms wrapping around me from behind.

"Is this ok," he asks.

"I'm too tired to care," I lie. Why did I have to tell him to get undressed? I should have just sucked it up about the kitchen clothes thing because now Raff is pressed against me in just his black boxer briefs. I'm hyper aware that his groin is curving around my ass. I shift slightly and he suddenly jerks back. "Sorry," I wince as I roll over to face him.

In the light from the street lamp Raff is gorgeous, even with his black eye, which has now fully blossomed. He has annoyingly perfect bone structure, only accentuated by his mustache and a little scar above his eyebrow. I study his face. Let my eyes indulge in the dip and glide of every familiar facial curve. He's doing the same to me. Taking stock in the subtle changes of the last few years.

"How's your shiner, Rocky," I ask.

The corners of his eyes crinkle as he smiles. "I've had worse."

"Jeez, humble brag," I huff.

He uses his bandaged hand to brush my bangs back slightly, exposing a sliver of my forehead. It's a tender gesture that makes my pulse race. It's both thrilling and dangerously vulnerable. He can sense my unease, so he doesn't make any other moves.

"What's with all the crap," I ask nodding my head towards the discarded items by the front door.

"I had this whole plan," he says shyly. "I was going to make you dinner and help you pack."

My eyes narrow. "Are you trying to get rid of me," I ask.

He shakes his head. "No. I'm going to bring you home."

My breath catches. A sudden shocking sensation fills me, taking me by surprise like a flash flood. I don't realize it's happening until it happens. I suddenly start to cry. Big fat tears spilling down my cheeks.

It's overwhelming and humiliating. I immediately bring my hands up to my face, ducking my head down and curling into myself. I want to disappear. I try to bite my lips closed but the sobs are escaping in gasping breathes. The more I attempt to hold the river of emotion in the faster it comes hurtling out of me. I can't remember the last time I cried, and I certainly do not want anyone to witness it.

I feel his arms snake around me, pulling me into his bare chest. My shoulders shudder with sobs as I continue to cry. He doesn't say anything, just holds me and lets the feelings pass. My body shakes violently. Something that would probably be terrifying if I was alone, but somehow seems bearable with Raff holding me. I'm not sure how much time passes. How long I lose control, the weight of everything breaking the surface.

"I'm so embarrassed," I finally eke out.

"Don't be," he says tenderly, smoothing my hair.

I continue to cry, to let the tears fall as he embraces me.

Then when I feel as if I've depleted myself, the well empty and nothing more to expel I try to pull back. He doesn't release me. He's rooting me to the bed. His arms the retrains that are keeping me tethered to the earth and preventing me from flying up off into outer space as the world turns on its axis.

"You can let go," I mutter. I feel his head shake a no on the top of my head. I laugh nervously. "God, I bet you do this for all the girls."

I feel him pulling me back, positioning me to look up at him. "Only you. Always only you," he says.

I feel like sobbing a second time. Maybe from the humiliation of it all but also this is not how we are—especially with each other. We are tough. We do not need to be cared for, to be treated gently. This totally goes against the Pirate's Code. I am unbreakable and yet in front of Raff, of all fucking people, I broke.

"You don't have to," I start but Raff stops me.

"I do. I know that I fucked up. I've been fucking up a lot, actually."

I look at him. His face is serious. I've never seen Raff like this before, stoic. Usually, he's twisting out of any uncomfortable situation with anger or humor. Just like I would be steadfast and unmoved when confronted by the undesirable aspects of life. He exhales in the way one prepares to make a declaration. He's mulling something over.

"I like you," he says finally.

Unfortunately, I laugh. "You said that yesterday," I reply.

"I know, but I just needed to say it again. And I'll keep saying it until you believe me. No. I won't just say it, I'll show you too."

My lips press as I consider this. I can feel the acid in my throat building, that uncomfortable unease when promised affection.

Raff rolls onto his back and pulls me into him. I'm too tired to fight so I let myself be dragged in close, my head resting on his torso.

"My dad sucked," he says.

I let myself luxuriate in the gentle vibrating reverb of his chest against my ear. "Everything was always everyone else's problem. One time on Valentine's Day he took my mom on a fancy date to that old seafood place on the water, the uh," Raff struggles for the name.

"Windjammer," I offer.

I remember it well. The kind of place that the Santa Luna Yacht Club types would take their wives for Mother's Day brunch and anniversaries. Cary took Van there on their second date despite knowing she was a vegetarian. We all marveled at her description of the bread and butter.

"Yeah, that was it. He ended up getting them kicked out because he screamed at some random guy. My mom said later that it was because the man looked like his boss. Who he hated."

I let my fingers come up to Raff's ribs. Let them glide over the curve of a familiar snake tattooed there.

"He was irate for the rest of the night. Came home screaming. Punched a hole in the bathroom door. Woke up Eleni and I. Caused this big stink. But the entire time he kept making it seem like it was my mom's fault. Like her not wanting to hold his hand when he was getting escorted out was the problem. And it just sucked. Nothing was ever his fault, and he could never just, like, be there. Own his shit and be what my mom needed. I realized today that I'm just like him. I gotta start owning my shit or I can never get what I want."

My finger pauses. "You're not your dad," I say.

Raff shakes his head. "Yeah, don't I fucking know it. I'd never beat up on women or little kids. But I also ain't doing shit to be there for the people I love either."

I still in his arms.

"Like Guy," he adds quickly.

I breathe out a laugh. "Oh good. I'm glad that you love Guy." I feel his arms tighten around me, like he's worried that I'm going to run away.

"Would that scare you?" he asks hesitantly.

My pulse is pounding. The sound is accentuated by my inability to recall how to breathe right now.

“Maybe,” I say after a long pause. Honestly, that’s the truth. I don’t know. “What if you decide that you don’t like me. You leave me holding the bag again,” I ask.

I feel the muscles in his neck and jaw work as he thinks about this.

“Well, my track record is shit. So even if I fucking say I won’t bolt what good does my word do, you know? I guess you’ll just have to trust me. And I’ll just have to show you that I’ve changed.” The last part hangs in the thick night air. I can hear his heart beating just as hard as mine.

“How,” I ask.

I feel him shift as he cranes down and kisses me. It’s soft and very tender. This is the antithesis of Raff. Bone-chilling is what I would have called it all those months ago. However, right now he’s expressing something to me. This kiss is a promise and it’s out of character nature is exactly what he’s expressing. He wants to go against how he’d acted in the past. He’s trying to show me that he can be different. He won’t leave me when I need him the most.

Unfortunately, the kiss is too short. I’m desperate for more but as soon as I let myself indulge in him, he breaks us apart. My mouth longs for the rough feel of his mustache against my upper lip. The scratch of his stubble against my chin.

Between his comedic smooch in the restaurant tonight to this declarative action, I want him worse than I ever have before. I crave him. I need to feast on him. Suck out the velvety marrow from his bones until I've consumed every unctuous last drop of him. My chest is heaving, a light shuddering pant escapes me as I attempt to get my breath under me again. "What did you bring me to eat," I ask on a whisper.

His lips curve up. "I was going to make you chicken pastina soup."

Immediately I feel myself salivate. I'm Pavlovian for this man. I bite my bottom lip. "Feed me," I say, my voice breathy with need.

Raff sets about cooking the simple Italian soup.

At first, I'm satisfied to just watch him from bed, propped on an elbow. However, that's not enough. I need to be closer. Experience the intense, energized focus and total immersion in the activity. Raff thoroughly enjoys cooking. He has an ease to him when he's moving around my kitchen.

I perch on the end of the bed and watch over his shoulder. He pauses from time to time asking me to direct him towards ingredients or utensils. Then turns back to his work, head bobbing as he hums a Sum 41 song.

However, it's me who's in too deep. I can't stop looking at him. Gulping down every aspect of his physique. His back is fucking stunning. I marvel in his shape. Surfing has given him broad, muscular shoulders that taper down towards his narrow waist. This is the evolved version of the Raff I knew in our early twenties. Fuck this man.

As the soup simmers, Raff pulls out the boxes. "I don't think it'll take long. You don't have a lot of stuff," he says.

I frown. That is actually on purpose. I never want to get comfortable. Planting roots is not really a luxury I let myself indulge in. Everything I own can fit into Belinda's trunk. I always have to be ready to leave when I wear out my welcome. "Are you sure about this," I ask.

He looks at me, face turning serious. "Yes," he says simply.

I pull my knees up to my chest as I feel the bubbling acid. "But what about Guy? Is this cool with him," I ask.

"Fuck Guy," Raff says. A common refrain in their relationship. "Guy will be stoked. And if he isn't, we'll move. Fuck it, I'll buy you a house if you want."

My eyebrows lift. "You can afford a house in Santa Luna," I ask dryly.

"Hell no," he laughs. "But, if you wanted one I'd figure it out. Silverstein is trying to get us to open a second location at this brewery he's building higher up the mountain. I'll construct you a cabin up there."

My nose wrinkles. "Slow down, Abraham Lincoln."

He stops folding boxes and sits next to me on the edge of the bed. "It'd be fun. I'd chop wood and shit, and you could bake bread in a hearth." I try to imagine living in a log cabin with Raff. In this fantasy I assume he's shirtless and rocking a stovepipe hat.

"Honestly, the baking bread stuff is what excites me more than the cabin," I say thoughtfully. "Baking is all I've ever wanted to do."

"Then I'll build you a bakery," he says.

Chapter 21

RAFF

Ash eats while I pack. It's oddly comforting to take care of her. She feels real. As if she's here for the first time since moving back to Santa Luna. I want all of her. Especially as she slurps and sucks spoonfuls of cheesy broth wrapped in my hoodie and only her underwear. I keep stealing glances at her body. Tan and tattooed. Lean and soft. I'm dying to rub my hands all over her. Feel her. Possess every inch of her. But I have to wait. I cannot fuck this up again.

Ashley is still raw and liable to bolt if I go too fast this time. Besides we're both slap happy with exhaustion.

"How are you not passing out," she asks me as she places her bowl in the sink.

"You've reinvigorated me," I say giving her a wide smile.

She furrows her brows. "You're worried that you have a concussion, aren't you," she asks flatly. Bingo.

We laugh and talk long into the early morning as we pack up her things. We sing Fugazi's I'm So Tired at the top of our lungs grabbing and swaying with one another like two drunks. Then collapse into maniacal peals of laughter when her downstairs neighbor thunks a broom handle against the floor.

“It’s Anita’s problem now,” she says smiling into my shoulder. It’s dawn when we toss the last of her clothing into a garbage bag.

She slides under the duvet, and I lower the blinds before climbing in behind her.

“Just a nap,” I assure her. I tuck her into me, letting our long limbs fold and tangle with each other. I wince when her feet make contact with mine.

“You’re freezing,” I say.

She responds by rubbing her toes up and down my shins. I attempt to move away but she continues her assault. My only recourse is to tickle her. She retaliates escalating us into a full-on wrestling brawl.

“Truce,” she wheezes after I’ve cornered her at the edge of the bed, her only option to spasm with laughter.

I’m tempted to ignore her plea but then she accidentally knocks into my stitches with her failing limbs. I recoil with a yelp.

We settle back into the center of the bed. Our bodies pressed against one another in a familiar knot of extremities. As we resolve into the quiet of early morning our breathing synchronizes. The sound of the sleepy neighborhood outside permeates the window. The world below waking up to begin the day.

"Good night," I whisper. I can feel that her chest is rising in long deep inhales. I think she might already be asleep. So, I tuck my face in close to the top of her head. I drop a kiss into her smooth dark hair.

The last thing I remember before falling asleep is the sound of Ashley murmuring back. "Good morning."

We don't sleep as long as either of us would have liked. She doesn't have blackout curtains, so once the early-morning fog lifts, the apartment is bright. Around nine a car alarm keeps going off. Perhaps it's karma for our late-night impromptu karaoke session.

Ash groans as I drag myself out of bed.

"Should we get moving?" I ask.

She rolls on her back, letting her lips buzz as she blows out a breath. "My car's busted," she says.

I frown. "How'd you get home," I ask.

She blinks at me, and I shake my head, eyebrows lifting. "The night bus," I scold blinking back.

Santa Luna has great public transportation. Fuck most Bay Area cities do. With the college so close and a booming population of eco-conscious citizens our's is one of the best. However, between one and five a.m., the multiple routes condense into one giant loop of the city that everyone just calls the night bus. It fucking sucks of you miss your stop because you have to jump on and take the loop in the reverse direction. It's main patrons are the intoxicated and the unhoused, so a ride on the night bus can be quite lively.

"I'll drive," I say.

Concern blossoms on her face.

"You're not too tired," she asks.

I shake my head. Why is she so worried about it? She's just as tired as I am. I don't dwell. I get dressed quickly and load up the car while she carefully brings down the contents of her fridge. It's not much food but she is careful and ginger in her handling of a glass jar containing a sourdough starter. I nod at it.

"That's Vanessa 2.0," she says with a mischievous grin.

"Mama," I ask, remembering the nickname. She winks at me as she slides into the front seat of my car, cradling the fermentation on her lap.

When we get back to Guy's, we find him on the couch shirtless in pajama pants with a bowl of cereal in hand. His hair is tasseled from sleep and Minnie is resting her head on his knee. When we come through the front door, boxes in hand she rushes over to greet us, tail wagging.

"You guys hit up a garage sale," Guy asks confused. Ash straightens as she hesitantly follows me down the hall.

“You unpack. Guy and I will get the rest,” I assure her. That impassive expression is on her face as she nods. I jog back towards the living room.

“Come help me,” I say to Guy as I lead him towards the drive way. He slips on a pair of well-worn Rainbows before following me outside.

“Ash is going to move in,” I say.

Guy’s eyebrows lift.

“Her place fell through,” I add which causes his brows to drop. Fuck it. Show up for her, I think. “I, uh, like her. A lot. And before you freak out. I am not going to fuck her over and blow it all up again. I’m trying to be better. I know that I was a dick to everyone, especially you,” I say.

“You fucking think,” Guy exhales. “What the fuck is wrong with you?”

I cringe. I knew he’d be pissed. Honestly, if I were him, I’d be more than pissed.

“You’re fucking serious. And just when things were finally starting to get good,” he says.

“I know,” I say throwing my hands up. “But they’re good because of her. And who I am around her. I can see that now. Guy, man, I won’t fuck it up. I know I have in the past but you just have to trust me.”

Guy studies me. There's a crease between his brows that wasn't there five years ago. Now it's etched into the set of his face. Guy looks tired. I can see that for the first time. He's been holding it all together. I want to lighten his load. I am ready to take responsibility for everyone.

"I promise you that I won't fuck it up again," I add.

Guy has been through some shit. Though you'd probably never know. He's so even tempered and, well, chill as fuck. However, he has his limits. It's not fair to push him to that point. Hell, the entire reason I discovered my love of cooking is because of Guy and Louise.

Neither of them knew their way around a kitchen. Louise would just order them take out or her favorite cold rotisserie chicken and potato salad from the deli counter. She never really ate much, enjoying a cigarette and very cold gin martini over actual food. Guy was just left to his own devices most of the time, which probably explained why he was such a chubby little fucker as a kid.

So, when I followed Guy home one day I felt like it was my responsibility to take care of these two people who'd shown me kindness. I pestered my mom to teach me how to cook. She never asked why, probably because she was so overwhelmed with work and raising two annoying kids by herself. She taught me all the Italian and Greek recipes she grew up eating. On my twelfth birthday she even bought me a copy of the Silver Spoon.

I'd take the lawn mowing money that I didn't waste with Guy at the arcade or skate shop to buy ingredients. I'd show up at Louise's door with a shopping bag in hand. Guy would sit at the dinette with one of his surf magazines and read to me while I tried my hand at carbonara or cacio e pepe.

Then we'd all eat. Like a proper fucking family around a proper fucking table. It felt good to show up for them. The same feeling I'd get when I'd pack Eleni lunch every day so she didn't have to stand in line for the free meal the school provided, or stock my mom's freezer with her favorite lasagna to eat when she got off shift. I guess maybe along the way between all of my shit I forgot that feeling.

Guy brings his fist up and I flinch. I wouldn't blame him for punching me right now. However, to my surprise he knocks me in the shoulder with his big hand. "I guess, congrats man," he says reluctantly. "So she's the girl, huh?"

I nod.

"Well, if you were willing to fight me about it yesterday, you must be serious." A smile spreads across his face.

"Yeah. I just hope I can show her that," I say relief washing over me.

"Those Lobo women are tricky. They'll never come right out and tell you how they feel," he says knowingly.

I exhale. "I'm totally fucked aren't I?"

Guy laughs as we both grab boxes out of my trunk. "You're about to be. Don't forget you have to ask permission from her Daddy," he says with a grin.

My mouth goes dry. Shit.

Chapter 22

ASH

Raff and I didn't discuss the logistics of where I'd be staying when I got to Guy's house. I assumed it'd be with Mac. However, when we arrived, he ushered me into his room. Fuck he'd even emptied out a drawer for me in the dresser. I stare at the empty rectangle of wood. The feeling of acid rising in my throat.

Suddenly I feel very exposed. The room is too bright and too big. I'm not sure where to start, so I just sort of crawl into a corner between his bed and the dresser. With my back against the wall, I pull my knees up towards my chest. I'm still exhausted from the weekend, but the precious few hours of sleep have given me some awareness. My hand might not hurt any more, but the memory of the pain still remains. This is dangerous.

I might be a fucking idiot. Raff is not to be trusted. That is something I know deep down. He's unsafe. Why did I just fucking agree to move in with him? This is the man who left me high and dry all those years ago, vulnerable to Cita and Lulu. The catalyst to my exile. Fuck me I even let him see me cry. My pulse is racing, and I tighten my grip around my knees. I should just take my shit into Mac's room.

However, as soon as I have the thought the bedroom door swings open. Raff and Guy walk in with my boxes.

“Here ok,” Guy asks as he eyes a spot on the floor.

“Uh, actually, maybe I should just put them in Mac’s room,” I say quickly, getting to my feet. The sudden movement makes my head spin. Raff and Guy exchange a look.

“Just put them there for now,” Raff says. Guy nods as he obliges and then heads back into the hallway.

“I’m going for a session with Marco and Justin,” Guy says giving us a tiny wave. “Probably won’t be back until the afternoon.”

With that he shuts the bedroom door behind him, disappearing.

Raff closes the distance between us, reaching out towards me. Instinctually, I step backward, a micro movement, but Raff notices.

“What’s going on,” he questions, an expression of concern on his face as his body curves in towards me.

I’m not sure why but my eyes fall to his shoulders. His clavicle is striking, and I have the sudden urge to run my fingers up his trapezius to the base of his neck. But I don’t. I just stare at him and swallow down a growing panic. “Sorry. I, uh, don’t think that I really thought this through.”

He doesn’t hesitate this time. He wraps his arms around me. “You’re freaking out,” he asks.

I nod into his chest.

"Do you want to stay in Mac's room until you've had some time to think about everything," he offers.

I tilt my head up towards him. "Fuck... you really are trying to change," I say in a disbelieving tone.

He laughs as he agrees.

Raff looks around the room. "How about we just pause?"

I wrinkle my brow.

Sensing my confusion he continues. "Fucking unpacking, both literally and emotionally. Let's just do whatever you want to do right now. If you want to go back to sleep, I'll give you space. If you want to shower or eat or, fuck it go to the movies, whatever. I'm here for you."

I can't make a decision. Raff is being so supportive. I'm still not used to it. I roll my upper lip between my teeth. My hands subconsciously falling to the hem of my black western-style pearl-snap shirt.

I haven't thought about what I'd like to do in a long time. I certainly have never asked for what I want either. Time and time again when met with the refusal of my basic needs I just learned to stop asking. To stop wanting. So the idea that this man is standing here, asking me what I want to do, is overwhelming. Sensing my unease Raff gently brushes my hair off of my cheek.

"I think I know what you might want to do," he says a shy grin spreading across his face.

I click on the overhead lights while Raff disarms the alarm. It's strange to be here at this time of day. It's even stranger to be here alone with Raff. He tugs me inside as he goes into the walk in to pull out some of the basics.

"Whatever you want, help yourself," he says disappearing around the corner to pull out dry goods.

I don't really have a plan. I just knew it felt right when Raff said we should go bake.

I love baking. The best part of my day was early mornings at Mother Wolf. I loved stretching and folding, laminating, scoring, and shaping. There is no better feeling than working dough. It's why I wanted to work at Princess Pizzarina. Whenever I'm stressed or overwhelmed, I can always ground myself by baking something. I love that anything is possible when you bake. Seemingly random parts culminate to create infinite possibilities. Something from nothing. The cook is only limited by their imagination. It is the pure freedom that I have always craved.

"What'll it be, chef?" Raff asks, pulling on his apron.

I scoff at his use of the word, remembering when I used it to get under his skin. I stare at the ingredients in front of me.

"How do you feel about morning buns," I say after a long pause. Then, thinking better of it, I start to backpedal. "But it takes a long time for everything to proof. Let's just..." I start but Raff stops me.

"We got nothing but time, baby. So, let's do it."

I set about making the dough. Princess has a spiral mixer, so it comes together very quickly. At Mother Wolf we usually use our croissant dough to make flakey morning buns that have a caramelized sugar crust. It's crunchy and buttery in such a delightful way. However, that would take way too long. We don't have two days to waste. So I make a brioche dough similar to a cinnamon roll.

As I pull it together, Raff blanches orange peels. Then as I set the dough aside to rise, I use the rest of the orange to make a simple syrup.

With these elements working, Raff looks at me with a coy smile. "Hungry," he asks raising an eyebrow.

I nod. However, I know it isn't food that I crave.

God damn. Raff is annoyingly attractive right now. Not just because he's being so considerate of me. His face is appealing in an old-school masculine way, with a chiseled jawline and classic, handsome features. Which is hilarious when you consider the juxtaposition that he's a total punk shit head with tattoos, mustache, and a black eye. My stomach tightens as I look at him. I take the flat bill of his cap and pull it down.

"The fuck," he says in response to my random gesture.

Raff makes an egg-and-tomato dish. I'd only ever known it as Shakshuka, but he explains that it's the Greek version called Kagiana. It's a bright and surprisingly velvety rustic dish that comes together quickly. He serves it on one shared plate.

Heads bowed low, faces conspiratorially close, we eat standing over the stainless-steel work counter in the kitchen. Forks scraping, jaws working, ice water rattling in our deli containers, there is an ease to the quiet familiarity that we share. My eyes drift down to the curve of Raff's mouth. I can't help watching the way his lips move as he eats. Delightfully slow and sumptuous movements that make me remember what it felt like to have them pressed all over me.

After we clean up, there's still time to kill before the dough has fully risen. We wander out through the swinging doors into the front of house. The roller blinds are down in the big front windows. The sun shining through the sheer navy fabric bathes the empty restaurant in an unnatural exposure. I walk along the row of long wooden tables, letting my fingers slide across the smooth finish. Raff disappears behind the bar, and within a minute, Minor Threat starts to play on the stereo.

We both start to dance. Playfully pretending to jostle and bash into one another in a mosh made of two people, until I accidentally trip over one of his feet. Raff grabs me, steadying our bodies close.

"Easy tiger," he says.

We're practically pressed together. His warm breath tickles my nose. I suddenly feel shy. Too self-aware of his proximity and how badly I want him.

I spin out of his grasp, ducking into the nearby photo booth. I swing side to side on the stool as Raff slowly stalks towards me. Anticipation of his arrival makes my pulse roar between my thighs. Reaching the entrance, he braces his forearms on the frame as he leans over me.

"Wanna take some pictures?" he asks slowly.

My eyes widen, and I nod eagerly. "Fuck yes," I squeal, my tone uncharacteristically eager. I love a photo booth. Always have and always will.

He leans over the bar again, returning a minute later with a key ring. After unlocking something on the exterior of the machine and flipping a few stitches within its ancient mechanical guts, the photo booth whirls to life. He extends a hand towards the screen in a go-ahead type of gesture before placing the key ring on the bar. I shoo him out of the booth, pulling the curtain closed with a dramatic swish.

I purse my lips, propping my fist under my chin. Flash. I turn my face to profile, adopting a stoic expression. Flash. I slide on my sunglasses on and muster my best Olsen Twins prune face. Flash. I pull the oversized sunglasses down to the tip of my nose, peering over the frames with a playfully coy smirk. Flash.

Raff peaks in through the crack in the curtain.

“Again,” I say, my tone similar to an overjoyed toddler.

Raff smiles, amused. “Sure. You want to see a cool one,” he asks.

I nod enthusiastically.

He curls his index finger at me in a come here gesture. I slip out of the booth, letting him occupy my space on the stool.

“Excuse me,” he says teasingly as he swishes the curtain closed in the exact flourish I had used earlier.

I exhale a laugh taking a step back and scooping up my photos that just expelled from the machine.

I admire my work as the four flashes go off in my peripheral. There is something so charming and a little mysterious about the grainy black-and-white images. In high contrast, the four vertical pictures share a genuine expression. Timeless but also historic in some odd way.

One of my most treasured possessions is a photo strip of Abuelita when she first arrived in Santa Luna. She’s at the beach boardwalk, her hair teased high and sunglasses on the top of her head. Despite everything she’d left behind and everything she faced, she’d found time to have fun. Even if it was just for the five minutes inside of that photo booth. She looked awkward and silly. Unsure of how to pose. In my favorite photo, her cheeks are raised with her mouth pursed mid syllable, as if she were caught off guard. It is the only time I’d ever seen her carefree.

Raff's photos thunk into the metal delivery slot. I greedily snatch them up then immediately toss my head back with a raucous cackle of laughter. The first photo is just Raff's arms pointed straight up in the air. The next, his arms still raised, portrays his head and shoulders, then his torso and finally his legs. The entire strip gives the illusion of Raff flying with his arms stretched high.

What is making me laugh, though, is his serious expression, only exaggerated by his shiner and mustache.

"Impressed," he drawls as he peeks through the curtain at me. I only realize now he's been watching me as I study his photos. I bring my hands together in a slow clap.

"Want to do more," he asks, drawing out the last word.

I nod eagerly.

He jerks his head, beckoning me inside.

"Ok, but don't tell Guy. This film is hard to get."

Raff pulls me down onto his knee. I tense at first when I realize how good the pressure of his leg feels between my thighs. Shit. Do not grind yourself on Raff, I scold internally.

"Serious," Raff says gruffly.

We both sit ramrod straight as we stare blankly into the camera. Flash.

"Silly," I command before I stick out my tongue.

Raff pulls his ears to each side, puffing up his cheeks and crossing his eyes. Flash. "Naughty," Raff singsongs playfully.

He purses his lips, bringing his index finger to the side of his mouth in an old-timey scandalized way.

Without thinking, I grasp the hem of my shirt and yank it up over my face, exposing my bra to the camera. Flash.

Raff's eyebrows are raised in a stunned but impressed expression.

"Last one," I squeal with hurried delight. I snatch his hat and put it on.

Raff, in turn, lifts the hem of his shirt over his head, bearing his chest in a mimic of my last pose. I fall against the wall of the booth, hugging myself as I laugh ridiculously. His cap falling to the floor. Flash.

In the panic between shots, I've moved entirely onto Raff's lap. He's practically cradling me as I'm draped across him. We're laughing, gulping down air as we hold each other, our faces swaying closer and then apart. Our eyes meet as we regain our composure. Now noses only inches away, we see each other. I pull my bottom lip between my teeth.

"Can I?" Raff asks in a low voice.

I start to nod, but he's already there.

Our mouths meet, soft at first but deepening quickly. Desperation has been building up, and I need him. I need all of him. I need to taste him. I need to consume him. I need to be with him.

Our hands find each other's faces, as mouths part open wide and tongues dance. Breathing deepens, and paces quicken. I shift myself so I'm straddling Raff's lap on that stool. The air inside the little photo booth thickens as our momentum increases. I can't help but roll my hips, grinding down on him. His hands descend on my neck and shoulders. I grasp the western shirt, ripping open the pearl snap front. Raff jerks his head back.

"Is this ok?" I pant.

He shakes his head. "Fuck yes," he confirms breathlessly.

Then we're back together, kissing and grinding. It's hard and frantic. Gone is the tenderness of the previous night. I start dragging my lips down his neck, but he's desperate to make contact with my shoulders and chest. It's clumsy and needy. We're like two starving diners at a banquet table, unsure of where to start but uncaring of what is being shoveled into our mouths. We need to consume.

Raff pulls the shirt down my shoulders and forearms. I struggle to get it over my wrists, letting it slap to the floor when I'm finally free. Faces crashing back together, I tug Raff's shirt up and over his head. Pressing and tugging, we are constantly coming together and then breaking apart as we clamor to connect with one another. I'm eager to get his pants off, finally expose him, but also unwilling to stop kissing him for the brief moment it will take.

Raff tilts me back, I brace myself on the screen of the photo booth as he undoes my jeans, tugging them free. My boots pop off with the momentum. I fall back into him, both of our heads ducked, replenishing our contact before finding his belt buckle. I'm yanking down his pants, he's holding my face and kissing me while he kicks them off. Tripping over his own shoes as he struggles out of them. All the while, the machine has whirled back to life.

Everything is chaos. Whole Lotta Love is ripping through the speakers. Fitting, I'll think later, but now I'm totally engrossed. I undo my bra as Raff yanks me back onto his lap. Flash. He's cupping my breasts, teasing my nipples, as I rub myself along his stiff cock. Flash. I'm gasping at the sensation of my softness pressing into the rigid center of him. "Condom," I whisper on a pant between full mouth kisses. Flash. He's ducking down for his wallet, returning with one between his teeth. Flash.

I keep myself satisfied rubbing long wet strokes against his leg as Raff rolls the condom on. His eyes raised to mine, studying my face. However, I have no time to overthink this. I'm consumed with my desire for him. I'm lifting and lowering. Feeling the sharp stretch and then the satisfying fullness of him as we both inhale jagged, gasping breaths. My hands find his shoulders that I was so desperate to touch before. He easily grasps my hips, his fingers sinking into my supple flesh. Slowly, I start to rock myself in oblong loops; up and down. Our gaze locked, he's guiding me, helping me build momentum.

Then, as I pick up pace, his mouth finds my neck. Hips thrusting, he's pushing up into me with each loop. Up, down, thrust. I'm feeling the pressure mounting as we both jostle to get closer to the other. Mouths still searching, sucking, licking, kissing. I'm bouncing up and down with him, our rhythm fast and pulsing. I nearly bang my head into the top of the booth. Raff is pulling me down close just in the nick of time.

"Ok," he questions, his voice ragged in my ear.

I nod, swiveling my hips. The feeling is incredible and overwhelming. With each thrust, a pressure is building in my core. "Harder," I beg desperate to not lose the sensation.

Raff hoists me up, and I make a strangled yelp as he slides out of me. He turns us, placing my elbows on the stool as he easily enters me from behind. I'm soaking wet, my entrance swollen and soft. I brace myself, and he fills me. This angle allows him to go deeper. With his first thrust, I cry out, it's a wounded sound. Not because it is painful, but because it is the ache of feeling an unfamiliar pleasure.

The pressure is nearly unbearable. My fingers curl around the lip of the stool as Raff fucks me. I hear the guttural sound of rhythmic whimpers, only to realize I'm making those noises. Dizzy at how out of control I am in this moment. The music blasting, the camera flashing, and Raff's thrusting is building a crescendo of tension deep inside of me. He slips one hand between my legs, finding my clit, and with the tiniest rub I'm unraveling. My body spasms forward as I gasp out my release. I feel Raff follow, his sex spilling deep inside of the condom between us.

He rolls his hips a few times slowly until he's sure that we've both finished. We've lowered ourselves to practically kneeling on the floor of the photo booth, bent over the stool in a quivering L-shaped mass. He drops warm sticky kisses on the back of my shoulders and at the nape of my neck. Then very slowly he draws himself out of me, careful to keep the condom in place.

I pant a little, and he helps me up. It's weird to be naked at work. It's even weirder to have just had sex here. Condom still on, dropping with its newfound weight, he wraps me up in a hug.

"You ok?" he whispers into my hair before dropping a kiss on the top of my head.

I nod and tilt my face up towards him. "I'll be right back."

We both awkwardly grab our clothing and slip into the bathrooms. I catch my reflection in the mirror. My hair is tussled, cheeks flushed, and lips a deep red. I look alive. Fuck, I feel alive. I quickly pee with the stall door open, unable to take my eyes off my current form. I feel in my body for the first time in a long time. Typically, I think of myself as a tiny alien piloting the spaceship that is me around all the time.

However, right now, I am me, with round hips, tapered waist, full breasts, and narrow shoulders. I take my time getting dressed, noticing how I feel the drag of fabric on flesh and where each garment hangs, drapes, or holds me. With my mussed hair teased high and smudged makeup accentuating my almond eyes in this greenish fluorescent lighting, I look like an extraterrestrial in a Barbarella movie. I smirk. Jane Fonda and Anita Pallenberg are queens. I'd be happy to inhabit their galaxy.

I find Raff sitting at the bar. He's chewing on the end of an orange swizzle stick, admiring a few photo strips.

"Hello, pretty-pretty," I coo, dropping into a stool next to him. "What's so amusing?"

He grins as he slides the pictures towards me.

"Oh shit," I say, studying the candid photos.

He taps the image of our blurry limbs as we grapple for closeness, mid sloppy kiss. We appear as feral as I had felt. I laugh.

"You imagine it looking more graceful in the moment," I say.

He shakes his head. "You're better than I imagined," he replies, leaning over and kissing my jaw.

My stomach tightens, which I willfully disregard. He sighs, sinking onto his outstretched forearm on the bar top.

I lean down, so we're face to face, cheeks pressed on the smooth wood surface. We stare at each other. Drink in the afterglow and timid postcoital silence.

"So... what does all this mean?" I say.

He lifts a shoulder and lets it drop. "Do you want to be my girlfriend?" he asks in a husky voice.

I'm shocked that he, of all people, would even suggest it. I feel a giddy pinch deep inside. However, I ignore the feeling as I blurt out, "Girlfriend? Are we in middle school?" Immediately, I regret how harsh that came out.

"Ok, if not girlfriend, how about wife?" he asks, which causes me to cough out a choked laugh.

"I do not aspire to become anyone's wife or mother," I say.

"Good," he says, sliding his hand into mine. "Cuz I got snipped a few years ago."

My eyebrows raise in surprise.

"Only Guy knows," he adds.

Do I tell him about my own precautions? Why the fuck not, I think. We're already in pretty deep at this point. "It's not that I hate kids. I just can't imagine having one. I've always had an IUD. Maybe you remember that?"

He dips his chin in agreement.

"Either way, I'd get my tubes tied, but I can't find a doctor who will do it."

He nods thoughtfully. "Fucking politics. My mom probably would have been a lot happier if she'd had her tubes tied. I had a shit childhood. My parents hated being parents. I'd never put anyone through what I endured. So, I eliminated the possibility. End the cycle and shit. I still, uh, use condoms though," he puts in quickly. "Just to be safe."

I try to fight the shy smile on my face. "Same. Plus, I don't know where you've been, you dirty boy."

He laughs. "Should we go get tested together?"

Fuck this man. The harder I try to convince myself that I don't like him, he finds another way to be on the same page as me.

"So if you don't want to get married, what is it that you want?" Raff asks, bringing his thumb up and brushing a lock of hair off my cheek.

The acid bubbles, but for once, I'm able to keep it at bay as I think about his question. Fuck it. I've already come this far. "To be free," I whisper.

A smile spreads on his face, the corners of his eyes crinkling slightly.

"To bake. Stay up late. Do what I want whenever I want. To fuck, especially like this afternoon. To get drunk and smoke joints. To lie in bed all day if I have the urge. Read trashy books and drink Diet Coke, even though I know that I should be consuming way more water. To eat nothing but torn hunks of sourdough and obscene amounts of French butter for every meal or leftover Indian takeout for breakfast," I say.

He leans forward and kisses me again. Soft but purposeful on the corner of my mouth. His mustache causes my nose to twitch, and I can't help but smile.

"But what about me?" he asks hopefully.

I exhale slowly. Fuck it. No bullshit, man.

"I want you so badly it hurts sometimes... which terrifies me. What if my desire for you traps me? Robs me of the few pleasures I'm able to attain in my dumb life. What if I convince myself that whatever you want is more important than me? Like, I give up cooking or something stupid like that? What if you leave and I'm stuck forever wanting you again?" That last part tumbles out in a strangled sound, and I immediately regret it.

In a blink, his expression is sad, but I turn my face downwards towards the bar top.

I feel his hands around me, pulling me off my stool and close to his chest.

"Ask me what I want," he says softly.

I hesitate, worried that the answer might break me. I shouldn't have been so honest. However, I oblige. My gaze is still downturned, so it comes out muffled against him.

"You," he replies. "Being with you."

I tilt my face towards him hesitantly. "Listen, I know I fucked it up last time. I was too young, and I totally freaked."

I smile at him. I'm all too familiar with his methods.

"But since then, I've just been running around trying to avoid you. Which is fucked because I realize now that you're all I've ever wanted," he says.

I wrap my arms around him and return his embrace. "That's kind of unhealthy," I tease.

He scoffs. "Fucking tell me about it."

Chapter 23

RAFF

We don't discuss it further. I don't want to push her. Which is hard because I'd typically be pretty fucking pissed if I'd laid myself out there like that and someone had turned me down. However, I don't think she's actually turning me down. Ash doesn't want labels for some reason. Hey, I get it. Labels can potentially make things complicated. Complicated would definitely send Ash running. Honestly, same... until now. We've made a lot of progress in a short amount of time. I just need to keep being patient.

So, I don't push. We finish making morning buns. They're fucking delicious. We soak them in orange simple syrup and top them with thick icing and the candied orange peels. We pull them apart in strips of soft dough. They're thick and syrupy. The contrast between the bun's puffy density and the bright flavors is rich. It's exactly what you'd want to eat on a Sunday morning... or Monday at 1:46 p.m. in our case.

We head back to the house after we clean up. She lets me hold her hand as we drive in my old Tacoma and sing along with the Red-Hot Chili Peppers. Guy's truck is still gone, so I'm hoping she'll hang out with me in my room. Fuck, I sound like a teenager. Whatever. That's what she does to me. I want to be young, dumb, and infatuated with her.

Unfortunately, when we come through the door, Vanessa and Mackenzie are sitting in the living room. Mac is nose deep in her laptop, which she is balancing on her knee. While Van is doing a weird contortion on the ground, dressed in a hand-dyed shirt that reads "Moon Collective Yoga" and a pair of very tight yoga pants. Both of them look shocked for a moment to see Ashley walking in with me. Then, the realization dawning on them, Vanessa leaps to her feet with a screaming battle cry.

"I *knew* you'd need a plus one for my wedding!"

Mac furrows her brows as she simultaneously says, "Bitch, how long has *this* been going on?"

Ash tentatively takes a few steps back, but Vanessa and Mac are engulfing her. Both rapid-firing questions. I understand now why she was so hesitant to define the relationship. I attempt to wedge my body between them, protect her as best I can. However, this only causes them to turn their attention towards me.

"What are your intentions towards our daughter?" Van asks in a playfully stern tone.

"Yeah, mother fucker? What's the deal?" Mac says. Her tone is not playful.

This is how we find ourselves seated across from Mac and Van at the dinette, like some strange aisatsu. Whatever. If I have to perform all the rituals of a Japanese marriage meeting, deep bowing as I beg Ashley's family for permission to woo her, then I will.

“You guys are being fucking ridiculous,” Ash says, glaring across the table.

“Are we?” Mac questions and Van echoes, “Yeah! Are we?”

Ashley huffs and crosses her arms. “Well, it’s not that serious,” she says.

This has my head turning. All three of us ask Ash, “Really?”

She can sense my surprise. There’s a quick look of something I can’t read before she steadies her expression. “I don’t know. It’s not like he’s my boyfriend.” Van and Mac turn to me.

I just shrug. “She’s right. Ash is not my girlfriend... yet.” I smile at her, and she rolls her eyes as Mac and Van fly into another barrage of questions.

Ash throws her hands up as she stands from the table. “You two are worse than Cita and Lulu,” she says, stomping down the hallway.

We all watch her stop, unsure of which door to enter. Then, much to my amusement, with a huff, she pushes into my bedroom, slamming the door behind her.

“They grow up so fast,” Van says.

“I should probably...” standing I wave towards the hallway.

Mac grabs the sleeve of my hoodie. "Be careful with her. She's not as tough as she looks."

I nod.

She didn't need to tell me that. I remember the aftermath of our original pop-up. I thought she'd call or text after I didn't show. Instead, I was met with silence. At the time, I thought it was good, easier really. Now I know she's still raw inside. Unable to trust anyone, partially because of my betrayal. However, I'm taking Mac's warning as a subtle gesture that she's accepting of this situation, which is good because Mac is scary as shit.

I wrap my knuckles a few times on the door before I enter. I find Ashley face down in my bed.

"What," she moans into my pillows.

"Can I come in?" I ask.

"It's your room," she says, turning to prop herself upright.

I'm almost about to say it's "our room," but I think better of it. That would probably send her jumping through the closed window. I'd just have an Ashley-shaped hole in the wall, like a fucking cartoon.

"This fucking sucks," she says.

I drop down on the bed next to her. "What does," I ask.

"This. You. All of it. If you were an ass, I could just fucking leave. When Anita wanted her apartment back, I could get in the car and just drive off," she says.

I know I shouldn't, but I can't help myself. "Your car's busted. Remember?"

She rolls her eyes and flops back on the mattress with an overly dramatic groan. "See! Fuck. Now I have to fucking deal with all of this shit!"

"What shit," I ask sharply, furrowing my eyebrows, which is fucking hard when you have a black eye. The skin on my face is still bruised and swollen in places.

She hesitates for a moment before blurting out, "My fucking feelings."

I know I shouldn't laugh, but I fucking do.

"Stop," she scolds. "I don't want to like you back. In fact, it would be really fucking better if I didn't."

I try to steel my face. However, I fucking can't. I can't help it. I'm God damn giddy.

I wrap her up in my arms. She wriggles as I drop kisses all over her face and head. "You love me," I tease.

Ash thrashes in protest. "I said a like you. Like you!" I don't care. This is fucking progress.

I suspect that this admission might be an understatement, but I am still going to celebrate. "So you'll live in this little shit-hole with me," I ask.

She sighs dramatically. "Fine. On one condition."

I stop my physical assault and stare into her almond-shaped eyes. Fuck she's so beautiful. "Anything," I say softly.

"Either of us can leave at any time. You just have to tell me. Please just give me a heads up." She looks worried. "Don't disappear again." She's asking this of me rather than making it a statement.

I realize she's still unconvinced that I've changed.

I lean over and kiss her softly. She doesn't push me away. I know she wants to make this work, we just have a lot of shit to overcome. Shit that I unfortunately put in our path.

"We can have a codeword," she says, breaking our kiss. "You just say the word saucier, and I'll know."

"We work in a restaurant. I'm going to have to say saucier every once in a while," I counter. I shouldn't be entertaining this, but the visible worry has left her. I want her to feel heard.

"Ok fine. How about gecko?"

She's acting so nonchalant, but I know she's being vulnerable right now. This is the girl who emerged after I pushed her away. The one who I made feel unlovable. However, she's still here, open to another chance.

My work is far from over, but I can see that if I just keep trying she'll come around. I'm going to show her how much I like her. She'll know that she can fucking trust me. I take her hand in my bandaged-up paw, giving it a shake.

"Deal." Then I toss my arms around her, dipping her back and kissing her hard.

Chapter 24

ASH

I'm not sure what I'd expected when I decided to move into Guy's house, but between a rotating door of my family coming in and out, we've totally taken over the place. It's only been a few days, and it's already feeling more and more like the blue house.

With the wedding two weeks away, Van has been spending most of her nights in Santa Luna, cuddled up close to Mac. The two of them have always been the closest of all of us. Now, with Mac acting as Van's wedding coordinator, it's gone to an entirely new level. Honestly, I'm getting a little worried for Mac when Van moves in with Cary permanently after the big day.

Then, of course, not to be left out Lex and Nat have been spending all of their free time at the house too. When we get home from Princess after closing, we usually find the pair casually swimming naked in the pool with the dog or lounging on the patio furniture eating oranges and avocados off the trees behind the garage, like they didn't just hop the fence and help themselves.

Then, when Nat got caught crawling through the dog door to use the bathroom inside, Mac put her foot down. "The neighbors are going to call the police on you two shady freaks," she'd scolded when she realized that this was a new escalating pattern of behavior.

So, naturally, Guy had a key made for them.

"Thank you so much, Step-Daddy," Lex had squealed when he presented it to her.

Mac shot him a glare, which made Guy shrug. "Aw, let me spoil the kid."

Besides the breaking and entering, Nat and Lex are both crafty. So, they've been helping Vanessa with the final details of the ceremony and some other weird shit for her bachelorette party. I've been so busy at the restaurant these past few days that I can't keep track of all their little projects. They've taken over the living room and dinette with their supplies.

I thought Guy and Raff would be more annoyed about the boxes of newspaper strips and scrap cardboard. However, they've seemed to enjoy the added activity. I woke up yesterday to the sound of hammering. When I peeked my head out into the garage, I found Guy and Raff happily constructing some sort of arch-type structure made out of aged driftwood while listening to Lou Reed and smoking a joint.

It also can't hurt that, between the five of us, we've been keeping them very well fed. Van shows up with reusable bags filled with random produce she's either grown or traded for with other CSA farm growers. Mac has extended her weekly sandwich order to include everyone, not just Guy.

Somehow, when you get more than one Lobo in a kitchen, we just immediately start cooking Mexican food: tacos, enchiladas, and pozole. Although Van's version of these dishes is typically vegetarian. Whoever works in the bakery that morning brings any leftover bread home at the end of the day. However, that's dwindling now that they're almost fully off the schedule and the new hires are taking over.

"So what's the end game here?" I ask while I watch Van and Nat cut some dyed muslin cloth.

"Table runners," Lex exclaims from where she's lying on the floor with a long strip of gauze in front of her.

"No. I mean... Mother Wolf," I say.

Normally, I wouldn't bring the topic up, but Raff and Guy are out surfing. It's rare to have a minute of just the five of us together since we've all left the bakery. Plus, this is nice. I've missed getting to be a part of the family again. It's terrifying to think that it's going to end soon.

Mac stops tapping on her laptop and looks up at me. The abrupt movement causes the dog on the sofa next to her to shift and sneeze in protest before resettling its head in Mac's lap. "We all have our issues with Cita and Lulu, but that doesn't mean they can take their shit out on you all the time." This has been her stance since she organized the mass exodus.

Van puts down her scissors and adds, "They need to know that we don't support the way they treat you."

I frown. "Listen, I'm grateful for that and all. But once you're done at the bakery, then what? Are you all seriously saying that you're going to cut them out of your lives? It's not a fun way to live. Trust me. Plus, what are you going to do after the wedding?" I ask, pulling my legs up under myself as I shift in the armchair.

"My mom has actually been understanding. I think she's just kinda worried about going against Cita," Van starts, but Mac quickly cuts in.

"Cita and Lulu are not the poor old victims that they want us to believe that they are. They need to realize that if they want all of us in their lives, then they need to make concessions for everyone. I personally don't want to work for someone who constantly dangles an opportunity in front of my face and then yanks it away to keep me in check. I want to build my own life. They can be a part of it if they can accept that it's mine to live." I'm a little stunned. I knew how Mac felt, but I've never heard her speak so openly about it. I think the distance away from our mom is helping her get clarity.

"But isn't Mother Wolf a part of that? Wasn't the idea that we'd all run the bakery together?" I ask.

"Together is the keyword," Lex says, rolling onto her back. "Also, this is way more fun. I like getting to make shit with you guys... the bakery was just the medium to do it. It doesn't always have to be."

We look at her as she lifts her legs up over her head in a plow pose and wiggles her toes.

"Hey, great extension," Nat notes. "But, Lex's right. What if you all just started your own thing? It doesn't have to be Mother Wolf, right?"

"Yeah," Van agrees eagerly.

I bite my bottom lip. I look over at Mac, who has a similar expression. She knows as well as I do that just simply starting our own thing would be difficult. Most restaurants fail spectacularly. We're all financially stable right now, but how long would it last if we take on that kind of commitment?

"Let's start a taco truck," Lex shrieks, unfolding from her inverted pose and using the momentum to rocket up to sitting.

"Girl, you're going to give yourself a nosebleed if you do shit like that," Nat snaps.

"I don't hate the idea, but let's keep thinking about it," Mac says.

"You know, Cary could probably help us with seed money," Van starts but we all shake our heads.

"No offense, but we don't need his blood money," Lex says.

"What about Step-Daddy?" Nat asks.

Mac and I exchange a look. Princess Pizzarina has been booming since the Log Jam. In fact, Guy confided to Mac that they were finally turning a profit, rather than just barely breaking even. We don't want to jinx their hot streak. "We'll figure it out," Mac says definitively.

"More importantly, how's it going?" Lex asks, waggling her eyebrows as she snakes her way over to the base of my chair.

"Huh," I reply, suddenly finding the felt I've been tasked to cut very interesting.

"She means your boo," Nat interjects.

"Oh, god," I say, rolling my eyes.

Now, as if they've rehearsed it, they all start clapping and chanting. "Details! Details! Details!"

"What do you want to know?" I sigh, setting my scissors aside. I should have seen this coming. For the past few days, they've given Raff and me a wide berth. After our formal sit-down with Van and Mac, everyone has just been operating as though it's a totally natural occurrence that we're together... or whatever we're calling it. However, every once in a while, I'd catch one of them staring at me from across the room or over Raff's shoulder with a mischievous smirk.

"Tell us everything," Van says.

"There isn't anything to know," I reply.

"Ugh, you're being a fucking cat. You're obviously going to be so lame, and all repressed about it," Lex says.

I furrow my brow, offended. "Repressed," I ask.

"Yeah, like all, oh, whatever. It's all fine. Nothing matters. But then it actually *really* deeply matters. You're such a fucking Scorpio," Lex says.

I kick her in the face with my bare foot, making sure to extend my toes for maximum impact.

"Ow," she whines and yanks my leg down towards the floor.

I cascade out of the chair on top of her. Our legs and arms flailing as I attempt to keep kicking her, but she's also trying to hit me in return. This gets the dog's attention, who's now in our faces, attempting to get in on the action.

"Stop," I yell as she sinks her nails into my skin.

"You stop," Lex hurls back, or at least she attempts to, but the wind gets knocked out of her as the dog leaps on top of us, a large paw stepping on her head.

Nat has grabbed hold of Lex, while Mac gets a grip on the dog's collar. I'm still wedged between Lex and the chair.

"Both of you stop," Mac declares as she pulls the dog towards the slider.

“Just admit that you like him, you butthead,” Lex says, wriggling out of Nat’s arms.

“I can’t,” I shout back still hot from our tussle. They all look at me.

“So, you’re just using him for a place to crash and some loud sex,” Nat asks.

My mouth pops open, jaw slack, before I shriek.

“It’s not loud, right?!”

They all give me a pitying look. I bring my hands up to my face and let my head fall forward. I can feel the cracks showing. I will myself to hold it all together.

“We’re just figuring it out,” I say quietly.

I feel Van’s hand on my back as she lowers down next to me. “It’s ok if you like him. We won’t judge you,” she says softly.

I hate that they’re forcing me to talk about this. I’d make a break for Raff’s bedroom, but I know they’d find another way to get me to confess. It’s better to just get it over with now.

“It’s just... what if he changes his mind again? What if I’m not enough?” I say. I’m so fucking humiliated right now, I can’t even bear to look at any of them.

Van's arm slips around my back as she pulls me into her. I feel Mac on the other side as she wraps an arm around me. Nat gives my leg a squeeze as Lex basically lays in my lap. The dog is there too somewhere. I can feel her hot breath on the bare skin of my arm, before the jingling of her license as Mac pushes her away.

"You're allowed to have good things," Van says carefully.

I shake my head, hands still firmly placed over my face. "But what about the curse? What if I let myself love Raff and something horrible happens to him?"

I feel my sisters tighten their hold on me. We never talk about Erik. Fuck I don't even refer to him as dad. I often wonder if Cita was kinder before he died. If losing him was the reason that she turned into the person that she is today. What was he like? Who was he? For someone that we barely ever discuss, his presence or lack thereof, looms large over all of us. He's the ghost that haunts all of our relationships.

"The curse is bullshit," Van says. "I love Cary, and we want to be together. I have to just trust that whatever is meant for me will be provided by the Universe."

"But aren't you fucking terrified," I ask. I feel the rise and fall of her shoulder against mine.

"Sometimes, but I can't control the future. So why waste my time worrying about what might be? It'll only make me miss out on what is."

I dare to lift my head and look at my beautiful cousin. She truly is a mother goddess.

"You know, when I used to do competitive dance, I was always scared as fuck of the judges. But I wanted to dance more than anything. So, I just had to do it scared," Nat rasps.

"Same's true for when I went skydiving with my art friends last year. Fucking terrified, but I still did it. And now I get to bring it up constantly," Lex adds.

"Fucking tell us about it," Nat says, rolling her eyes.

I venture a glance at these two gorgeous weirdos. They stare up at me like Dickensian orphans from Mars, with their hopeful eyes, tattoos, piercings, and pink hair.

"I hate scary movies, but I still went with Guy to that anniversary showing of The Lost Boys at the La Paloma," Mac says.

I nod at her. The girl is tough, but she seriously has no threshold for horror movies. The screening had been midday, but for a month, she'd still run every time she had to go from the car to the house in the dark. Terrified that a teenage Kiefer Sutherland might grab her while she was most vulnerable. Until she ate shit tripping over her Swedish clogs and broke a strap. She decided that to ruin handcrafted leather was worse than being taken by a gang of vampires from the 80s. Yes, it is that ridiculous.

“Shit is going to happen. You can’t control it. But you can control going after what you want. So if you want to pursue a relationship with Raff, do it scared,” Mac says.

A jolt shoots up my back, fizzing out through the branches of nerves in my shoulders. They’re right. I can’t deny that. “But if he fucks you over again, I’ll cut his dick off,” she adds matter-of-factly.

“Same,” Lex says.

“Oh, we’ll totally make him eat it too, babe,” Nat rasps with a mischievous smile.

“Let’s save it to sacrifice under a blood moon in exchange for fertility,” Van pipes up.

“Thanks,” I say softly and they all lean in closer to me.

This is what I’ve been missing in the years that I’ve been away. A deeper sadness settles in the pit of my stomach. This is what I’ve lost because I was too afraid to deal with Cita and Lulu head-on. Fuck. I guess I’m going to have to do it all, even if I am scared.

Chapter 25

RAFF

When we walk into the house, Minnie jumps up to greet us. All of the Lobos are in a heap on the floor in the living room. When they see me enter the room behind Guy, they all immediately start singing Isn't She Lovely by Stevie Wonder. This is now a commonplace occurrence whenever I encounter them. I guess, since Guy is Step-Daddy and Ash is their teenage daughter, then, by some logic, this has made them all refer to me as Baby Girl. So now some swooning Motown song precedes any interaction I have with Ash's family.

"Why can't I be a dude?" I ask, crossing my arms. Minnie is immediately sniffing and licking the dried saltwater off our feet.

"We're already the twin brothers," Lex says, waving an index finger between herself and Nat, the only non-Lobo.

"Well, then? Can I be a cousin?" I say, pushing Minnie away.

She immediately starts to nose Guy's ankles and calves. "Ew. You can't be my cousin," Ash says, wrinkling up her nose.

I throw my hands up.

"Yeah, if anything, you'd be, like, the crotchety old neighbor," Nat says thoughtfully. This causes all of them to hum and nod in agreement.

"No! I'm staying as Baby Girl," I huff and walk towards my room.

Though we clumsily towel-changed out of our wetsuits in the parking lot before heading back, I need to shower off the ocean water. I strip out of my clothes just as Ash is slipping into the room behind me. I stand naked in front of her. Something feels off. My heart starts to race.

She looks nervous as she whispers something inaudible. Shit, what's happening? I close the distance between us, trying not to let her see my panic. She's leaving me. That's the only thought that's rushing through my mind. I've already started the shower spray in the Jack-and-Jill bathroom, so it's hard to hear what she said when she entered the room.

"What," I ask, coming in close to hear her.

"Alright," she mumbles into my bare chest.

I left my arms to encircle her gently as I look down at Ash in confusion. She steadies herself, her soft lips tickling over my skin as she leans up closer, brushing herself against my exposed flesh.

"Ok. I'll do it. I will be your girlfriend," she says.

My breath catches for a moment as I process what she's saying to me.

"Is that still ok?" she asks with a slight stammer.

I don't reply. Just let my overwhelming need to devour her take over. I notice that her bottom lip is quivering slightly as I press my mouth into her's. The kiss is deep and hopefully confirms her feelings.

"Hell yeah, it's ok," I say breathlessly as we break apart. However, it's only momentarily. I'm scooping her up and over my shoulder. She shrieks, but I ignore her protests as I bring her into the bathroom.

I set her down, kissing every inch of her as I pull off her clothing.

"What are you doing?" she asks.

"Getting you naked," I say before sucking on the skin at the point of her elbow.

She laughs slightly.

I drop to my knees, mouth dragging along her stomach. I find the button on her jeans, as I rub my mustache and upper lip along the sensitive skin above her waistband. She shudders at the sensation, bringing her hands to the top of my head. Her fingers twisting into my hair, my name escaping her lips in a pant.

"I need you," I say, tugging off her jeans and nuzzling into her center. I'm too eager for her. I must taste her, feast on her as soon as possible. She's agreed to be mine. My need to consume her is impatient. The gnawing screams echo in the cavities of my skull. The primal part of me has taken over. I hunger for her. So as soon as I've discarded her pants, I press my mouth into her underwear, letting myself rub through the cotton of her thong.

"Raff," she exhales. On my hands and knees in the bathroom now, like the feral animal I am, I use my shoulders to nudge her stance wide as I continue to drag my face over her entrance, kissing her vagina through her panties, giving the soft skin a light squeeze with my lips. I feel the muscles of her stomach tighten at the sensation.

"So fucking sensitive," I murmur into her.

"Yeah, right," she lies as she attempts to straighten, but I softly run the tip of my tongue over her sex from the bottom right up to the clit. I'm rewarded with the musky smell of her arousal. Contrary to what she says, Ash is wet and ready for me. She lifts her hands to take her underwear off, but I catch her wrist.

"What are you..." she starts, but before she can finish, I'm dragging the fabric down with my teeth.

I have a firm grasp on her thighs, providing her with stability but also using my thumbs to massage circles into her hips. I kiss my way down the insides of one thigh and then back on the other until my mouth is at her entrance.

"Raff," Ash says, her tone a little more desperate.

"What?" I ask coyly as I gently bite the flesh just below her pussy.

She gives my hair a yank.

"Ok, ok, brat. So impatient," I say before I languidly lick my lips. Then, making my mouth into an "o" shape, I find her clit and suck hard. It's a good thing I'm holding her up, because she immediately buckles under the pressure of my embouchure.

Ash can't stop moaning and squirming in my grip. Though I know she's not inexperienced by any means, there are moments when we do these more intimate acts that I feel as though this is the first time she's let anyone get this close to her. I'm sucking and releasing the pressure rhythmically. Pulling her clit in and out of my mouth. She's curling around me as I gain momentum. Moaning, her eyes squeezed shut, she grips me tight. Just when I think she's nearing a release, I slip two fingers inside of her. She's clenching like mad around me as I gently curve my digits upwards in search of her G spot. Ashley comes with a scream that rivals the gnawing in my brain.

As her voice echoes on the bathroom walls, I feel a light gush of liquid against my mouth and chin. Holy shit... did she just fucking squirt? That's a first, even for me. I smile into her center as I back off a little to let her ride the wave. She's shuddering as she holds onto my head and shoulders. God, she's fucking gorgeous. I can't help myself. I shape my tongue into a wide flat surface and gently lap up her juices as they run down.

"What the fuck was that?" she gasps when she regains her senses.

"I needed to taste you," I say with a smile as I lower her down into my lap. She rolls her eyes as we sit on the tile floor. Then, with my arms wrapped around her, she leans in close and drags her tongue up my arm. She smacks her lips as she takes in my flavor.

"How'd I taste?" I ask.

"Salty," she says.

"Funny, so did you," I reply.

She gives my bicep a swift punch, which causes me to laugh.

"Sorry," I say. She turns in my lap, so we're face to face. She's draped both of her legs around me and the head of my cock is dangerously close to her entrance. We both feel it. The heaviness of what comes next. The air is thick with anticipation as we study each other's gaze. Then, leaning past me towards the cabinet, Ashley pulls out a condom from under the sink.

"Should we rinse off?" she asks, her voice low and husky.

She doesn't need to ask me twice. I summon all of my strength, because honestly, if I fall right now, it will be so fucking lame. I move both of us to standing in one motion. She squeals, which is good because I think I made a very uncool-sounding grunt. She's kissing me, legs still wrapped around my center as I step us into the shower. The water is too cold, and we both gasp, as I frantically feel around for the knob. Then, when the temperature evens out, we're on each other's mouths again.

She rolls on the condom as I lean my back against the shower wall. Then she's back on me, locking her arms around my neck. Water is hitting us at all angles as it drips down our faces and into our open mouths. We don't care, just continue to consume each other. Her legs are firmly wrapped around my waist as I rub myself against her entrance. My cock is painfully hard, desperate to be inside of her.

The water makes our bodies slick as she slides onto me. My head pressing into her until ever so slowly she's fully seated. I brace her with my forearms, giving her leverage as she uses her feet to push back and forth against the wall. She's in control, but hasn't she always been? Ash sets our pace. Rocking her hips, she sets the movement and depth of our pleasure. I'm just here to support her.

Ashley's movements are deep. She's full of me and going to make sure that we both feel every inch of our connection. The fury of the shower spray underscores the unfathomable desire we share in this moment. She's licking and kissing my wet sink, sucking in every last drop of me. The pressure grows between us until I can't hold on any longer. With a whimpering shudder, I'm coming, just as she's reaching up to the ceiling of the shower to push down onto my cock. She grounds out her release with a loud moan.

My legs shake as she falls forward into me. The water continues to fall on us as we pant into each other. "Fuck," I whisper.

"Fuck," she confirms.

"You should become my girlfriend more often," I say, smiling into her neck as she lowers herself to standing.

She shakes her head. "You're so fucking annoying," she says, her mischievous smile spreading across her face.

We finish showering and reenter the living room to discover that Guy has taken her place. He's surrounded by her family as he cuts crooked lines into felt. Upon seeing us, her family begins to applaud and rise to their feet.

"What the fuck," I say. Ashley immediately brings a palm to her forehead.

"They're giving us a standing ovation," she moans, her cheeks flushing bright red. "You guys suck so much," she says as she walks into the kitchen. I follow her, trying to hide my smile. I've never been in a relationship before. It's both weird and flattering to have an entire room of people clapping about it.

"So does this mean that Baby Girl and Regular Girl are a couple?" Lex calls after us.

"Can it, Pinky," I warn.

Ashley opens the fridge, ignoring her sister.

"Come on, we're all waiting with bated breath," Nat chimes in.

Ash straightens from the fridge with the Britta filter in hand. She rolls her eyes at them before letting her head drop onto my shoulder.

"Hey, leave my girlfriend alone," I call back, wrapping my arms around Ash.

Immediately, there's another irruption of cheers from the other room. Guy even wolf-whistles, which causes Minnie to howl.

"Oh, God. You're in for it now," she says into my chest.

Right on cue, her family is spilling into the kitchen. Everyone, Guy included, is wrapping us in a big group hug. "One of us! One of us! Gooble gobble! Gooble gobble!" They all start chanting.

"Enough, you, freaks," Ash says, attempting to push them off. Which only spurs them on to change their chanting to "Kiss! Kiss! Kiss!"

Despite her protests, I take Ash in my arms and plant one on her. In an overly dramatic movement, I dip her back and kiss her deeply. They all cheer. The Britta sloshes water on our feet and all over the kitchen floor.

“We accept him, we accept him, one of us, one of us,” they repeat.

Wow. This group really likes to chant. This is the weirdest family I’ve ever been a part of. However, there’s something that is making my chest tight when I realize that I’m a part of it. It’s not just Ashley but this entire strange gang who wants me. I’m going to do everything in my power to make damn sure that I don’t ever fuck that up again.

Chapter 26

ASH

I'm hesitant to even admit this but things are actually going really well... Which is very uncomfortable. However, I'm learning to trust it. It's just like being on the line, keep your head down and cook. You can handle anything that's coming for you if you just take it one dish at a time. So, I'll gladly accept this happy feeling, even as the wedding looms heavy over us all.

Lex and Nat have basically been camping in Guy's living room. Rather than driving back to Nat's apartment after a long night working on wedding prep, they simply flop back onto the sofa or shag carpet. Even the dog curls up with them. All three in a cozy puddle until Lex or Nat have to wake up to either take or teach a class.

Van has been a ball of nerves getting everything ready and also shuttling herself between Cary's townhouse and what feels like the endless last-minute obligations that always seem to pop up with his family. In these times of chaos, it's Mac who usually is the grounding force.

In one instance, sensing an impending meltdown, Mac gingerly took a pair of scissors out of Van's trembling hands as she stood before the bathroom mirror, talking herself into trimming her own bangs. Mac swiftly sent her to bed with a quarter of a blueberry-flavored CBD gummy.

At the slightest sign of overwhelm or stress, Mac steps in to help make decisions, remind everyone to drink water or eat something, and generally just assumes any unclaimed responsibility. I think this is why, in the few short weeks she's been working at Princess Pizzarina, Mac's gone from training as a bar back to practically running the managerial duties with Guy.

For my part, I've been living for the work environment at Princess. The crew is tight. We're operating on all cylinders every shift, which is good because business has been booming since the Jam. With the fall semester starting soon, the students have returned to town plus the last few weeks of tourist season have pushed us to maximum capacity.

There's a line nearly every night. However, despite how busy it is, Raff has created an atmosphere of both efficiency and ease. Everything flows, and though there are still moments of difficulty, we somehow manage them easily.

Gone are the days of walking on eggshells, nervous that Raff's mood will suddenly shift. He's really stepped up to assume his role as head chef. He's not pushing us away anymore. It's fun to work with everyone because he's made it that way.

Occasionally, he'll throw out a hypothetical question. We'll spend an entire shift debating the complex absurdity of which celebrity we think has paid to have sex with a dolphin (Nicolas Cage) or what inanimate non-food object you'd attempt to cook and eat for a million dollars (brand new leather belt sous vide until tender and finished in a butter base with fresh herbs). Honestly, it reminds me of my best days spent at Mother Wolf with my family.

We dance to music and joke around, but there's one major difference between Raff and Cita. Raff trusts us to cook to the best of our abilities. Several times, I've heard him challenge Nora to "show me what you got, chef." This is usually accompanied by a fist bump, which she is desperate to accept.

It's a small gesture, but he's letting her take creative liberties where there's room to express her unique cooking style. A huge vote of confidence you wouldn't typically find in most professional kitchens. This is what makes Princess awesome. It's always been Raff's ability to say yes and take a chance on a chef, whether he knew he was doing it or not.

I love that he has always liked experimentation and creativity. It's how we connected all those years ago. We'd spend hours making weird shit in the downtime at the bakery or venture over to his mom's apartment and raid the cabinets for mystery ingredients, usually bizarro things she bought at the Greek Market in Millbrae. This is why I wanted to work for him when I moved back to town. Raff has always embodied freedom.

That's what I lost when he suddenly ghosted me. More than just friend and lover, he was my coconspirator. He'd barged into my deepest secret part and tore a Raff-shaped hole wide inside of my entire being. Then left me to figure out how to suture the tear when he unceremoniously pushed his way out of my life. We were so close, and then he was gone, dragging a trail of my innards in his wake.

Being with Raff made me feel like anything was possible. I mistakenly chopped that sensation up to being young. However, with age and distance, I know now it was him. He supported and encouraged me. It was fun to just be myself with him. To waste time experimenting and trying new things. It was vulnerability that I would never let myself experience with anyone again. He'd given me a taste of what I'd craved and then abruptly cut me off. Raff's full attention is my favorite meal.

I'm not the only one who feels this way. Nora looks at Raff with little hearts in her eyes. She fidgets nervously when he's at her station and typically finds any reason to seek out his approval. She's still quick to give her opinion before anyone has asked. However, her dough mishap did curb her pedant attitude.

Raff has also been focused on trying to teach and encourage her, rather than dominate, like he probably would have done in times gone by. So, I try not to get jealous when she gets too close to him or laughs shrilly at his jokes... Or I should say attempted jokes. I'm discovering that work Raff is corny as hell. But then again, Nora just might not have a sophisticated sense of humor. Either way, it's not her fault. I haven't really told anyone at work that we're a couple yet.

Laurel guessed, of course. Literally the day after the Jam, she was giving me the look that told me she just knew.

"What," I said, attempting to sound nonchalant.

She sucked her teeth and eyed me. "Nice hickey," she retorted before squirting Diet Coke into my cup.

My hand immediately shot up to the side of my neck. I did not, in fact, have a hickey, but the movement was its own admission of guilt.

"It's about fucking time," she'd mused.

I just shook my head. How do bartenders always have a sixth sense for this shit?

"Just give me a heads up if there's trouble in paradise. I want to win the betting pool. Raff usually goes scorched earth on his sous chefs around the five-week mark," she'd teased.

I laughed. I fucking had to laugh. What other choice did I have? One dish at a time. Though that didn't prevent the sinking pit in my stomach. I can't control Raff. He says he's into me and he wants to be with me. I just need to trust that. He's free to leave at any time. Do it scared and whatever. However, as another week winds down, I start to get anxious. The constant simmering anxiety that I feel has slowly increased to a rolling boil.

Maybe that's why I was so on edge tonight. My body is humming with some strange sense that something was about to happen. It was my third time working the large pizza oven in the front of house. Now that we all are working at the top of our game, Raff doesn't need to be precious about where he schedules us.

I saw them immediately. Tattoos, glasses, and, in Davey's case, a big bushy beard. This was the crew I'd worked with in San Francisco a few years ago after I got back from New York. The restaurant was called The Bamboo Clam and was a total vanity joint for some rich Marina family. I worked pastry until the place got shut down. The family was more concerned with keeping up appearances than actually paying their vendors. So, despite our killer menu, eight months in we folded. I loved working with Davey, Carlos, and Mariana.

Mariana waves in my direction. I return the gesture and stick out my tongue at them. She is robust and funny as hell. Her wild curly hair and huge personality make her always easy to spot in a crowd. Davey is her husband, tall and stoic. However, he'd roll up next to your station and hit you with a cripplingly funny snarky remark when you'd least expected it. Carlos and I had worked at a few places together, both before and after the Clam. He is a very sassy young man from Juarez. Often, the first person I texted when I came across a stockpile of clean kitchen towels squirreled away in a secret space by another chef.

"Hey, Chef," Mariana says, jumping up from their place at the long table in the center of the dining room.

"What are you guys doing here?" I ask, leaning around the edge of my station and giving her a very sweaty hug.

"We had to try this place. Everyone is talking about it." I smile at her reply, genuine pride oozing into my chest.

I glance up at Guy running between tables just past us. I call out to him, and when he turns, I point towards my friends. "Comp," I mouth, and he gives me a confirming nod before making his way back towards the bar.

"I got tickets, but can you guys hang out," I ask.

She nods vigorously. "Heard, baby. We're staying down the road, so we can chill all night."

I've cooked with this particular group of chefs for countless hours without ever batting an eye. However, standing in full view of them right now, I'm hyper-aware of their presence. I don't even wait for them to order. I start firing some of our most popular pizzas and send it out. Guy strikes up a conversation with them immediately. He's opening a bottle of wine and pouring glasses. They're laughing and joking like old friends when I glance up from time to time. Good. I'm glad we're making a positive impression.

"How's it going?" I hear a deep voice ask behind me as I slide a pie off my peel. I turn with a smirk.

"Better now," I say.

Raff gazes down at me, returning my expression. We're living in the precious moments before everyone at work knows that we're together. It's like an exquisite secret. Once we say anything, it is no longer just ours. This must be what expectant couples feel like in the first months of pregnancy.

The inches of distance between us feels painfully far right now. However, this isn't the time or place to come together.

"Hey, can I introduce you to my friends?" I ask shyly. His eyebrows raise in surprise.

"Hell yeah," he says.

Raff helps to get me ahead at my station before following me out to the table, where Mariana, Davey, and Carlos are working their way through a cacio e pepe style pizza that I may or may not have made extra swanier to impress them. When they all see us approaching, they throw their hands up and cheer.

I'm trying to sequester my nerves and perhaps sensing this Raff slips a steading arm low around my hips. So much for keeping our secret.

"Hey, uh, so this is Raff. He's the chef here and also my, um, boyfriend," I stammer out, suddenly feeling extremely self-conscious.

Raff chuckles as he shakes hands with Davey. "I'm surprised that she didn't add 'or whatever' after that sentence," Raff muses.

I can tell that Carlos is delighted. He bites his bottom lip as he gives Raff an appraising look. "Girl, I've known Miss Lala here for a long time, and I've never *ever* met anyone that she's introduced as her boyfriend before. So, you must be very special," Carlos says, extending a hand in a very Victorian manner to greet Raff.

My face is now molten lava. I would like to climb under the table and die. My corpse melting into the concrete slab to be inevitably reclaimed by nature. Even the tops of Raff's ears are red from secondhand embarrassment.

"She's also very special," Raff replies, which makes everyone preen and chatter obviously charmed.

This is not the Raff that I was reintroduced to when I returned to town. This Raff is the person I knew all those years ago. He's kind and welcoming. Sure, he can be a shithead, but only when the situation warrants it. This is the person I've been subconsciously searching for after he abruptly left.

I know that this should make me feel happy, but my anxiety is now at maximum temperature, with violent, large, and fast-moving bubbles that are erupting with acidic tension throughout my entire body. My face is set in an easy smile, but I'm not inside. I'm somewhere above everyone looking down, observing from a safe distance.

My friends are hanging on Raff's every word as they swap resumes and compare mutual former coworkers.

"Oh shit, you know Tara," Raff asks, and I can sense that there's some story there.

Carlos hums dramatically in the affirmative. "She actually warned us about you," he says teasingly.

I suck in air and gather the courage to glance at Raff. How will he respond? However, he just throws his head back and laughs.

"Probably rightly so. I'm an asshole, or at least a recovering one," he says.

I unconsciously release the breath that I'd been holding.

We're still really busy, but Raff promises after-work drinks to my friends as he excuses us from the table. The rest of the shift passes in what feels like both one minute and one hundred years. My friends eat and drink, standing to wander around the space several times. They basically endear themselves to everyone who's working tonight.

By the time last call is being given, they're helping to clear glasses and bus tables. I know I feel happy, but I don't think I'm experiencing it. Not fully. Right now, the world is in high-gloss, and I'm stuck in a muted matte finish.

Raff has Laurel pour everyone on shift a drink. We all hang out after closing. Then, when it's clear the party isn't going to stop, we all walk down the block to the nearest bar, Broken Promises. I should feel happy, but I can't relax. I get stuck sometimes. The acid fizzing, my brain gets caught in a loop of the worst-case scenario. He leaves. I was too much to handle.

On the walk, Raff slips his hand into mine. I'm so out of my body right now, I startle slightly at the gesture.

“Hey, you ok?” he asks gently as he guides us towards the bar.

“I’m fine,” I start, but he doesn’t let me finish.

“No, you’re not. What’s up?” he asks, halting us.

We’re at the back of the slow-moving throng of people. So no one notices that he’s pulled me into an alcove between buildings. “No bullshit, remember?”

I’m about to argue, but to my surprise, my voice cracks. “It’s nothing,” I say pathetically.

“Hey, it’s ok,” he says, bringing his arms around me.

My body is rigid.

“Did I do something wrong?” he asks.

I shake my head, stuffing back the overwhelming emotions. “No. I’m fine. I swear.”

I feel his hand brush my hair off of my cheek as he kisses the top of my head. “I hate when you use that word. Stop trying to keep it all bottled up. Seriously, I can handle whatever you’re feeling,” Raff says.

My head dips slightly in the motion of a nod, but I’m still stiff in my movements. I am somewhere between outer space and my body, but Raff is holding me tightly to the ground.

He's here. He's got me. I can touch him. I let myself lean into my most favorite parts of him. I touch the muscles of his forearms that are wrapped around me. I slide my hands up the broad expanse of his back. I feel the rise and fall of his chest pressed against my face. Then he exhales slowly, and without realizing it, I mimic him. Our breathing has synchronized, and I'm finally able to let him come into full focus.

"It's ok. You're just feeling shit." I shake my head slightly. I don't want to feel this shit. I want to just muscle through all of my anxieties. Except right now I can't.

"You're ok. I got you. Tell me what's going on," he says.

I keep breathing, matching him.

"You're being too nice. It's really freaking me out," I blurt. My sudden admission is so weird that I immediately flush red. Too much, girl. Embarrassed, I'm jerking back.

However, he holds on firmly to my upper arms, not letting me escape.

So, I just freeze and stare at him. Total deer in the headlines. He blinks for a moment. I blink back. Then we both start to laugh. I cover my face with my hands. "That's so dumb. I'm sorry. I'm just worried that you're going to figure out that I suck and then you'll leave like..." shit. I trail off, but the words last time hang in the air.

He leans down, evening our gaze. "Homie, I don't think that you suck. I know that you do," he says, cupping my chin in between his index finger and thumb.

"Rude, ass-hole," I shriek, slugging him in the shoulder.

"Ow," he laughs and rubs at his arm. "Just tell me that you're feeling insecure. It's not a big deal. So, you get freaked out sometimes? Me too. Let's just be freaked out together. I don't want to guess what you're feeling all the time. Otherwise, I'm gonna spin out and do some bad shit like fight Dre again."

I run my thumb over his healing black eye. Van has been giving Raff arnica balm, which has actually been helping. Only a light-yellow bruise remains.

"That was because of me," I ask.

He shakes his head and catches my hand in his. "Nah. It'd be a cop out to say the fight was because of you. It was because of me."

My eyebrows raise. "Shit. Did we just become smarter, Rat?"

He grins as he closes the distance between us. "You enlighten me," he says before pressing a hard kiss on my lips.

I love the way his stubble rubs my face. I melt into him slightly until Laurel pops her head into the alcove.

“Oh, shit. I totally called it. Jorge, you owe me twenty bucks,” she calls over her shoulder. “Are you guys coming or what?” she asks.

Raff nods. “Yeah. Just give us a sec.”

When Laurel disappears around the corner, I move to follow her, but Raff stops me, his eyebrow arched in a questioning look. “We’re good?”

I nod. “Yeah. Sorry, Rat. You’ve just broken me open, and I can’t keep all of this shit inside anymore,” I say sheepishly.

An easy smile spreads across his face.

I roll my eyes. “Don’t look so smug. It’s embarrassing. I don’t know how to handle it,” I snap.

He slides his arms around me again. “I get it. When things would get too heavy with my family, I’d feel like I was in some other place. But then I realized if I wasn’t experiencing it, I couldn’t help my mom and sister. So now when shit gets real, I just focus on things that are actually there.”

He looks around and then points to the wall behind me. “Like the bricks in that wall are chipped in a shape that looks like an old man laughing.” I turn my face to see the distinct outline of cracks and fragments in the facade.

“Or that if you listen really closely, you can hear the music from whoever is playing at The Belly Up tonight.” He raises a finger as if he’s willing all other noises around us to cease.

We both instinctively close our eyes and lean towards each other slightly until we can hear the faint metallic sound of a faraway speaker at the nearby music venue.

“Or, that you have a tiny mole on the inside of your lip. It’s faded a bit with time, but it’s still there.” He gently and painfully slowly drags his nose along the line of my mouth. I do my best not to melt into him but his strong arms hold me upright as my body relaxes.

“Thank you,” I say when our eyes meet.

“You got it, Miss Lala,” he says with a mischievous smile. “Now let’s go get drunk with your friends.”

Chapter 27

RAFF

Night stills the world around us as the merriment winds down. Her friends came back to Guy's for more drinks after Broken Promises closed up shop. I like Ash's friends. They've been regaling me with stories about Ash in her early twenties.

It's comforting to know that she had a whole universe outside of Santa Luna. That she wasn't just caught struggling in her family's orbit all this time. She built something for herself. I find myself stealing glances at her periodically as the night marches on. I don't dare insert myself into her conversations or plaster my body to her side. I let her linger in discussion and mingle with her friends.

Ash can be quite reserved. If you didn't know her, you would think that her superficial, stony exterior is the real Ash, but she has a depth of warmth and humor when she feels comfortable. Tonight, she's finally back into her full self. I don't want to diminish that by hovering too close. So, while we're at the bar I hang back and simply bask in her radiance.

Someone has either made or bought falafel. Either way, I find myself eating it by the tahini-dripping handful with my legs in the pool next to Ashley.

"So are you going to move back to SF to open that tapas bar with your friends?" I ask.

Her lips curve wryly as she uses her feline tongue to lick a long streak of sauce that races from her wrist towards her elbow.

"And miss out on all this," she says, gesturing towards the backyard full of dwindling intoxicated people. The movement, paired with the soggy peta, causes her to clumsily drop her half-eaten falafel gyro into the chlorinated water. A round of applause sounding from the few coherent enough to see the catastrophe unfold.

She makes a whimpering noise and juts out her bottom lip. "I've dropped my balls," she laments.

I cannot control my laughter as I take in her pathetic expression. "I bet Raff will lend you his," Laurel calls from somewhere just outside the halo of the patio lights.

"It's not funny," she says.

But I can't hide my amusement as I toss my own half-eaten gyro over my shoulder, its contents splatting on the concrete.

I wrap her up in my arms, dropping brutal kisses on her face and head. Someone wolf-whistles from some unknown space in our periphery. She's struggling and reaching towards the water for the remnants of her food that slowly bobs further away.

"Let it go. I'll make you a million falafel. As long as you stay with me," I say between kisses.

"So needy," she teases. That devilish grin is curling up her lips. However, she's not flighting me anymore.

I run my mustache along the tip of her nose. This causes her to squirm, but she still pecks small kisses along my jawline. Fuck. I really like this girl.

Though my question was innocent, the thought of her leaving me is still horrifying. I can't lose her again. Maybe I'm just stuck in limerence, but this girl makes me desperate for her.

"Nah. I can't get used to it. It's weird," she says when our embrace stills, eyes studying each other.

I'm acutely aware of the sound of the lapping water splashing against the nearby filter inlet. The slight waves of our movement drenching the rolled cuffs of our pants. "What," I ask.

"You're being too nice. It's still kinda freaky."

"Would you rather I be meaner?" I say. She immediately bites her bottom lip, dipping her chin in a slight nod.

"Don't tempt me with a good time, chef," she purrs.

From behind us, I hear the slider open. Minnie is immediately next to me, sniffing and gobbling down my discarded food. However, I don't break my gaze from Ash as action continues at the mouth of the door.

"Yo, we're taking off," Mariana calls out.

"Coming," Ash says; however, her eyes are still fixed on mine. Finally, our connection breaks as she moves to stand, but I hold her in place for a moment.

"Go in there and say goodbye to your friends. And then you're going to meet me in the bedroom like a good girl," I say in a low tone.

Ash's mouth opens in surprise. Then a hedonistic smile crosses her lips. "Yes, chef," she says before slowly getting to her feet and disappearing into the house.

Ten minutes later, I open the bedroom door to find Ashley in her underwear, seated on the edge of the bed. A sharp exhale escapes me as I take in the supple curve of her form, perfect in the dim light of the room. My eyes stop on her black bra and mismatched pink strawberry panties. Strawberries... a stark contrast to the all-black tattooed tough exterior that she usually presents.

I close the door behind me and slowly saunter over to her. No words are exchanged. We just watch each other with rapt anticipation. Then, when I'm right in front of her, I bring my hand up the back of her neck, dragging my fingertips up along the sensitive nape until I find the base of her long ponytail.

I take a handful, wrapping her hair around my fist. She lets out a gasp as I gently tug her back, head craning upwards. “Is that what you wanted?” I ask sternly.

Her breath is heavy as she pants out. “Yes.”

My lips twitch. I didn’t realize I’d like this so much. She seems to be beyond turned on as I can smell her arousal saturating the small bedroom.

“Yes, what?” I ask.

She shudders as she corrects, “Yes, Chef.”

I release her hair. “Good girl. Now you’re going to get on your knees in front of me.”

Her tongue pushes out from between her lips as she drags it across the pillowy surface. Without breaking eye contact, she lowers herself to her knees in front of me.

“So obedient. Now you’re going to take me in your mouth and suck me off,” I command.

I hold my breath momentarily as she hesitates. However much to my relief, she simply bites her bottom lip before reaching up to unfasten my dickies. I’ve been hard since she left me by the pool. So, when she unzips my pants, my straining dick immediately presses forward against the loose fabric of my Jockeys.

“So eager,” she teases, looking up at me with a coy smile.

"Hey, you little brat, I thought I was the mean one here," I reply.

She giggles to herself as she takes one nail and runs it down the length of my cock over my boxers. "Sorry, chef," she replies.

I suppress the full-body shudder that sizzles through me at the sensation. She's not gone down on me yet. Well, not since all those years ago. Our physical relationship back then was brief and, in retrospect, sophomoric compared with the deep feelings we share now.

We both were inexperienced by comparison. In the time that we've come back together, I love exploring her body. Feeling how familiar it is, but also the newness of its absence. Like meeting a long-lost friend, with both a lifetime and no time having passed simultaneously. I cannot get enough of her.

She tugs down my pants and boxers. A little clumsy in her movement as she's still drunk.

"You ok?" I murmur momentarily breaking character. "We don't have to do this if you're too fucked up."

She giggles again, biting her bottom lip and looking up at me. "You're doing it again," she warns.

Shit. When did I get so nice?

I know the answer. All those times before, I wasn't actually intentionally being an ass. I was just freaked. It's why I didn't show up on the day she needed me the most. Just simply disappeared. Couldn't handle anyone getting close. Close meant that people could hurt you. Or leave you. So, I was always the one to fuck it up first.

Quick to fight. Quick to turn off. Quick to leave. Get out before I found myself on the wrong end of the situation. But right now, Ashley is worth the hurt. I want to feel her. All of her. And if that means getting fucked up by her because I let myself love her, then I guess I'm about to get fucked. Hard.

"I'm sober enough to give you a blow job. Stop being so nice."

I scrub a hand down my face because fuck. I'm going to cum right now if she keeps teasing me like this. Then, still looking at me, she parts her lips, sticks out her eager tongue, and drags a slow-moving path from the base of my cock to the sensitive head.

"Fuck," I groan out. It's met with her giggling reply. "You like that," she asks.

"Yes," I say, feeling around the wall to steady myself.

Then she draws me into her mouth, gently dropping her head down to take my full length before pulling back slightly to create suction. The sensation is insane. I am going to cum fast if she keeps this up. She's cupping the base while moving me in and out of her mouth, pausing every now and then to do some sort of swallowing motion that has me seeing stars. God damn, how did she get so good at doing this?

She's an expert. I wasn't prepared for how well she'd take me.

"Easy, baby," I say, but the words are labored as I try to hold back my release.

"Yes, chef," she says, continuing to stroke me and tonguing the straining tip. She slides her free hand up, letting it trace my hip flexor.

I shudder out another breath as she continues to face fuck my cock. Pressure is building, and I can't contain myself. "Where do you want me to cum," I growl out.

She releases me with a pop, dragging her swollen lips around the head. She doesn't answer, just continues to move me ever so lazily around her mouth and face, softly tracing her skin against me.

"Quit teasing me, brat," I scold.

"Sorry, chef," she replies with her devilish smirk.

"You want to taste me," I ask, getting desperate as my release builds.

"Yes, chef," she replies.

I take her ponytail in my grip and tilt her back to maintain eye contact. "Good. Then keep those eyes on me as you swallow." I can feel the shiver of desire that travels down her. She opens her mouth, and I slide inside.

With our gaze locked and her hair twisted in my hand, it only takes a few pumps before I feel myself explode inside her mouth. Just like when she was eating my pasta, she moans and swallows in a deviously sensual way that has me clenching my eyes shut and bracing myself on the nearby wall. Then, as if I wasn't already a goner for this girl, she has the audacity to rock back on her heels, bring her thumb up to the corner of her mouth, and slowly drag its tip across her bottom lip.

"Delicious," she says with a satisfied grin.

In one swift movement, I hoist her up and onto the bed. She squeals as she bounces on the mattress. "You're mine, brat," I growl as I climb on top of her.

She's thrilled at my sudden dominance. "Yes, chef," she smiles into me as I cover her mouth in a rough kiss.

I'm unclasping her bra, pushing it down until I have access to her soft breasts. I'm hungry to taste her supple flesh. I give her shoulder a bite as I work my way to her chest. She gasps at the sensation. Her pelvis rolling underneath me. I can feel her little strawberry panties dampening.

Her nipples are hard as I let my tongue swirl circles around one. I massage the other with my thumb.

"Raff," she exhales, encouraging me to continue.

I roll the stiff peak between my teeth, gently tugging, and she jolts with a gasp. "Too hard," I ask.

She shakes her head. "Sensitive."

I do it again, and she shudders.

"Hey," she chides.

"Sorry, I thought you wanted me to be mean." She brings her mouth up and returns the gesture. Biting me hard on the nipple. I gasp and jerk back.

"Tit for tat," she says with a wicked grin.

I shake my head. "That's it. You're in for it now, brat."

I shift and flip her over onto her stomach. I'm still over her, tilting back and straddling her thighs. My hand slides down and rests on her adorable pink-and-white panties. Then slap! I bring my hand down to make contact with her ass. A sudden, surprised noise follows the loud smack. "Do you like that, brat?"

"Yes, chef," she whimpers.

The rolling of her hips underneath me is confirmation that she's turned on. She's seeking friction. "Do you deserve another?" I growl.

Her breath is getting heavy as her arousal deepens. "Oh, God," she pants.

I rub my hand over the fullest part of her perfect butt. Giving her a taste of her own medicine. She's squirming, attempting to find some relief for her excitement.

"Please," she begs as I let my hand tease across her backside again without the reward of pain. "I want you," she starts, but I surprise her with another slap.

God, she's amazing. Despite having just cum, I'm aching for her. My stomach tightens with anticipation. I need to fill her. I drag those damn strawberries down, exposing the now reddening bare flesh below. I love seeing how wet she is for me. She's quivering from the suspense of my cock. Just as ready for me as I am for her.

"Raff," she urges as I bring her underwear up to my nose and take a long inhale. Musky and sweet, just like Madagascar vanilla.

I slide back, lining myself up with her. However, I don't enter her immediately. It's more fun to tease her a bit. She cranes around to see what I'm doing, but then is surprised when I bring my dick down to give her a few swift taps. The small smacks of my straining erection on her waiting pussy have her moaning again. Her arms stretched out toward the top of the bed, fisting the sheets as her desperation reaches a fever pitch.

"Stop teasing me, Rat," she says through labored breath.

I chuckle as I lean over towards the bedside table to retrieve a condom. "Cross your ankles," I order as I sheath myself.

"What," she's starting to say, but I'm too impatient. I lean back and adjust her legs.

"Good girl," I say as I position myself on top of her.

I slide in between her legs, and we both groan at the tightness. With her ankles crossed it's a snug fit as I push deeper. Her grip on the sheets strains as I enter her to the hilt. "You good," I whisper, my mouth brushing against her ear. All she can do in reply is whimper and nod. The sensation is overwhelming.

"Fuck me," she begs.

So, I do. Deep long thrusts that have both of us making guttural noises. I use one arm to brace myself over her. While I slip my other hand under her pelvis, pushing her back to meet each downward press. The pressure is intense. I know that I must be kissing her G-spot with my tip by the way she's sucking in sharp inhales with each move of my hips.

Her breath is quickening as my tempo increases. She's getting close as she starts to mutter my name under panting exhales. Then, when I know she's on the edge of release, I duck my head low and whisper in her ear. "Scream my name when you cum on my cock." I feel her clench around me as she climaxes.

"Raff," she calls out. The sound of my name on her lips as she comes undone has me following suit.

We collapse to the mattress, panting. Then I suddenly realize I'm probably crushing her into the bed. "Shit," I say, rolling off of her. "I didn't mean to squish you."

She smiles at me, cheeks flushed and makeup smudged. "I like having you on top of me. It just reminds me that you're there."

Chapter 28

ASH

The wedding is two days away. Raff and Guy have let us turn the Princess kitchen into a make-shift flower shop. Van and Mac rolled in with ten large plastic buckets, filled to the brim with the numerous blooms Van had grown in the yard of the blue house. It's incredible to see the fruit of her hard work. Literally, she handed me a few loose figs she'd harvested when they cut the flowers this morning.

So, while Raff, Guy, Van, and Mac break down stems and foliage, I'm making a stack of crepes with caramelized figs and mascarpone cheese. I'm just setting out the large serving platter when Raff wanders up towards the prep station closest to me. He has a humongous, fluffy purple dahlia tucked between the band of his backward hat and his ear.

"Aren't you pretty," I say as he leans towards me, fluttering his lashes.

"Not as pretty as you," he says, extending a spiky light pink Aster towards me.

He flourishes the flower, presenting it as though he's in a silent melodrama. I fain a swoon, clutching my heart before accepting his gift. It's moments like this that I relish in the silliness of this brutish man, the delightful juxtaposition.

He comes around the metal prep counter that separates us, tucking the flower behind my ear. Then, as my cheeks burn with embarrassment, he drops down to brush a soft kiss on my lips. "Can I take you on a date?" he asks.

An involuntary scoff escapes me.

"I want to take you out. Let me romance you. I don't want you to think that I'm just keeping you in the kitchen or my bedroom," he says.

Again I laugh.

"But those are my two favorite places," I retort matter of factly.

He brushes a wayward lock of hair off of my cheek before bringing his hands to cup either side of my face.

"I'm serious," he says. "Let me outdo any other date you've been on."

This guy. I ignore the weak sensation behind my kneecaps. "Well, that should be easy," I laugh. "I've never been on a date before."

His mouth parts, and he stares at me in utter disbelief.

"Cursed, remember," I say pointing an index finger at myself and grimacing. He blinks.

"Seriously? Not even some awkward middle school dance or, like, a group hang at bowling or mini golf?" I shake my head, eyebrows raising.

"Nope. Can't say that I have."

His hands drop to my shoulders, and he proceeds to shake me in an overt manner. "You're telling me you never held any tween's sweaty palm while you wandered up and down the boardwalk?"

I'm leaning into the shake, placating his exaggeration of the movement.

"I need to change that immediately," he says with mock urgency.

"I don't want to hold some kid's hot hand," I say wriggling free when the shaking subsides.

"Ashley, let me show you what you're missing. I'm going to take you on so many dates, your head will spin," he says.

The heat of his gaze settling on me causes my blood to pool and pulse in my core, mainly because I'm still getting used to having all of his attention.

I pluck a quartered fig off the nearby plate and bring it to my mouth. Not because I'm hungry, but rather to have something to focus on.

"Fine," I say flatly. "After the wedding. You can traipse me around town. Or whatever it is that you want to do."

With a smug grin, Raff settles in next to me. "Great. Be sure to wear your traipsing shoes."

Leaning against the prep station, he also picks a fig from the platter. While maintaining eye contact and that stupid smile tipping the edges of his mustache upwards, he brings a halved fig to his mouth and runs his tongue along the inner syconium of the fruit. He lets out a little moan for good measure.

"You're so gross," I tease.

His expression turns devious. "What do you mean? I just like eating your fruit," he says with faux innocence. I'm about to give his shoulder a shove when the Feist song playing on the speakers is interrupted by my ringtone.

Van and Mac immediately turn their heads, all too familiar with this specific alert. They stop what they're doing and walk towards me. I stare down at the phone cradled in my hand, unsure of what to do.

"It's Cita," I say as Raff peers over my shoulder.

"You gonna get it," he asks unplugging the dock cable.

I glance up at Mac, who gives me a slight nod. "Up to you," she says gently. With a shaky hand, I hastily tap the screen and bring the phone to my ear. "Hello," I start but Cita is already breathless and annoyed.

"Where are you?" she asks.

I look at Van and Mac, lifting my shoulders and shaking my head in confusion. "I'm," I try again, but she butts in. "You're late. I'm not making this cake on my own, you know," she snaps. Then she abruptly hangs up.

When I first came back to Santa Luna, part of my contribution to Van's wedding was to help Cita bake the desserts for the big day. After the blow-up, I'd assumed Cita would prefer that I didn't assist her. Apparently, I was wrong. "I guess, I'm going to Mother Wolf?" It comes across more as a wooden question than a statement.

Van and Mac exchange a glance. "You don't have to go," Raff says but I shake my head.

"Nah. I can't avoid her forever. Plus, I'm going to see them at the wedding. It's better that Cita has whatever reaction she's going to have in private, rather than hijacking Van's day," I shrug.

Wordlessly, Van comes around the counter and folds me into her arms. "Thank you," she whispers, holding me close to her breast. My heart sinks. As much as I've loved having my family around me, I know that I contribute to their stress by being here. I'm the source of conflict and anxiety. This was exactly why I'd begged Mac not to go through with her plan. I'm the stone causing a riffle in the stream of their lives. Despite Van's reassurance, I hate myself in this moment.

Raff tucks me under his arm and escorts me out the back rolling door towards our cars. However, as we pass Mac, she catches me by the wrist.

"Don't hold back," she urges, eyebrows furrowed.

I nod. Then she releases me.

Raff gives me a little squeeze as we continue outside. "Do you want me to drive you?" he asks. I shake my head.

"I'm fine." I'm unbreakable. Or at least I used to be. Now it seems that the cracks are more evident than ever, and I can't contain myself.

"I should take my own car in case I need a quick getaway," I say, attempting my most reassuring smile. Not that Belinda is either fast or reliable by any means. She's barely hanging on after Guy got her restarted. However, just knowing that I can escape is a comfort.

"I'm sorry I won't be able to help with shift prep today," I say when we get to my car.

He shakes his head before planting a long, firm kiss on my lips. "Don't worry about it. Everything's covered. I'll see you tomorrow morning after the bachelorette," he says.

Suddenly remembering I pull the Astor out of my hair and hand it to him. He takes it reluctantly, giving its withering stem a twirl. The heavy head of the bloom slumps to one side as a discarded strand of my dark hair tangles around its neck. We stare at each other for a brief moment. Neither of us is saying what we want to. I squint up at him in the late August sun. A scrub-jay screeches nearby, breaking the long pause. "I'm fine," I say. Then I climb into my car and make the five-minute drive to Mother Wolf.

Cita's bandana is tied tightly over her wiry hair as she measures dry ingredients into mixing bowls on a scale. As I study the paisley swoops on the worn-out cloth, I contemplate how long she's been covering herself with that thing. Cita never changes, I think, as she grumbles about punctuality. Always correcting some minor mistake I didn't even realize I'd made. Retying my flimsy apron for what feels like the fourteenth time, I glance around the bakery.

Mother Wolf also never changes, I think, until my eyes land on a speed rack tucked off to the side. I know better than to ask Cita outright, but the items on the rack appear to be day-old. This is strange. Mother Wolf rarely has leftovers at the end of a shift. We typically have a consistent number of turn each day. You could practically set your watch to it. Have they been struggling in our absence? I don't flatter myself with the thought.

A sore spot between Cita and I has always been what to do with unsold pastries. I'd suggested ways that we could repurpose them into new menu items: bread pudding, croutons, and croquettes monsieur. However, Cita insisted that we never change her menu.

Instead, Lulu would drop off any leftovers at a food pantry or, later on, at a youth yoga camp that Van ran in the summer. A good cause, but I couldn't help feeling like she was doing it to punish me. "Don't be so selfish, Ashley," Cita had scolded when I'd asked if I could set something aside. And now here the speed rack sat on full display. Mocking me. My pulse quickened.

"You don't look as tired," Cita says, handing me the scale. This is what it's like to work with my mother. You're one part scrub nurse, expected to know exactly what she needs when she needs it without any instructions, and one part mind reader. By saying I don't look tired, she's implying that I was looking haggard before. Sort of a back-handed compliment.

"You know me. Love to sleep," I say flatly. That isn't true. I'm notoriously a horrible sleeper. However, one time Cita walked into the living room when I'd dozed off after an all-night study session in high school. She'd since assigned me the characteristic of being lazy.

Cita grunts out a laugh as if to heartily agree with my statement. We continue to work in silence. The air is getting thick with the unresolved tension. I'm dying to talk about it. The roiling and bubbling in my stomach is almost unbearable. However, she has home-court advantage. We're firmly playing by her rules here. Make no mistake Cita is always in charge.

Then, when I think I'm about to burst, she sighs. "So I hear that you're sleeping with that man," she says.

I stifle a laugh because the sincerity in her disdain for Raff is so overt that she sounds like she's on a telenovela. Plus, when she makes this dramatic declaration she can't bring herself to look at me. Just sort of spits it out towards the wall in front of her. As if to say that my working at Princess Pizzarina is the biggest betrayal of her lifetime.

Cita's not a man-hater by any means. She has male friendships. She worships Uncle Ray, the Vietnam Vet with one arm who does maintenance at the bakery. She can't stop gushing about Cary and how proud she is of Van. Hell, though she never talks about him, I like to imagine that she even loved my father.

I remember sneaking into her closet to look at photos of them. Smiling faces, easy postures, so blissfully unaware of how it all would end. I almost didn't recognize my mother the first time I'd seen these images. That wasn't the Cita I knew. She scowled and always kept her arms braced for the next disaster. I guess, you'd have to love someone profoundly to have been changed so deeply after losing them. Had I changed in the years post Raff?

Cita hates Raff and, by proxy, Guy. I think that this is because she's jealous. In her mind, we took Raff in, and then he stole all of her secrets. This is a very silly idea because half of the time, while working in the bakery, Raff would get me to make the recipes for him. The other half of the time, he'd be screwing around and flirting. She just doesn't like that he didn't give a shit. Didn't get down on his knees and kiss her ring.

I don't dare roll my eyes, regardless of how dramatic she's being. All Mexican mothers possess an eerie sixth sense. Despite not looking directly at you they'll always know when you roll your eyes in their general direction. "He's my boyfriend," I say calmly. Good. Keep it together. You're unbreakable.

She sucks her teeth, bobbing her head in a deep nod. "For now," she says simply.

Ok. Ouch. However, I know that Cita isn't done yet. Which is why I really can't help myself. Fuck it. Mac is right. We need to just have it out finally. "Sure," I say in my best neutral tone. "Then one day he might be my husband."

I don't want to get married. I doubt Cita knows this, though. Why would she? She's never once taken an interest in me.

She immediately whirls around, eyes wild, mouth agape as she glares up at me through her smudged glasses. "Ashley, you cannot be serious."

I cross my arms and stare at her. In her mind, only Van is capable of a happy ending. She's always been the one the twins deemed worthy. "Cita. This is my life. I don't see how being with Raff affects you."

She's huffing now. Rage simmers inside of her as our close proximity has unintentionally cornered her in the back of the kitchen. "He will leave you. They always do. Just like last time, he's going to get what he wants and make a fool of you."

I throw my hands up in response. I don't usually react when pushed into these sorts of fights with her. She's just as surprised as I am and takes an involuntary step away from my uncharacteristically emotional display. "I am the one who wanted to do the bakery pop-up. Surprise! I'm the one who wanted to prove to you that I could run a bakery and that my ideas were viable. Not him. I wanted to prove to you that people would like *my* food," I say.

If she's shocked, she doesn't show it. She just squares up to me, crossing her arms, her thin lips pressing into a hard line.

"Raff didn't steal your secrets and then try to destroy Mother Wolf. I did. I'm the one who put my own spin on your menu. I'm the one who went behind your back. And guess what, you were fucking right. It failed spectacularly."

Cita scoffs but I keep going.

"You were right, Cita. Is that what you've been dying to hear this whole time? There! I'm sorry. Can you please, please stop punishing me for it now?" I beg. My face is hot. I am positive that it's flushed crimson, but I don't dare take my eyes off of Cita.

Her expression is still stony, unmoved by my words. I gulp down a few breaths, letting the register of my voice descend the octave it was pitched up.

"All I ever wanted was your approval. And all I ever got was your disdain," I say, attempting to sound composed.

The acid is back. Those last few words choke in my throat. I swallow down the vomit that is threatening to follow my admission. However, Cita's lack of reaction is making my breathing shallow. I can't get enough air in the milliseconds of silence, and I can feel my head starting to spin. Then, when I think I'm about to split open, she exhales.

"You must think I'm the worst mother in the world," she wails. This is a classic Cita move. However, it's more potent when Lulu is here to really sell the emotion.

I don't relent. Sensing that she won't get any pity from me, she immediately begins her lecture, all sentiment replaced with contempt.

"I don't disdain you. I just want better for you. I've been trying to raise a wolf. You should be a savage, strong, and independent. Instead, you're following some man around like a puppy. Men will betray you, Ashley. They'll leave you. I'm just trying to save you from some stupid mistake."

"But it's my mistake to make," I shout back. Ok. I have to work on my volume control. I'm still getting the hang of this whole expressing myself thing.

"You know what your problem is, Ashley? That you even wanted my approval to begin with," she says.

"You're my mother. Of course, I do. I have only ever wanted to be good enough for you."

She scoffs again as if it was the most ludicrous thing for a child to want from their parent.

"What do I have to do to be worthy of your love?"

She turns back towards her batter. Apparently deciding that my question is unimportant of her time. “You’re so dramatic. Not everything is about you, Ashley. There are more important things right now,” she says, turning one of the bowls out into the stand mixer before clicking it on.

“You’re right, Cita,” I say, straining to be heard as the padel whirls to life. “I don’t need your approval. I love Raff.” I stutter at my own admission. Fuck. My stomach sinks. That’s definitely something that I should be telling Raff and not Cita. However, I keep going as the power returns to my voice. “He loves me. And not because I did something that he deemed worthy. Just me.”

Cita shrugs. “Oh yeah. We’ll see,” she says. “You said it yourself. I’m always right.” I stare at the back of her head. The stupid swoops of paisley covering her coarse hair. She doesn’t look up from her work. Just gently pushes up her glasses that teeter on the tip of her nose and keeps mixing.

The whooshing of blood in my ears is overwhelming. I can feel my consciousness leaving my body. It’s somewhere above us, staring down at the all too familiar kitchen. The kitchen that I wanted so desperately to run one day. I see myself standing behind the woman that I wanted to become.

Let it be known that somewhere high above what will soon become a horrible memory, I somehow find some fucking perspective. “You’re never going to change,” I say. However, I think it comes out as more of a whisper. Volume control.

"Huh," Cita grunts but I don't hear her. I'm already watching myself walk out the back door of Mother Wolf. This, I know, will be the last time that I am in that kitchen with her. I no longer desire to prove to my mother that I am worthy.

When the fresh ocean air hits my face, I take a gasping breath as though I've suddenly surfaced from a deep-sea dive. My lungs burn, and I have to fold over to brace my hands on my knees. I stagger the few steps to the car and, with trembling hands, get the door unlocked. Then, without thinking, I drive.

Chapter 29

RAFF

I try to put Ashley out of my mind as I do the prep for the evening shift. Mac and Van also do their best to pretend that they aren't hyper-focused on her absence right now. Fuck she's brave. I like to think that literally nothing scares me, except maybe Ash's mother. She's ferocious, untamed, and liable to bite. I wouldn't want to face her alone. Yet Ash simply put on her armor and walked into battle.

The girls get a cryptic message from Lex about forty-five minutes after Ashley has gone. She's also been summoned to Mother Wolf. My stomach dips when they read this text and no word from or about Ashley follows. Once they've finished prepping their florals for tomorrow's arrangements, they safely tuck everything into the walk-in and head back to the house. I look at my phone. Still no word. I know I should feel good, but I can't ignore this new gnawing deep in my guts.

When prep is done, Guy and I are discussing ducking into Roberto's for a burrito before the team starts arriving when he gets a text message. She's at the house, it reads. I'm immediately out the door and booking it to the car.

"Dude, we have less than thirty," Guy yells.

However, he's on his feet too, following me out the back. Much to my annoyance, it takes Guy what feels like a fucking eternity to lock up. Though in reality, it's probably only a few minutes. I consider leaving him, but I think he's just as invested as I am. How did we end up adopting this group of loud-mouthed girls? I shake my head. They're part of the crew now. We're back at the house in no time. My car sliding to a stop as I pull the break and jump out.

Ash is sitting in the backyard. Legs dipped in the pool, despite her pants not being rolled high enough to avoid the surface of the water. Minnie's upper body is draped over her lap. Ashley, who isn't really a dog-person, has her arms wrapped around Minnie's neck and face buried in her white fur.

When I approach, Mac and Van give her some space, allowing me to slide down next to her. "Hi," I say with a cautious murmur.

She peeks up at me through her lashes. A soft smile spreads across her face, which immediately quells the gnawing that I've felt over the past few hours. "Hi," she says back.

"Are you ok?" I ask.

She nods. I run a hand up her arm, attempting to hold her. However, she still cradles the dog. So we sit in an awkward embrace. Whatever. As long as I can feel her pressed into me. Know that I can support her.

"How was it?" I say, deciding to jump right in.

“Horrible,” she replies with a slight chuckle.

In the glow of the late-afternoon sun, Ashley’s tan skin and light dusting of freckles are on full display. I can see the golden flecks in her dark eyes. A serene expression still fixed on her face. She’s beautiful. She looks at me for a long time, like she’s about to admit something. However, she must think better of it and bites her bottom lip instead.

God. This woman. I use my long index finger to brush that determined strand of wayward hair off of her cheek.

“You didn’t have to come to see me. I’m totally fine,” she says with a slight shake of her head. She doesn’t need to pretend to be ok. Who fucking cares?

“Can it. I’m here because I needed to be. So, you can save the ‘fine’ crap for someone else,” I say. Her laugh hits me square in the chest. Good. I turn her towards me, nudging Minnie out of the way. I need her. I have to be as close as possible to her. I desire her.

“I got you,” I say low in Ashley’s ear. “What did I tell you? Give me that messy shit. I love it. I’ll handle it, ok?” I have to pull her back to earth.

I hear a whoosh of air leave her lungs as I crush her tiny body against mine. There’s something that she isn’t telling me. I can feel it in my bones and it’s raising my hackles. I need her to know that I’m here. That I’m not going anywhere this time.

"You don't have to say that," she says but I don't let her finish.

I'm pulling her back and kissing her. Long and hard and as deep as I can, while Mac, Van, and Guy awkwardly disappear inside the house. The sound of Minnie's collar jangling as Guy tugs her with them.

"I don't want to scare you," she says when I finally release her.

I shake my head. "The only thing that scares me is losing you."

Her smile widens. "Fuck you," she says with lazy amusement. "Why do you have to be such an ass and say things like that, Rat?"

"You better get ready. I'm going to say so many nice things to you because I—," I stop myself. Fuck was I about to say something without thinking? My chest tightens. Because I love you... I guess I've known for a long time.

I was about to say it so casually. It would have flowed like water off of my tongue and she would have bolted. Skittered away into outer space. She crinkles her face at me. "Because you're worth it," I amend, pulling her close and peppering her head and face with kisses.

"That's too much," she protests.

"Then would you rather I show you?" I ask, an eyebrow raised.

She rolls her eyes and looks away, attempting to conceal the expression of embarrassed delight on her face. "Always."

There's the sound of a throat clearing behind us. We turn to see Guy looming in the doorway.

"Sorry to interrupt," he says. "We have to head back."

I wrap my arms around her tightly, ghosting my lips over her mouth. Guy awkwardly looks away.

Mac is in the door now. She's waving what appears to be a large blue phallic object.

"Oh, Ashley. Quit being gross. We have a bachelorette to celebrate," Mac scolds. She waves what I now can see is, in fact, a vibrator, complete with a big pink bow wrapped around the base.

Guy does a double-take at the silicone dick Mac is holding, and he steps away, shaking his head. "Not going to ask," he mutters.

I give Ash a look. "Daddy is very invested in making sure Mama gets off," she says.

"Of course she is," I say, and I can't help but kiss her again. God damn, she's cute. I don't even care how weird it all is. "Have fun tonight," I whisper, attempting to kiss her just one more time. She pushes me off.

"You're ridiculous." I'm in love, I think with a stupid smile.

"Alright. Come on, lover-boy," Guy says, heading towards the side gate. "Ash, tell him to behave. You're the only one he listens to now. You've tamed the Rat King," Guy adds over his shoulder.

She takes one long look at me, shaking her head. "Nah. He's the one who broke me," she replies.

"Mackenzie, be careful where you point that thing," he says to Mac before slipping through the gate and pulling it shut behind him.

I stand tugging Ashley up, our hands locked. "You'll call me if you need help," she asks, eyebrows lifting hopefully.

"Nope. Unfortunately, you're going to have to do whatever bizarre activities Mac has planned."

We glance over as Mac is twisting the device on. Its tip spins and vibrates as internal beads tumble around.

"Save yourself," she says nervously. I plant a kiss on her lips before jogging to catch up with Guy.

I turn back to look at Ash before sliding through the gate. She gives me a guarded smile. I feel better having seen her, but there's still the slightest niggle in my gut. What isn't she telling me?

Chapter 30

ASH

"Bacchanal! Bacchanal! Bacchanal!" The chant rings in my ears as a middle-aged surfer with a pronounced sunglasses tan dip his head backward on the bar top, and Lex pours the boozy honey lemonade out of her growler into his open mouth. All night, her poorly constructed toga has been slipping down her shoulders. Mac yanking it up before her boobs tumble out.

"The Grecians didn't have bras," she'd declared as we all were getting ready for dinner.

Laurel's friend Sammy, who sometimes worked in the wardrobe department for the Santa Luna Shakespeare festival, had lent us some incredible Greek gowns from last year's production of Troilus and Cressida. Lex decided to modify the neckline of her toga, or whatever they're called, and was now dealing with a potential spillage issue. Either way we were all decked out in flowing gauzy dresses and custom floral head wreaths to celebrate Vanessa's bachelorette bacchanal ball... or bash. Honestly, I'm like a hundred shots in at this point, so call it whatever you want.

Sure, the night had started innocently enough, a fancy dinner at Nick's Taverna, a Mediterranean spot on the water. Raff knew the owner and hooked us up with the coveted reso. Of course he did. He's just so... so looking like

Greek goddesses, we took over the patio. Incredible vegetarian dishes came out in waves: zucchini cakes, moussaka, dolmas, and spanakopita. Plus, alcohol. Lots and lots of it.

We ate, laughed, and watched the sunset over the receding tide, the perfect meal to celebrate Van. We later found out that Guy and Raff had picked up the tab too. Something that made Mac feverishly text them an annoyed "thank you, assholes." While Van sang them some random song she'd made up over voice memo to declare her gratitude. And I just...

The five of us, plus Van's two soon-to-be sisters-in-law, feasted to our hearts' content while we all told stories about how much we loved Vanessa. Serena and Blair... or whatever their names are... didn't stay long. They also chose not to wear a toga. Instead, dressing in pastel ruffly maxi dresses that reminded me of Easter. We were informed that these dresses were *Lily Pulitzer*. This must have meant something important because they both nodded eagerly after they'd said the designer's name.

When they quickly realized that there were only so many photos of a potato-shaped toddler that we could stomach. Or that none of us had engagement rings to compare with them, they stopped trying to contribute to the evening. Despite knowing Van for however many years she'd been with Cary, neither of them had a single story to share about her.

One tried. She mentioned that Van had been horrible at skiing when the family went to Aspen a few years back.

That was it. Van had fallen while getting onto the chair lift and then again when getting off. We all nodded thoughtfully at her story, while she and the other one chortled. Then we moved on, Nat telling us all a story about a German woman who'd stalked her for two weeks post tongue fucking after a 2019 Ani DiFranco concert she'd attended in Santa Barbara.

Our wild antics seemed to only make their well-mannered sneers pucker. When dinner concluded they politely excused themselves, claiming they wanted to rest up for the weekend ahead. "Gotta get back to the baby," Serena or Blair had said.

To which Van clutched both hands over her chest and said, "Oh! Of course. Give Dabney a kiss for me. I'm going to officially be her aunt soon!" Both women had exchanged a sideways glance before reassuring Van that they would. Liars.

A sense of relief washed over all of us once they had left. For whatever reason, I'd felt uneasy when they were with us. Like everything we were doing and saying was being reported back to Cary or his mother. But then again maybe my unease was coming from my inability to act.

Why didn't I tell him? When he came to the house, I wanted to blurt out "I love you." Scream and cry and hold him the way that he was holding on to me. Wrap my arms around him and whisper his name a thousand times until I had no voice left. However, that's not what happened. I just sort of froze.

I take a long pull from my growler. "Hey, those are for our unsuspecting victims," Nat scolds.

I roll my eyes at her, dragging the back of my hand across my mouth. Mac and I had made a shit ton of Vodka lemonade infused with a rosemary-and-honey simple syrup. Kinda Greek-inspired, I guess, but then again, I doubt they'd had vodka.

We'd filled up a few glass jugs Silverstein lent us, and post-dinner we took to the street. We follow our queen Van from bar to bar, pouring libations for anyone who falls to their knees in front of her to pay tribute to her beauty and virtue. Basically, when drunks bow down before her or buy her a shot, we dump alcohol into their open mouths. It's kinda sloppy and grotesque and totally fun.

Between Laurel, Mac, and myself we know all of the bartenders and owners on Jupiter. We've worked out a deal so they turn a blind eye while we serve their customers homemade moonshine from our unmarked bottles in exchange for free pizza. Again, thank you, Raff and Guy. My chest squeezes thinking about him. I need to tell him. I *will* tell him... just when the time is right. When I'm not going to scare him off. I'll tell him on our date. Yeah. Good idea. Perfect.

"I want a drink from that one," a thick frat boy with a crew cut says, thumbing a finger at me.

I snap back into reality and give him a nod.

"Come on over, Cleopatra," he hollers, lowering down into more of a crouch than a kneel. He gives Van an inebriated cascade of his upper body before cracking his mouth open wide. I hesitate for a moment, staring at his fillings.

"You heard the man," Nat says, giving my hip a bump with her ass. Admittedly, I'm drunk at this point. So, my gentle pour comes out as more of a clumsy slosh, sticky golden liquid splashing down his chin and chest.

As I right my bottle, he surges to his feet, scooping me up in a wet hug. The entire bar cheers. "Careful, she's taken," Lex warns over the din.

He places my stiff carcass back down, turning to Van and pulling her up into some sort of two step. She throws her head back, laughing, as he turns her about the room. She's incredible. Tall and willowy, she has an ethereal quality that is only complemented by her Greek outfit and flowing brown hair.

I understand why Cary would want to marry her despite their drastically different backgrounds. There's an intangible essence about Van that you immediately want to possess. I imagine it's the same feeling you'd have if a hummingbird were to land on your shoulder. Something wild and delicate is choosing to trust you.

When we make our way to the next bar, Laurel and a few other friends of Van meet us. "How was it?" I slur out over the noise.

"Nora made a weird rice-a-roni thing for family meal," she replies, mouth practically pressed into my ear.

I know exactly the expression on her face. I've seen it a million times after Nora has done something both pretentiously and poorly. I close my eyes and hum before slightly bumping my head into her. I love the Princess crew. This is exactly what I'd hoped to build when I came back. The kind of place my family and I created without even trying. That has always been my legacy at every restaurant I've found myself in.

I'm suddenly hit with a wave of anticipation. I love Raff. I want to see him. Tell him so badly it's making my chest ache. Noticing the strangled look on my face, Laurel reels back.

"You're not going to puke, right?"

I shake my head. A smile crosses my lips, and I remember that night at the beginning of summer when Raff held my hair. Despite my inability to accept it, Raff treated me with reverence. Fuck. I am such a goner for him.

I secretly hope that he'd stop by, however I know better. Mac would probably kick their asses if Raff or Guy came to the bars. Since we'd all be gone, they'd talked about having friends over after closing. My mind wanders to him... what he's doing now. Maybe he's sitting on the roof, smoking a joint, and thinking about me too... God. When did I get so sentimental and lame?

We continue our bar crawl, party expanding as we pick up more women, until we end the night at The Tide Water. Much to my surprise, Mac talked Raj into letting us in. He has a strict no-bachelorette policy. However, I think we're the only women in all of Santa Luna that would ever host a bachelorette party in this dive. Our levels of drunkenness are reaching a fever pitch.

We're hanging all over each other, swaying and stumbling. Everyone is singing to music that isn't what's playing on the jukebox. Laughing at nothing and everything we encounter. I produce a fistful of Sharpies so we can all draw on the bathroom walls. When we emerge from the world's grossest restroom, it is clear that the bubble is about to burst. Lex, whose toga is now basically around her waist, is dancing topless to Closer by Nine Inch Nails. The usual crowd of salty regulars hoot and holler, Nat pouring shots into their gummy maws.

Mac, who'd usually be stopping them, is distracted by Van, who is threatening to join in. She's attempting to peel down the top of her dress, but Mac holds the collar firmly. She shoots me a withering look. I bring my fingers to my lips and unleash a loud chiflido. The high-pitched whistle brings everyone to a halt.

"Órale," Mac commands, tossing a handful of bills onto the bar and ushering us all outside.

I freeze when I step out and spot the Dodge Ram Van parked in front of The Tide Water. I hesitate in the doorway as the back doors swing wide and intoxicated women climb inside.

"Relax," Mac says, giving my shoulder a nudge.

Imani, Van's college friend from Santa Clara University, is five months pregnant and volunteered to be the designated driver. She and her husband got into town this evening. Imani picked up the van from the blue house before meeting us four bars ago. God, what a trooper to have endured this sober. But that's the thing about Vanessa, she brings good people together. Somehow, tonight has us acting like old friends, despite most of us never having met before. Sisterhood.

Mac sits up front, helping Imani navigate the winding road. After a few nail-bitingly tight turns, we make it to the clearing up the mountain. The yurt is illuminated with solar string lights and a few of these cool LED pathway lanterns that look like glowing rocks. Apparently, Imani's husband runs a company in Oregon that makes them. Lex and Nat, with a little help from Lex's art school friends, transformed the Moon Collective Yoga space into Van's bachelorette bacchanal bonfire.

The interior of the yurt is covered in plush lambskin, Mexican Thunderbird blankets, and bolsters. Perfect for all of us to crash at the end of the night. They've stocked a cooler with jugs of Lulu's famous sun tea and water, both coconut and still. Additionally, I immediately notice a basket overflowing with every gas station snack imaginable. Hell yeah.

I snatch a bag of nacho cheese Doritos and walk out the back to where Imani is helping Laurel light the bonfire starter that Guy prepared yesterday. He'd done it more out of self-preservation.

"Please don't burn the mountain down," Guy had warned. Lex and Nat had just saluted him.

Lex adding, "Only you can prevent forest fires, Step-Daddy." So now, with a whoosh, the pyre they'd constructed inside the rock-lined pit is engulfed in flames.

I take a deep breath of the cool mountain air, noticing notes of fragrant herbs like dried rosemary, sage, lavender, and mint. I turn to Van, who stands beside me, inhaling deeply.

"It's a natural mosquito repellent," she says.

I nod at her. "Smart," I reply. I'd hate for her to walk down the aisle on Saturday covered in bites. Then it hits me.

"What?" she asks, sensing my eyes on her.

"Mama, you're getting married," I say, disbelief in my tone.

She scrunches her face to suppress an adorably giddy grin. "Crazy, right?" she says, slipping her arms around me in a sort of side hug.

"Are you scared?" I ask.

I feel her shake her head against mine.

"I'm finally getting what I want. I feel like my life is going to start," she coos softly.

I bring my hand up to rest on her cheek. "Can I tell you a secret?" I say absently.

"Yes, please," she replies.

I blow out a breath. The tension in my chest easing slightly at the prospect of finally admitting my revelation to someone. "I'm in love with Raff," I say quickly as if the words are made of steam that will burn my mouth on the way out of my body.

Van's eyes go wide, and she shrieks.

I shush her, looking around to make sure we're not drawing attention. However, she's jostling me into a tight hug.

"Oh, Ash! I'm so happy for you guys. What did he say when you told him?"

I grimace and her eyebrows flatten.

"You haven't told him," she says, disappointment dripping in her tone.

I shrug. "There hasn't been a good time," I say.

She looks at me with a knowing smile. "There's always a good time to say I love you: big moments and little. You have to say it as often as possible," she says. Fuck this radiantly beautiful woman.

"Ok, so when?" I ask.

She shrugs. "Now?"

Drunk people should not encourage other drunk people to declare their love. I'm highly susceptible to doing it. Especially now that this magical fire and a million drinks are thawing my frozen exterior. I am about to make a huge mistake, but I'm dumb and emboldened by too many alcoholic beverages and Venus herself reassuring me. A decision only made worse when Laurel uncorks a bottle of 2023 Domaine du Pelican Arbois and begins to pour slugs of impressive red wine into reusable enamel camping cups.

Thus, orange Dorito dust on my fingers, I dial Raff, bringing my phone up to my red wine-stained mouth. There's a static crinkle as the line rings. My heart is racing, but I've already done it. No turning back. "I love you, Rat," I yell into the receiver as soon as I hear the phone connect.

"Who is this?" a female voice gasps with excitement, and I panic.

I immediately hang up and take the few stomping steps backward through the native ferns at the perimeter of the clearing. Acid tickles the back of my nose, and before I can stop myself, I'm twisting around and vomiting into the nearby tree line.

When my stomach clears, I feel a vibration in my hand. Shit. I look down to see that Raff is calling me back. I sink into a wide squat, the stretchy nylon of the toga easily spreading with my position. I'm so fucking dumb. Without fully processing, I answer the call.

"Who was that?" I blurt stupidly.

"Just some girl," Raff says. My head is spinning. I feel hot tears prick my eyes. "Marco brought her over. I'm in our room now," he says. *Our room*... an unfamiliar feeling of jealousy surges through me. I can hear through the crackling, poor connection that the background noise has lessened on his end.

"Are you ok?" he asks, alarm in his low tone.

I nod, which is dumb because he can't see me.

"Ash," he says, and maybe something else, but it's cutting in and out.

"Fine," I grunt back.

"There's the fucking word again. What's going on? Do you need me to come get you?" he says.

I, like the intoxicated mess that I am, shake my head. He can't see you, you drunk bitch. When I don't give him a verbal response, he snaps again.

"Ash, I'm getting an Uber."

I stop him, the line crackling with my next admission. "I need to tell you something but I'm worried it's going to make you disappear," I whimper.

There's a brief pause. Then I hear him exhale. "What is it?" he asks softly.

I can hear the concern in his voice. It's now or never girl. I take a deep breath and go for it.

Chapter 31

RAFF

I can barely hear Ashley. Service up the mountain is spotty. Not to mention the sound of Shania Twain and debauchery in the background. My heart is racing. Did she do something? Something that we won't be able to withstand... or maybe it's worse? She's changed her mind. Found out that I like her too much. That *I'm* too much. She's leaving. I steady myself as I wait for her tinny reply.

A reply that doesn't come. "What was that?" I say, panicked. I'm moving around the room, tripping over our discarded laundry, holding the phone in different directions, attempting to improve the quality on her end.

She says something that comes out strangled this time, but still inaudible.

"Fuck," I say quickly.

Now it's her turn to be panicked. "Really," she asks.

"Really, what? You're not making any sense," I repeat into the crackling connection.

There's a long pregnant pause. "Did I lose you?" I ask.

More static silence.

“I shouldn’t have told you,” she says, her reply choppy and partially audible.

My pulse is racing. What is going on? “Ok, fuck it. I’m gonna get that Uber,” I say, looking for my jacket.

“No,” she replies sharply. “Sorry. I just, um, you need to be careful. It’s really late.”

I glance at my watch, nearly three in the morning.

“Please don’t risk driving up here right now,” she says softly.

Then I think about her dad. Guy had filled me in after I’d told him how weird she was at the idea of driving tired. “I won’t,” I promise her. “But we’re going to talk when I get you back in the morning,” I say. I can’t hear her reply. So, like an idiot, I repeat it.

“Sure, Rat.” That’s the last thing I hear before those three beeps signaling that the line has gone dead.

Sleep does not come easily. This is the first time I haven’t had her in my bed in weeks. Her absence is immense. What if the last time that I held her was the last time? I want to feel her tiny body pressed into mine. Tangle myself around her and know that she is here, safe on the ground with me. I’m impatient to see her again.

When the time seems reasonable, I jump out of bed. Then I quickly realize that I’d be a total creep if I just rolled up on their slumber party at this hour. That would only push her away. Anxiety is fraying my nerves, so I go for a run. The blue haze of morning makes the familiar neighborhood look frozen in time. Same as it ever was. I get back and shower, but the hour is still ungodly early. I have to settle this gnawing. Stop the emotional free fall I'm in. So, I do the only thing I know that I can control.

Guy stumbles into the kitchen about twenty minutes before the girls are due back. "Need help," he asks, hair a wild mess and sniffing awake. Minnie's nails ticking against the tile floor behind him before flopping down in her bed. I put Guy to work using Louise's vintage espresso machine. Mac had pulled it out of storage in the garage. Between the two of us, Guy seems to be the only one who knows how to use it. As a kid, Louise had him make her cappuccino when she needed to sober up.

"I think I fucked up," I sigh over the rumble of the machine.

Guy grunts as he immediately stops the appliance. "What'd you do?" he asks, turning towards me wearily.

I know he's anticipating the worst from me. Calculating in his head how he'll correct my mistake this time. I always mess shit up. Guy always has to clean up the mess.

"Not on purpose," I snap.

"So, what's the problem, man? Everything seemed fine." Fine. There's that fucking word. I shake my head as it all tumbles out of me in an anxious deluge.

"Fuck, dude. I don't know. Everything was good until yesterday. But now I can feel Ash slipping through my fingers. I'm not trying to fuck up. I just am."

He narrows his eyes at me, then bursts into laughter. "Holy shit, Raff. You're scared. I've never seen you get worked up about anything. It's been one day, and honestly, nothing catastrophic has happened," Guy says.

Rage simmers. "Hell yeah, I'm scared. I'm in fucking love with her," I shoot back.

Guy blinks at me in surprise then, with a wide grin, he thumps his big fist against my chest. "Then if she tries to slip away, or whatever, don't let her." He turns back to the espresso shot he's just pulled. He sips it with a slight hum. "Damn. Never thought I'd see the day. Glad you finally pulled your head out of your ass and stopped sabotaging yourself. You've come a long way," he says, tipping his cup towards me.

I furrow my brows. I don't fucking sabotage myself. Right?

"C'est parti," he says after the last swallow of espresso.

I shake my head. Whatever.

"You got this," he nods.

Anticipating major hangovers, I've instructed Guy on how to make something called a Fridge Cigarette. It's basically a double shot of espresso poured over a Diet Coke and some caramelized cara cara syrup I made, courtesy of citrus grown by the bride, plus sugar and cardamom. Fucking delicious. Exactly what I'd want to knock back if I was fighting for my life after an epic night of drinking.

When they arrive, I'm putting the finishing touches on thick-cut toast topped with zesty lemon Greek yogurt, shredded sautéed kale, poached eggs, and a homemade chili crisp with fried shallots. I complete each plate with a crispy squash hash brown and a side of toasted sesame mayo. It's earthy and greasy. Precisely what will absorb all the alcohol. My hands are shaking as I set out the plates. I can't help it. My stomach is practically in my throat as anticipation courses through me.

"Hi," I hear from behind me.

My breathing stops. I turn to see a very disheveled Ashley standing in the doorway. Hair pulled back, she's wearing a black tank top and leggings. She tentatively stares at me through oversized sunglasses, her armor.

I close the distance between us, wrapping her up in my arms and kissing her. She lets me, but despite our close proximity, I can feel the vast distance between us. Don't let her, I think pulling her nearer.

"Ew. Please don't make me barf again," Mac says pushing her way into the kitchen. Minnie is up on her feet to greet everyone.

Lex is taking a long sip of the coffee concoction. "Shit, that's delicious," she says.

"I would fuck this drink," Nat agrees with her.

As if nothing has occurred out of the ordinary, they all slip into an easy cadence. Mac running through the day's schedule, Van gushing over the dish I made, and Lex and Nat laughing about something that isn't even remotely understandable. Guy is inspecting the mountain of vibrators Vanessa received as gifts from last night.

"Why'd you give her so many? She can't use them all at once," he ponders out loud.

Mac pats him on the forearm with a pitying look. "A girl likes to have options," she says.

Everyone is laughing except Ash and me.

I stare at her. She avoids eye contact with me. Keeping her head down as she takes small bites of eggs, chewing and swallowing quietly. I watch her eat, but not savor the meal like she typically would. Ashley may be an expert at hiding her emotions, but there's one place where she can't conceal her true feelings: when she's eating. She's unable to lie about how a dish moves her. Right now, she's in pain. Something is preventing her from putting herself into the experience.

"Come here," I say low in her ear.

She glances at me, fear sizzling across her face. A guilty child being summoned to the principal's office. She gets to her feet and follows me down the hall. When the door closes, she can't even bring herself to look at me.

“What happened,” I ask.

Worst-case scenarios running through my brain.

“What do you mean?” she says, but the pretense is written all over her face.

“That call,” I say, my tone getting more urgent. I’m not trying to push but fuck it. I can’t let her slip away.

She hesitates for a second. “What are you talking about,” she asks. “I don’t remember calling you.”

I study her face. “Well, you did,” I say.

She doesn’t reply. Just stares at me. “Oh, sorry,” she says coolly.

I scoff. Ok. That’s how she’s going to play it. “Yeah. Me too,” I say ruefully. I’m about to just ask her, beg her to tell me what she said but there’s a sharp knock at the door.

“Yo,” Mac’s voice booms. “We need to head out.”

Ashley nods at her sister and turns back to me. “Was that it?” she asks, still avoiding eye contact.

What the fuck is happening? “Sure,” I say, watching her leave.

As the door closes behind her, electric waves of panic wash over me. They start at the top of my scalp and run down my entire body, grounding out through my feet into the shag carpet. She's slipping. I need to get a fucking grip.

Chapter 32

ASH

I am such a fucking idiot. The rejection still looms over me. It's a heavy hand wrapped tightly around my throat. I should not have called Raff. I had no business laying myself bare to him. "I love you," I'd practically screamed into the phone.

I presented my sensitive mushy underbelly, and for what? Sure, the connection was bad, but when you tell someone that you love them, the typical response is anything other than "fuck." But that's how he fucking answered. He's probably thinking of spectacular ways to end this relationship right now. I am just happy that I was able to avoid him breaking up with me this morning. I could see it in his eyes when he took me into the bedroom. "Gecko," was written all over his lips.

Luckily, Mac had a laundry list of tasks we needed to get through before the rehearsal dinner. I just have to steer clear of him. He can't dump me if I'm not there. Maybe it would be better if he just disappeared again? I could pretend that we were still together. Save myself from the inevitable grief of losing him.

We were at Princess while Raff was at the house, and then vice versa when we needed to get ready to leave.

"Why are you so fucking jumpy?" Mac had asked, eyeing me suspiciously as we sliced veg for tomorrow's post-ceremony crudités. I open my mouth and then close it. Mac doesn't need this on her plate right now.

"Is it Cita?" she asks, a familiar crease setting between her eyebrows.

I grimace. Ah, yes, our mother. I'd forgotten that for the next forty-eight hours she'd be unavoidable. I shake my head. I know that I should be worried about her causing a scene, but Raff weighs heavily on my mind at the moment. He's all-consuming. The pain and embarrassment that I feel are overwhelming, passing over my entire being in constant waves that remind me of my stupid actions. I can't shake the radiating hurt that I am about to lose him because I was too much. I couldn't just keep my mouth shut.

"Listen, if it comes down to it, I'll kick her out," Mac says.

I snap back into reality, and a sudden surprised chuckle escapes me. Mac is always taking care of us.

"Thank you, Daddy," I reply, leaning my head into Mac's shoulder.

She jerks away. "Stop. You're freaking me out," she replies, focusing on halving the purple carrot in front of her.

The rest of the day passes in a blur. I'm pretty numb to most of it. Just turning that one word over and over in my mind. Fuck. Fuck. Fuck... I'm so out of sorts, I can't even disassociate. Just stuck somewhere deep in the pit of my stomach, unable to ascend above it all. Something that would've been very helpful when I came face-to-face with my mother later that evening.

Cita is wearing a red dress, a knit shawl, and a deep scowl when she sees me arrive at Sarafina, the fancy French restaurant where Cary's parents have elected to host the rehearsal dinner.

"I hope you apologized to your sister for that little stunt you pulled," Cita whispers when I pass her. She's alluding to the fact that Lex had to help her with the desserts rather than myself. I don't reply. She wants a fight that I don't have in me anymore. I give her a nod and continue into the party.

Cary looks uncomfortable. Rigid and sweaty. I'm assuming this is because of the golf trip his brothers took him on the day prior. Van coos and fawns over him while he struggles to stay upright. The back of his neck is an angry red. Beads of perspiration gather on his upper lip.

Lulu suggests a remedy that borders on witchcraft. She's up, asking for a dishtowel and a clear glass of water before anyone can stop her. Moments later inverting the glass and folded towel on top of Cary's head. Trickles of liquid streaming down the sides of his face and soaking his Oxford. "The bubbles rising to the surface mean it's working," she'd exclaimed, mistaking Meredith Phillips's expression of horror for curiosity. Fuck. Fuck. Fuck...

A key characteristic of the Phillips family is a stern yet bewildered expression. A perpetual incredulous gaze as if one of the servants has just informed them that there is no more caviar to serve at the luncheon. No one embodies this stare more fully than Cary's father, Charles Sterling Phillips III, followed closely by Cary's oldest brother, Charles Sterling Phillips IV, aka Court.

Cary's father and two older brothers are a sort of Darwinian evolution into what Cary can anticipate in the years to come. His tall, muscular frame softening and hunching as he pursues a life of white-collar upward mobility. Get a job, take a wife, have 2.5 children, hoard wealth, die with the knowledge that you were richer therefore better than everyone else. Apparently, this is the type of stability Van craves. The type of life Cita and Lulu have deemed prestigious and worthy of her.

As I listen to Charles address the crowd, touting the virtues of his son, directed mainly at Cary's groomsmen and their wives, I'm struck by a thought... this is safety. Despite their differences, Van trusts that Cary will never leave her. There is no risk. Unlike Van's father, Cary isn't going to simply go AWOL. Cary is going to give her the family and security she so desperately craves. Regardless of how wildly mismatched they are or how much Meredith Phillips probably wishes that Van were someone else, Van will never have to struggle like the rest of us again.

I look at her from across the room. Wearing a tailored vintage jumpsuit, she's nestled into the crook of Cary's arm, easily reclining into him. She's absolutely stunning and effortlessly chic. She'd often get called 'Jane Birkin with a tan' by Cita and Lulu. They were so struck by her beauty. Even now, I watch them beaming. Van is perfect. She will be the one to do everything that Cita and Lulu could not. Van has been chosen. Van will be the one to break the curse. Not me. She will never be too much. Cary will never disappear. Fuck.

My time with Raff was brief, a few months of bliss. I'm grateful for the time I spent relaxing into the comfort of finally being wanted. I guess I'm also happy that I never let myself fully accept it either. It will be easier to let him go when he inevitably leaves. This is how it always goes. When I lower my guard, I'm immediately reminded that I do not belong. I'm too much to be able to exist. Not at Mother Wolf. Not at Princess Pizzarina. Not in Santa Luna. Fuck. Fuck. Fuck...

I catch Cita's eye. Elbows firmly planted on the table, she slathers a dinner roll in butter. When she's sure that no one is watching, she brings it to her mouth, biting off a hunk with her exposed teeth, and then she points the tip of her knife at me.

"I'm always right, just you wait," the gesture seems to say. She's so dramatic it's honestly funny at this point. I gaze down at the napkin in my lap and swallow down a smile. Fuck. Fuck. Fuck it.

When Raff and I break up, I won't be able to stay at Guy's anymore. I certainly can't go back to the blue house. Maybe I should go back to San Francisco. Find a sublet and get a job with the old crew at that tapas place. There's a sudden tightening in my chest. I don't want to leave. I know it deep in the depths of my core. I want Princess. Fuck. I want my family. Fuck. I want Santa Luna. Fuck... I want Raff.

Something is opening deep inside of me. It's that Raff-shaped hole. The quick onset of that familiar, terrible wound. Grief. I recognize it immediately. The sudden hardening that I saw in my mother. The agony of losing the best feeling in an instant. The curse. Why did I think I could outrun it?

I'm up on my feet. The chair scraping as I push away from the table mid-speech. Mac looks at me with alarm. Nat attempts to grab my wrist, but I brush past. I'm outside into the cool August air. Sarafina is only a few blocks away from Mars. The Friday night crowd is bringing the street to life. Everyone is desperate to soak up those precious few days of summer. The electricity of change is humming.

I'll cut up Fifteenth and be at Guy's house in a few minutes. Throw all my stuff in the trunk. I'll get a hotel tonight and leave after the reception tomorrow. They'll understand. Van will be married, and everyone will be moving on.

It's that strange time of year when the sun is about to go down, but the moon is in full view. A new reality is about to dawn. Van had planned this wedding around something called a Cazimi.

"Big beautiful changes are coming," she'd explained excitedly. "A rebirth."

The sun sets while I'm walking. By the time I get to the front door, early evening shadows have stretched to engulf most of the walkway. The automatic lights have yet to kick on, so I'm stumbling up the pavers in my chunky heels. Just as I reach the threshold, something out of the corner of my eye moves, and I stagger back with a gasping yelp.

"Sorry," a tentative voice says over Minnie's muffled barking from within the house.

Back pressed to the exterior entry window, I squint until my eyes adjust to the low light. A woman in her early twenties is at the door. She tucks a lock of blonde hair behind her ear, and I notice that she's wearing too much foundation. When the porch light clicks on above us seconds later, I realize that the cakey makeup is covering the bumpy skin of youth. Shit. This woman is practically a teenager. Then my heart sinks when I look down, noticing her most defining feature: her pronounced, protruding pregnant belly. Fuck.

Chapter 33

RAFF

My jaw has been tight all day. I can feel the pressure radiating in my teeth from root to crown. Focus on what you can control. We're at max capacity tonight. So, I've been hustling. I had Nora out front because I just want to put my head down and fucking cook. I'm on the line with Chuy and Miguel. I'm hyper-focused. Tickets come in. Food goes out. Simple. I can't let myself think because if I do, I'll think about her. Complicated.

Ashley is all-consuming. She is just out of reach, but I feel like the more I try to grab hold the further she slips. Guy doesn't seem worried. Fuck Guy. He's never worried. Or at least he never shows it. Well, Guy's not the one who is about to lose her again. He is right about one thing, though. I'm not going to give up without a fight. She's been avoiding me all day. So, I know whatever she's about to tell me is bad. Fuck it. I've been dealing with bad shit my entire life. I'll deal with whatever she's about to send my way.

The kitchen vibrates with activity around me. I keep my head down. Ground myself into what's here in the moment. Miguel is expediting, calling out tickets in bursts of Spanglish. Waiters run in and out, yelling at one another. The dishwasher's pre-rinse sprayer drums on the metal basin of the sink. It's all just noise. That's why I don't hear my name being called over the cacophony of sounds.

When I look up, I see Guy. For the first time in years, there's an expression of concern on his face. My stomach drops. I don't think, just start moving towards the back door where he's standing. I rush outside and immediately see her. Her face is twisted in anguish. That doesn't stop me. I'm holding her, wrapping my arms around her.

"What's wrong?" I ask, urgency oozing. She shouldn't be here.

She's crying now. My guts clench as I continue to hold her. Guy has closed the door behind us.

"Baby, what's wrong?" I say again, bringing my hand to cradle the back of her head. She feels tinier than usual. God, what was she trying to tell me last night?

"I'm about to ruin everything," she whimpers. The vice currently twisted around my insides tightens.

"It's ok. Just tell me," I say, trying desperately not to beg.

It takes her a minute to calm down. Then, fighting another wave of tears, she motions to someone standing just off to the side of Guy. "That's Madison," she mumbles.

I have to do a double-take. Ash gestures to a young girl awkwardly resting her hands on her distended stomach. I'm at a loss for words. Ash is too overwhelmed to explain, and I am stunned with confusion. Thank God for Guy.

"Are you hungry?" he asks her with a warm smile.

Five minutes later, Madison is eating a margarita pizza on the loading dock while Guy, Ash, and I are huddled in the office with the door closed.

“We have to tell them,” Guy says somberly.

A shuddering whimper rips through Ash. I squeeze her hand.

“They were so happy. It’s going to destroy her. And I’m the one who’s doing this to them. I always ruin everything,” she says.

“Fuck that. You didn’t do shit,” I snap.

Guy shoots me a warning look. “Ashley, you didn’t fuck the intern at your tech start-up,” he amends my statement. Ashley could never ruin anything. However, with her admission, I realize that we are the same. Always carrying around the burden of our trauma. Feeling right in the moment and then wrong in the long run because we did what we had to do in a world that wasn’t set up for us.

“This isn’t on you. You didn’t ruin everything. You’d want to know if it was you, right?” I say.

She studies me, perhaps debating in her mind if I was capable of a betrayal this horrible. I squeeze her hand again hoping to pull her back down. She nods thoughtfully.

“Ok,” Guy says. “I’ll drive.”

She starts to protest but Guy just puts his hand up. "You're not doing this alone."

I interlock her fingers in mine and echo Guy. "We're a crew. We got your back."

She stares at us, a hard set to her gaze. I know she's fighting back overwhelming fear. "Ok," she concedes.

Chapter 34

ASH

Time moves at a strange pace, both too fast and not at all. The drive to Sarafina feels like both an eternity and twelve minutes. Raff is next to me every step of the way. He sits in the back of the truck, long slender fingers linked with mine. When I needed him, he came, no questions asked. Hell, he even still had a kitchen towel tucked into his apron, which he didn't take off until we were nearly halfway there.

Guy opens the door of the restaurant, the rehearsal dinner should be just wrapping up. My stomach dips as I suddenly realize that we might have missed them. However, even worse, there they stand at the center of it all. Surrounded by close family and friends with their cameras raised. Van's long arms draped around Cary's thick neck as they sway to a cover of All Of Me that one of Cary's frat brothers is plucking out on an acoustic guitar.

Everything is in slow motion. I see Mac notice us first. She turns, brows furrowing in a question as she realizes that I'm with Raff and Guy. Then she cuts a glance back to Cary. Despite his raging sunburn, all of the color has drained from his face when he sees Madison. Like the coward that he is, so concerned with appearances, he continues to dance as the final notes of the song twang out. In those precious few seconds, I'm contemplating what to do next, but the decision is quickly made for me.

Madison, who had been timid up until now, suddenly pushes past us. In a few swift stomps, she's in Cary's face. "You said you'd called the wedding off," she shrieks. From the moment her tiny fist makes contact with Cary's fat red head, utter pandemonium ensues.

Cary attempts to block her blows while screaming at Guy. The groomsmen activate and come running to Cary's defense in a clumsy clump of polo shirts and button-ups. Court and Carson grab Guy by the shoulders. Raff jumps over a table to come to his aid. The imitation Ed Sheeran swings his guitar wildly. A storm cloud of bodies, yelling and punching. It is like watching a cartoon fight.

Not to be outdone, Cita and Lulu insert themselves into the fray. Squawking and demanding answers from Meredith Phillips. Who decidedly looked unsurprised by Madison's presence. Charles Sterling Phillips has tolerated enough of the Lobo twins and quickly ushers his wife towards the exit with Cita and Lulu hot on their heels. The potato-shaped toddler, Dabney, wails despite the shushing of Serena or Blair, while the other wives film the ongoing brawl.

And then there is Van. Even now, somewhere in the future, when I close my eyes, I will never forget the look of heartbreak on her face. She stands in the middle of it all and watches the life she'd been promised burn to the ground. Mac rushes to her side and, with a few gentle urges, tugs her from the wreckage of her dream. Instinctively, I follow them towards the door. Though I don't look behind, I know that Lex and Nat are with us too. In that moment, we are a pack.

She doesn't make a sound the entire ride. Barely even breathing. Just sits looking straight forward until Mac's Volvo station wagon comes to a stop. In the dim internal overhead lights of the car, we stare at her blank expression. A familiar fixed gaze that I recognized as someone trying to come to terms with everything breaking them apart. Just as Mac is about to say something, Van whispers softly. "Cazimi." Then the cascade of tears begins to fall.

The familiar Victorian looks like a vintage dollhouse left out in the garden, slowly being reclaimed by nature. Overgrown bougainvillea explodes around the blue exterior. The vining plants nearly cover the entire outside of the house. On the veranda, homemade wind chimes clatter above handcrafted terra cotta pots filled with flora in various stages of life between thriving and death. Hand-painted rocks and found sea glass line our way towards the heavy yellow door.

I don't think. Just help Mac and Nat get Van out of the car. We guide her up the creaky porch steps and into the house. Lex is grabbing our bags as she closes doors behind us. There's no way we can get her up the stairs to her bedroom on the second floor. So, we steer her into Abuelita's room, a converted sunroom off the dining room. She always liked to be the closest to the kitchen.

She's been dead for over twenty years, but her room remains an untouched, stale reminder of the matriarch who inhabited it. Van immediately sinks onto the full bed with the carved wooden headboard, which wobbles and jerks violently against the wall. Listening to her muffled sobs, I'm reminded of my childhood. Those nights after the accident. When we all sought refuge from our reality in the safe confines of Abuelita's tissue paper soft embrace. Suzy, the papillon, curling up by our heads as we snuggled into Adela Lobo's too crowded bed.

When Lex clicks on the bedside lamp, I'm suddenly overcome. The shadows are exactly the same as they were those nights long ago. The darkness never changes. My eyes follow the curve of light up the ceiling and across the room, landing on the familiar stone carved sculpture. Two striped primitive dogs dance on their hind legs. Teeth bared in a brutal smile as they waltz to unheard music. I always thought that the Colima dancing dogs were not lovers but rather twins. Two halves of the same whole, who never needed anyone else.

I make for the door, but Van quickly bolts upright.

"Where are you going?" she asks, a little panicked.

Away, I think. They don't want me here. I've already ruined things. However, I'm surprised by what she says next.

"I need you," she murmurs pathetically.

My breath catches. I've been so concerned with being wanted. I've forgotten that I'm also needed. I can't just run away this time. So, I climb back into the dam of bodies encasing the flood of Vanessa's dissolving emotions. I support her despite my own insecurities.

Mac doesn't let us dwell for too long. She leaves Lex to lie with Van, ensuring she takes sips of water as the three of us get to work. Mac pulls up the guest list on her phone and immediately begins the arduous task of dialing. Nat, Mac, and I lean against the kitchen island, phones in hand, as we all inform the invited that there will be no wedding tomorrow. We could sit at the long dining table, but none of us has the patience. Instead, electing to slant or pace as uncomfortable feelings bubble up and burst inside.

Lulu and Cita come home less than twenty minutes later. So consumed with concern, they kick Lex out and replace her as Van's bedside nurse. It's in moments of great distress that I'm reminded there's often very little that one can actually do. Mac continues to call and cancel the well-laid plans for tomorrow. Lex and Nat ferry supplies into the bedroom at Cita's direction. I go into the kitchen and set to work in the only way that I know how.

Besides the stacks of containers holding components of dishes that will go unserved at tomorrow's reception, there's not much besides condiments. In the crisper, I find a few wilting items that should do the trick. In the pantry, I spot the can of cannellini beans, and on the counter, the half loaf of country bread that will complete my dish.

Cita wanders into the kitchen, following the deep smell of roasted garlic and sautéed cauliflower, potato, and spinach. I've just dropped the hand immersion blender into the sink, and I clutch a healthy pinch of salt hovering above the roiling soup below. Without permission, she takes a spoon from the nearby drawer and dips it into my pot. Bringing the utensil to her lips, she blows and slurps the contents. I ignore her intrusion, instead raising the lemon in my hand.

"Needs acid," she's saying before she realizes that I'm already squeezing.

"Yes, chef," I say with a placid nod.

She huffs before giving the nearby pan a toss, flipping my crisping florets and potato skins in the hot oil.

"Go ahead and say it," she says after another rapid push and pull of the skillet.

My brows furrow in confusion. "Say what?" I ask, not lifting my eyes from the pot.

Her face crumples into an agonized expression before she says, "I was right."

In that moment, I feel Cita's genuine pain for the first time. I drop the handle of the long wooden spoon I'm using to stir and turn to embrace my mother.

As I hold her, I realize that I've never actually seen Cita cry before. Not really. I've heard the real sobs throughout the blue house. I've perceived her crocodile tears shed when she's pushed into a corner. But now, for the first time as they soak into my shoulder, I feel the tangible proof of her humanity, the unbearable weight of her grief. "We're cursed," she mutters.

I bring my hand up to caress her wiry hair, uncovered for the first time in a long time. I think about Raff. How I told him I loved him. Strangely, I don't feel the acid. I think about how the anxiety of being loved was outweighing the joy of getting to love. Even if he cannot return my feelings, I don't regret how I feel about him. I'm experiencing something profound that I never would have pursued if I truly believed deep down that I couldn't be loved by him. That it would have been a waste.

"No," I say, quickly turning off the burner under the skillet.

Cita sniffs, watching me as I carefully remove the potato skins and florets from the pan and place them onto a waiting rack.

"We're not cursed. You're not always right either. We can love and be loved." I take another pinch of salt from the nearby ceramic dish, lifting my hand high, letting it rain down onto the crackling vegetables below.

"Then why does this always happen to us?" she asks.

I shrug as I pull down bowls from the open shelf.

"Life is unpredictable. You can't control it. But you got to experience love, Cita. Or at least I hope you did. Even if you lost it, it was yours and no curse can take that away from you."

I ladle the soup over a few washed cannellini beans, then top it with a crescent moon of crispy florets and potato skins.

"Love and curses are what you make them," I say. Then I turn the grinder of the pepper mill.

Cita sputters, her bristles raising slightly.

I know that's not what she wants to hear. She wants to believe that she's always the victim of fate's cruel hand.

"You sound just like Erik," she says with a roll of her eyes.

I smile. I suddenly realize that in all of these years since losing him, this is the first time I've heard her say his name.

"Good," I say as I slide a piece of toasted bread onto my bowl and move towards the bedroom.

Even the thickest ice can melt. Healing is possible. I have hope. Now I serve the soup that may go untasted, but it's my turn to take care. To show the love that I was so desperate to receive. The pain of losing it is merely proof of how much it meant.

Chapter 35

RAFF

When we get back, the house is dark. After we escaped the mayhem, Guy pointed out that despite everything, we still needed to return to close up the restaurant. So that's what we fucking did. We know that the crew had our backs while we were gone, which is why, ripped shirts and bruised bodies, we walked back into Princess and finished out the final few hours of the shift.

When I took my spot on the line, Chuy just shook his head, letting out a low whistle. "You should see the other guys," I said, cracking a sly smile. This got them all laughing. Good. They were definitely in the weeds but still in high spirits.

I was able to catch them up from the nearly two hours that we'd missed. Then Guy stopped service exactly at midnight.

"Let's pack it up," he'd hollered.

I could tell he was anxious to check in with Mac. Her phone had been busy all night. His only clue was a single text that read: Handling shit at blue house.

My stomach sank. Was Ash ok? If I found out that her mom had somehow spun this shit back onto her, I'd kill the old bitch. "Should I go get her?" I asked Guy as he locked up.

“They don’t need us there,” he replied simply.

So we just went home. The house felt empty without any of those loud-mouthed girls. There was a vacant feeling despite the garage and living room still filled to bursting with all the crap we’d constructed for a wedding that was no longer happening.

Minnie didn’t immediately greet us when we walked through the door. Something that had Guy on edge, clicking his tongue and searching.

“She’s here,” a voice said from down the dark hallway.

My feet were moving. I had to get to her.

“Ash,” I said, pushing the door open.

She stood abruptly from the bed, still wearing the black dress and heels from earlier. Minnie stayed to jump and bark twice before trudging out of the room to find Guy.

“Hi,” she said as I pulled her into my arms.

In our haste to hold one another, forgotten were the tentative, awkward feelings of the day prior. I ran my fingers through her long, messy hair, bringing her face towards mine and kissing her. She was matching me, drinking in my desire. Her lips pressed hard, her mouth parting as I coaxed her open with my tongue. Then, as if remembering something, she suddenly stopped, pulling back.

"Listen, I know you don't feel the same way, but I have to just say it. And I'm going to keep saying it until maybe one day you can return my feelings." I'm trying to make sense of what she's talking about when she exhales the next words like a prayer.

"I love you, Rat."

My eyes widen and my mouth parts open, confusion written all over my face. "I love you," I demand. "Why wouldn't I ever feel the same?" I'm furious. I've been bottling up all of these feelings that she'd been concealing this entire time. Was she worried I'd reject her?

She shakes her head. "I told you on that call, and you were so weird," she stammers out.

"I knew you remembered it," I say. I'm laughing now, giddy with relief. "I couldn't hear what you were fucking saying."

She's squeezing me. An unspoken expression of the tense and overwhelming significance of our admissions.

"Shit, Ash. This whole time, I've been dying to tell you that I love you. Waiting desperately for when I was sure you wouldn't bolt."

We're kissing again, gulping down each other with needy lapping mouths. It's sloppy, but neither of us is able to care. We need to consume one another. Stop time in this moment and swallow every particle of the experience.

I'm pushing her back towards the bed. Slipping my fingers under her hem, I drag the tips up her soft thighs. She shudders at the light touch, hands coming to meet mine and we pull her dress up and over her head together. Before the backs of her knees connect with the edge and we tumble onto the mattress.

She's in her underwear and shoes. Tan skin and tattoos on full display below me. She's gorgeous. Despite how exposed she is, she gives me that wicked grin as she impatiently pulls at my clothing.

I smile as I take her hands in mine. There's still so much to sort out. So much that we need to discuss. However, right now in the dark, quiet house, there's only one thing that matters. I'm in love with Ashley, and she loves me.

My stomach tightens. The gnawing is ready to be satiated. I'm looking forward to my last meal. "What's the rush? Now that I know you're mine, I'm going to take my time," I say, lazily kissing either corner of her pillowy lips.

"You're such an ass," she says, unbuckling my pants.

"I'm your ass," I correct.

"Hell, yes," she exhales.

We're both naked now. I thrust into her languidly. Enjoying having her in my arms and feeling the deepest, most exposed parts of her. We lock eyes, no one running away from the intensity. I push deep, and she widens to accept all of me.

Certain moments demand to be savored. The first time I tasted Ash's freshly baked croissants when I arrived at Mother Wolf lingers in my mind. They were still warm out of the oven. The top layers were impossibly flaky. I burned my fingertips as I pulled back the ribbons of lamination in long strips. Dangled the crispy parts into my mouth and crunched through the exterior. Rewarded with steaming soft buttery dough beneath. The flavor and texture were unrivaled by any other baked good I'd ever tasted. I could have eaten an entire tray. Just continued to experience the moment again and again.

This is how I want to live with Ashley. I will pull back all of her layers. Enjoy the crunch, even if it burns my fingertips in the process. I will get to savor all of the exposed softness underneath.

"I love you," I say as our heads fall back onto the pillows, climaxes reached and hunger satisfied. A smile stretches across her pillowy lips.

"I love you too, Rat."

I brush my finger through her hair, pushing it back to expose her face to me. "I'm going to keep saying it. You'd better get ready," I muse. I still can't quell this giddy feeling.

She entwines her fingers in mine under the blanket. "Same," she replies sleepily.

Tonight, we will sleep. Tomorrow, who knows? We just have to take it one dish at a time.

Epilogue

RAFF

September is Santa Luna's best-kept secret. Most tourists have returned to their lives, school begins, and the mundanity of routine creeps back in. However, that first month of fall hides unseasonably warm weather and sweeping Pacific Ocean breezes that make conditions perfect for summer activities without the vacationing crowds.

So today, on one of the final days before it closes for the season, Ash and I take our seats in the front pew of The Big Dipper, the rickety wooden rollercoaster at the end of the beach boardwalk.

"You ready?" I ask with a knowing grin.

She's about to reply when the coaster takes off like a rocket. Well, not a fast-moving rocket per se, it's more of a shaking, jolting type of propulsion. The cranking rise and plummeting falls have us sliding into one another, flesh and bones clanking into rusty metal and splintering wood, sweaty hands clasped tightly as we both scream.

When we exit the ride a few minutes later, we're clutching our asses.

"I don't remember it being so painful," I wince.

"I haven't been on that thing since I was maybe twelve," she admits, staggering into the warm afternoon sun. Her dark hair pulled up into a messy ponytail, oversized sunglasses on top of her head, and dark denim cut-off jeans display her slender legs. She is gorgeous.

"What should we do next?" I ask, taking her hand again. I will never let her go. "You decided, as it's your first date, after all."

She rolls her almond eyes and scrunches up her nose cutely. I know what she's thinking; what a fucking lame-o.

She considers a cotton candy stand for a moment before pointing a finger at the bank of vintage photo booths.

"You dirty girl," I tease with a coy smile.

Her face immediately flushes. "Whatever, I get it. You want to add to our collection." Ash laughs and tugs my hand forward.

These are the best types of days. The lazy ones that remind me that we have time. No one is running. No one is afraid. We get to be. After the night of the rehearsal dinner, we made a promise to each other that we weren't going to be so worried about everything ending that we'd forget to enjoy what was already there.

"A life lived in fear is a life half lived," Guy had said through a mouthful of Fruit Loops when I told him the next morning. It's from some movie Mac had dragged him to at the La Paloma as revenge for The Lost Boys. He's right. We can't control any of it. All we can do is love each other.

The promise was just words, but Ash doesn't want to get married. So, these are our vows. Our commitment to the here and now. To stay grounded with one another.

It's late afternoon when we get back to the house. We decided that our first date should be on a Monday. This way, we wouldn't have to rush back for work. I love Princess Pizzarina. Gone are the days of my rage and fear dominating the place. Ash has ushered in a new era. It's her restaurant just as much as it belongs to myself or Guy.

I hope she feels pride in its success. I plan to have her work with us as for long as she's interested. Which should be a while, because now that business is consistent and the team is capable, we're starting another restaurant at Silverstein's new brewery.

"Pizza," Ash asked when we told her and Mac about our plans after our date.

Guy shook his head.

"We're thinking about something new," I'd said.

"What do you think about sandwiches?" he'd asked, venturing a glance at Mac.

"You two would help us develop the menu. Bake the bread and all that shit."

They'd both looked stunned. Surprised that we'd trust them to put their stamp on something new.

"We want to give you the freedom to create," I'd told her. That's what I plan to do for the rest of my life.

"Thank you," she whispered before kissing me.

"Where's my kiss?" Guy had asked Mac with a teasing smile.

She just huffed, adjusting her dark-framed glasses, but I noticed that the tips of her ears were turning red. There was a sound down the hallway that had all of our heads turning.

Van appeared at the end of the dinette. She'd been splitting her time between Mother Wolf and our house, a walking ghost living her former life over the past month. We didn't mind the addition to the fold. We were happy to take care of her. Guy and I never talked about it, but I was certain that we felt the same. They were our family now.

"Mac is going to kiss Guy," Ash said, turning towards Van.

"Fuck you," Mac said, swiftly slugging her sister in the upper arm.

Ash gasped and reeled, rubbing at the impact point on her shoulder. Van smiled, but it didn't change the determination in her expression.

"I've made a decision," she declared.

Ash and Mac exchanged a glance, but Van continued. “I’m going to have a baby.”

About the Author

Odette Azul — Is a writer living in Los Angeles with her husband, son, two cats, and a pug.

www.ingramcontent.com/pod-product-compliance
Lightning Source LLC
LaVergne TN
LVHW010637110826
845149LV00014B/2866

* 9 7 9 8 9 9 5 8 0 9 6 0 9 *